THE QUANTUM WEIRDNESS OF THE ALMOST-KISS

AMY
NOELLE
PARKS

WEIRDNESS
OF THE
ALMOST-
KISS

AMULET BOOKS • NEW YORK

Cataloging-in-Publication Data has been applied for and may be obtained from the Library of Congress.

ISBN 978-1-4197-3972-9

Text copyright © 2020 Amy Noelle Parks
Jacket illustration © 2020 Andi Porretta
Book design by Hana Anouk Nakamura

Printed and bound in U.S.A.
10 9 8 7 6 5 4 3 2 1

Amulet Books are available at special discounts when purchased in quantity for premiums and promotions as well as fundraising or educational use. Special editions can also be created to specification. For details, contact specialsales@abramsbooks.com or the address below.

Amulet Books® is a registered trademark of Harry N. Abrams, Inc.

ABRAMS The Art of Books
195 Broadway, New York, NY 10007
abramsbooks.com

For Perry. My best friend. For always.

CALEB

"I AM NOT IN LOVE WITH EVIE BECKHAM."

I'd like to be more emphatic about this, but Leo and I are twenty minutes into a sprints workout, so I can barely talk at all, much less with any intensity. I drop to the ground and lie flat on my back.

"Not time to stop," Leo says, checking his watch.

He is smack in the middle of his soccer season, but I am a pitcher, and baseball is still months away. I'm only here because I felt bad about his solo workouts. No one should have to endure this torture alone, and despite the searing pain in my lungs, I didn't mind all that much until he started up about Evie.

"Feel free to keep going," I tell him.

Instead, he sits beside me. "You and Evie—you're always together."

"We're friends," I say, although that doesn't begin to cover it.

Evie and I grew up in each other's pockets. When we were five, she came home from kindergarten to a locked house in the dead of winter because her absentminded parents (a mathematician and a psychologist) briefly forgot they had a daughter. My mom and dad rescued her, and we've been inseparable ever since.

Almost four years ago, she talked me into applying to Newton Academy, the ridiculously selective math and science boarding school she, Leo, and I now attend. I agreed only because I thought I had zero chance of getting in, unlike Evie, who turned in her screening exam in half the allotted time. Her flex probably improved my chances, since it intimidated the hell out of everyone else, while I expected it.

When, to my everlasting surprise, we both got acceptance letters, I tried to talk Evie out of going. Despite the rosy picture she painted of days spent coding and building robots, I hadn't wanted to leave my family in Wisconsin for what is practically an all-boys school in downstate Illinois, wear uniforms, and work my ass off. My plan had been to coast through high school into my inevitable role as valedictorian, because while Evie will win the Fields Medal for mathematics someday, she will never get anything above a B in an English class.

But Evie had opened her big gray eyes, laid her hand on my arm, and said, "Please?" And so six months later, I packed my bags. Not that I regret it. I could have taught the coding classes at our high school back home, but our instructor here actually worked for Microsoft.

"Do you think I have a shot?" Leo asks, interrupting my thoughts.

"Maybe," I say. The answer is no.

Evie is not a fan of new experiences. She eats about twelve foods (half of them beige), doesn't like talking to strangers, and at seventeen years old is still so afraid of learning to ride a bike that when we're at home, she uses her scooter for trips to the library—a habit that is both irritating and adorable.

So far, Evie has shown absolutely no interest in dating and has discouraged all comers with brutal efficiency.

A typical encounter usually goes something like this:

Gabe: You want to see a movie sometime?

Evie: I don't like movies. As soon as I figure out who everyone is, they're over.

Gabe: Well, the movie isn't actually the point.

Evie: I'm going to do my physics now.

I find these interactions hilarious, but the victims of her unapologetic refusals tend to be less amused.

"Why Evie?" I ask Leo. Because I am protective.

Like a brother.

Or a cousin.

Or a concerned citizen with no familial relationship whatsoever.

Leo's quiet for a moment. Then he says, "I like how you can tell she's thinking so much more than she's saying, and how she never backs down with Dr. Lewis. And the way she bites her lip when she's working on a problem? My physics grade dropped four points since I noticed her doing it."

There's nothing I can reasonably object to here. No hint that Evie is just some challenging level on a video game he'd like to be the first to unlock.

"If you're really not interested, you could talk to her for me?" Leo says.

He is not the first to ask for help jailbreaking Evie's code, but I never provide tech support for my classmates. I like watching them crash and burn.

Because let's face it:

I am totally in love with Evie Beckham.

EVIE

THESE ARE THE STORIES OF MY CHILDHOOD:

Georg Cantor, the inventor of set theory, spent much of his life locked within the walls of an asylum.

Kurt Gödel wrote two of the most famous theorems in all of mathematics and then starved to death when his wife got sick, because he refused to eat food prepared by anyone else.

And game theorist John Nash disappeared into his own head.

I could go on, but the last time I saw Anita, she told me I needed to stop perseverating on ill-fated mathematicians. She said fixating on their troubles is unproductive. I wish someone would tell my mother.

Today, Anita invites me in before I have a chance to start my homework. The living room of the turn-of-the-century house has been converted into a therapist's office, including the requisite lounge on which to recline and French doors that lead out to a walkway so patients never have to encounter each other coming and going. This system is supposed to protect my privacy, but it just makes me feel as though I ought to be ashamed to be here.

The one consolation is Anita herself. She has a big smile, wild curly hair traced with gray, and feels more like an aunt than a doctor. She is the first therapist I found myself.

Mom, who wrote her dissertation on the relationship between mental illness and mathematical genius, sees my visits as preventative maintenance, and she picked a psychiatrist for me when I came to Newton. But I left him last year when I started to feel more anxious about going to appointments than I did about staying away.

"How is everything?" Anita asks, taking one of the chairs in front of the French doors because I refuse to lie down on that ridiculous couch.

"Bex and I finished our applications for the University of Chicago." We applied because it has a top-notch theoretical physics department for me and an amazing med school acceptance rate for Bex. Knowing we'll be together makes me less panicky about the whole thing.

"And Caleb?" Anita asks with a smile.

"Still making up his mind."

"Would it be okay with you if he went somewhere far away?"

I think about it. "He won't."

"You're very certain," she says.

And I am.

My fears are legion. All the normal ones—eight-legged creatures, enclosed spaces, speaking in public, dolls that talk, and overly enthusiastic elementary school teachers. But quite a few unusual ones as well—frogs (why do their legs bend like that?), bridges, empty swimming pools, full restaurants, and Jell-O (touching or eating, which Caleb says is entirely rational).

But I am not afraid that Caleb will go to college far away from me.

"We've been friends our whole lives." The simplicity of this statement doesn't capture everything I mean, but I'm not sure what to add.

"Sometimes friends grow apart," Anita suggests.

"Not us," I say, but I don't like the flicker of doubt that flares up at her words.

"I hope not. But it might be a good idea to widen your circle a little. Beyond Bex and Caleb. Get some practice getting to know people while you're somewhere you feel safe."

"But people are boring."

"You go to a school with 120 math and science prodigies," Anita says. "Find a couple more who are worth your time."

We finish by reviewing each trigger that set me off this week. My doctors before worked on my anxiety only through cognitive behavioral therapy and medicine, but Anita's gone deeper, helping me see that my anxiety isn't only the product of my own brain. She taught me the words *situational anxiety* and helped me see that growing up in my hometown was a bit of a situation.

With her help, I got off my meds last spring. I'm grateful for the space they gave me to get better, but I don't need them every day anymore. Mom is not quite convinced this is the right path, but Anita keeps reminding me that I am in charge of myself.

"Keep up the good work," she says when our time is up, and I exit through the doors of shame.

The walk back to Newton in the bright October sunshine is quick. The school's grounds hug the university campus and are sprinkled with giant concrete statues of mythical beasts—unicorns, dragons, and sea serpents—which I have always thought an odd choice for a school focused on science. The main building is Gothic in style though it's less than a decade old, with panes of glass that are artfully cracked and leaded to give them the appearance of age. Caleb says this is so they can charge more in tuition, which doesn't make sense, but I've learned to trust him on this sort of thing.

The dorm, more prosaic in construction, is connected by a corridor off the main lobby and hidden from view. There are three floors of single rooms with girls on the top floor, reflecting the two-to-one ratio of boys to girls. The admissions office says this mirrors the applicant pool. Bex is skeptical.

I open my door to find Bex sitting cross-legged on my bed with her bio notes spread around her. Her look today is Geek Princess. She's wearing a white button-down under a cobalt-blue sweater-vest with a pleated plaid skirt in Newton's signature blue, black, and gray. Her mahogany-brown hair is pulled into high pigtails, and chunky black glasses frame her eyes. Tomorrow, despite the restrictions of the dress code, she'll look completely different.

I wear pretty much the same thing every day—black hoodie, blue T-shirt, and pleated plaid skirt. According to Bex, Newton's uniform restrictions are like the rules of a sonnet: disasters for most people, but magic in the hands of the right poet. (I think all sonnets are disasters.)

Bex is the youngest daughter of a wildly popular television minister, beloved by the right because of his politics and because he's Latinx, which makes his mostly white audience feel less racist. Bex essentially blackmailed him and her mother into letting her come to Newton, threatening to act out in far more embarrassing ways than her attending a science academy if they refused.

I hang my coat and bag on the hooks by my closet and place my notebook and felt-tip pens on the edge of my desk, running my finger along the bottom of the row to line them up. (I don't have a fear of disorder. It's an aversion. Like with cottage cheese.)

"I was going to ask if you talked all the crazy out, but clearly there's still some work to do," Bex says.

"Organization is not an illness." I give her papers a significant look.

She gathers them into stacks.

"Why are you here, anyway? And how did you get in?"

She tilts her head, flutters her eyelashes, and speaks in a breathy voice. "Evan, I left my biology book in Evie's room, and if I don't get it right now, I'm going to fail our quiz tomorrow."

I snort. Bex would have to get hit on the head with an anvil to fail a bio quiz, but she is so pretty that she is consistently underestimated. Evan, a college student who serves as one of our dorm's resident assistants, is one of Bex's many followers and would not only give her the master keycard but would hand her my laptop if she asked.

"Do you ever think those big brown eyes and deep dimples constitute an unfair advantage?"

"Yes, Evie—as a brown woman in the sciences, I worry daily about my unfair advantages," she responds. "You know, if you ever want to play up that English rose thing, I'm here to help."

I inherited my British father's fair coloring: light brown hair, gray eyes, and pale skin. From my mother, I got my lack of height, wavy hair that runs to curls, and a mild disappointment in most of humanity.

Sitting next to Bex, I ask again, "Why are you here?"

It's not that Bex never camps out in my room, but she knows I am protective of my space. I like my things just so, and my favorite part of the room—a giant whiteboard with my current work splashed across it in vibrant colors—is not something I like to share.

"I got a belated birthday present from my parents," she says, holding out a small box. Inside is a thick silver ring. It's simple but pretty. When I look at her, she says, "Read it."

Inside the ring is a tiny line of cursive script: *You are not your own.*

I don't know what that means, but even so, a shiver runs through me.

"It's from the Bible," Bex says. "It means your body doesn't belong to you. It's kind of like a purity ring. I promised I wouldn't date when they let me come here, but I think they can tell I'm wavering."

Sometimes I wonder who is more damaged: Bex, with her father who takes so many of the worst parts of the Bible literally, or me, with my mother who thinks the *DSM-5* (the official book of all mental disorders) is a parenting manual.

I snap the ring box closed and put it in my desk drawer. "If you need it when you go home, you can get it then," I say. "Let's go get cookies."

Moonbeam Bakery solves all our problems, big and small. I get the same thing every time—chocolate chocolate chip— while Bex asks for the unfailingly odd monthly special— currently pineapple orange coconut—which maybe says everything anyone needs to know about us.

We head back toward Newton with our cookies wrapped in brown paper.

When she finishes eating, Bex says, "Can I ask you something?"

"Anything."

"What were all those drawings on your whiteboard?"

Surprised, I turn toward her. This is not what I was expecting.

"Usually your board is full of equations, but today you had all those crazy pictures." Her eyes roam across my face, and I look back, searching for the hidden meaning in her question.

Occasionally I find it challenging to read emotions in other people, although the better I know them, the easier it is. Bex's approach to this failing of mine is pragmatic—she often narrates the feelings that flash across people's faces for me and calls it "doing emotional subtitles." But it doesn't help when she's the one I'm trying to read.

Finally, the word *crazy* tips me off. She's worried the drawings on my board are the products of anxiety.

"They're adinkras," I say, hoping to reassure her.

"You realize that's not an answer?"

"Long version?" She nods, and I explain. "The first adinkras are these story symbols from Ghana. They're kind of like hieroglyphs, because they pack all of this information into tiny little pictures. Here." I pull out my phone to show her a picture of a square drawn around what looks like crooked railroad tracks. "That means 'wind-resistant house,' and it's a symbol of strength in the face of treachery."

"What was the big one on the top of your board—the sideways fleur-de-lis?"

I smile. "That's my favorite. It means 'The hen treads on her chicks, but she does not kill them.' It's advice for parents—nurture, but don't coddle."

"The Beckham family motto," Bex says.

"Close enough," I agree.

"But why are you interested in them?"

"Because this is the genius thing," I say. "You can make math adinkras."

"The spaceship things you drew?" Bex asks.

"Yes. The black and white dots, the different colors, the dashed and solid lines—all of that encodes information. You can cram a bunch of equations into one drawing."

"Why do you want to?"

"It lets you model some pretty complex things."

"So you're not turning into Newton's own Unabomber?"

"No. I am not."

I don't bother to tell her his name or his mathematical expertise, although I know both.

CALEB

AFTER GRABBING BREAKFAST, I THROW MY TRAY on the table across from Bex and Evie and eat scrambled eggs, drink coffee, and review my physics homework all at the same time. It's efficient but not pretty.

Evie's drinking tea, while Bex stares mournfully off into space. She's wearing a navy dress that's too long on her and a high-necked white blouse that looks like she stole it from a nun.

"I hate that outfit," I tell her.

"That's because you can't see my legs."

"No," I say, although Bex's legs are very nice. "It's because you only wear it when you're sad."

Evie looks at me like I did a magic trick. She finds feelings mysterious.

I check out the crowded cafeteria. "Is there someone who needs a lesson in manners?" I ask Bex. She is beautiful and smart, and because of some Faustian deal with her parents, she does not date. Unfortunately, some of my classmates see this as a challenge. Last year, I nailed Mason Plowman in the shoulder with a baseball because he put his hands on her, and I would be happy to do it again.

But Bex smiles and shakes her head. "No, but thank you for offering."

"I live to serve," I say. "We'll see you in humanities?" Bex nods, and I get up. My eggs and coffee are gone, although the homework could use some more attention. "Ready, Eves?"

We dump our trays and head toward physics.

"What's going on with her?" I ask as we head down the hall.

"Home. Her parents gave her a scary birthday present."

I raise my eyebrows but don't ask. "Can you imagine growing up like that?"

"No," Evie says.

"Probably worse if you're a girl," I say, holding the door for her. We take our regular desks. Although we don't have assigned seats, we gravitate toward the same places each day. There are only fourteen of us, all the seniors who chose physics as a major or minor. Biology, with its premed hopefuls, and coding, with all its nascent Google employees, are almost twice as big.

With a flourish, Dr. Lewis enters the room and plugs in an old-fashioned digital clock. It flashes "24:00:00" and begins counting down.

"Midterm tomorrow," he says by way of beginning class. "Review today. Study tonight. Because you know what they call physicists who fail?" No one takes the bait. "Engineers."

Dr. Lewis is a little hard-core.

He goes over the relevant equations for the test tomorrow. I'm frantically copying them down, but Evie isn't even paying attention. Instead, she sketches some little design in the corner of her notebook that I hope has nothing to do with our exam, because I have no idea what it is.

Dr. Lewis flicks off the projector and says, "Before we go over the homework, I want to remind you that the deadline to submit to Frontier will be here before you know it."

Evie goes still. Frontier is like a combination of the Nobel Prize and the Academy Awards for high school physics. You submit a paper that must include at least some original mathematics, and finalists are invited to a conference where they present their work to judges. An invitation to the conference practically guarantees you admission to the best universities in the country. Finishing in the top five means scholarships.

Evie's paper got picked last year, but she had a freak-out before the conference, so she never presented. I wonder what she's thinking.

Dr. Lewis collects our homework—a multistep problem

about spinning tops of various sizes—cuts our names off our papers, and starts pinning them up on corkboard strips around the perimeter of the room.

I look over at Evie and smile in sympathy. Last year, when we began to solve more advanced problems, Dr. Lewis started these gallery walks. He posts our papers by number and asks us to choose the best solution. The goal, he says, is to evaluate each other's work in ways that go beyond right and wrong.

Evie hates it, both because she is unimpressed by the solutions of others, which are never as thoughtful as her own, and because she always wins, which means public conversations with Dr. Lewis.

I stand and pull Evie out of her seat, giving her hand an encouraging little squeeze before crossing to the other side of the room. As always, I recognize her solution immediately. It uses half the steps of anyone else's and draws on equations we've never talked about, but her answer is exactly the same as mine. I'm writing her paper's number on my Post-it when Leo, who's standing behind me, says, "This is gorgeous."

He trails his fingers across Evie's paper, and I have an irrational urge to yank his hand off the page. Instead, I look over at Evie, who is transfixed by the paper in front of her. I have a bad feeling about this.

Going back to her, I say, "See something you like?"

"Look at this, Caleb. It's lovely." She puts her fingers on the paper with the same reverence Leo showed for hers across the room. I cannot believe I am being forced into a front-row seat for Evie's meet-cute. I have done nothing to deserve this.

Instead of answering, I return to my seat. When I look back over at Leo, I see him watching Evie, and although it kills me to admit it, she's watching him too. The papers are anonymous, but Evie knows no one else could have produced the solution she's so taken with.

Leo, whose blue eyes and shaggy brown hair make him look like one-fifth of a boy band, transferred to Newton at the beginning of this year and hasn't quite found his place yet. I liked him fine up until he declared his interest in Evie, but I am now questioning my judgment.

When Dr. Lewis herds us back to our seats, he announces that Leo's solution received the most votes. "As Mr. McGill's work demonstrates, mathematics should achieve a particular purpose. Communication. Clarity. Even beauty. It's not enough to be merely correct." He tears one of the papers off the wall and drops it on Blake's desk. "Although that would certainly be a nice start, Mr. Winters."

Then he has Leo talk through the problem before asking for questions. Margot Hannah raises her hand, tossing her dark hair over her shoulder and opening her big blue eyes wide as she smiles at Leo. I was briefly caught up in Margot's beauty freshman year, and I'm hoping Leo might suffer the same fate, but he ignores her, as does Dr. Lewis, who says, "Any real questions?"

Leo says, "Is it against the rules to ask who paper three belongs to?"

"That's Ms. Beckham's work. Ever efficient."

"It's more than that," Leo argues. "It strips away every bit of unnecessary information." He turns to Evie. "It's an elegant solution."

She does not blush or look away but says, "Thanks" with a pleased smile.

Kara whispers to Margot, "I guess you should have spent more time on your homework and less time on your hair."

And I think, *You and me both.*

EVIE

CALEB AND I HAVE FIFTEEN MINUTES BETWEEN classes, which we nearly always spend in the senior lounge, consuming various forms of caffeine.

"So," Caleb says, "how does it feel to be dethroned as Queen of the Gallery Walk?"

"I can take it. I'm sure Dr. Lewis was glad to have someone who's majoring in physics win."

"Not to mention someone who's male," he adds.

"I didn't think you noticed that part."

"Maybe I wouldn't if it were anyone else, but it's you. Sometimes you answer a question and he looks so surprised. Like someone trained a monkey to do calculus."

I laugh. "Thanks. It makes me feel better to know I'm not imagining it." Despite my grades, Dr. Lewis treats me with a quiet contempt that is hard to understand as anything other than an objection to me being a girl who's good at math.

"I probably should have felt some solidarity when Dr. Lewis blew Margot off," I say. "But honestly, I didn't want to hear her question—which was not going to be about physics—any more than he did. Does that make me a traitor to my gender?"

"I don't think you're obligated to like every girl in the world." After a pause, he adds, "Especially the ones batting their eyes at Leo McGill."

"What does that have to do with anything?" I say, confused.

Caleb smiles. I don't know why. Boys like Margot. It doesn't have anything to do with me.

Instead of answering, he says, "Tell me what you're working on for Frontier."

He must have seen my sketches. I shouldn't have been doing them in class, but I can't get my adinkras out of my head. Still, Caleb ought to know better than to take it seriously. Last year, I was thrilled when my paper got in. But the closer Frontier got, the more the idea of standing onstage in front of a room full of strangers in a place I'd never been weighed on me.

In the end, I never made it to San Diego, much less to the conference. My parents and I got to the airport, but at the gate, I started to shake and sob. I couldn't get on the plane. It was one of my worst breakdowns in years. And I can't go through that again. Not when I'm finally feeling in control.

To Caleb, I say, "You know I can't go to Frontier. I tried. It didn't work."

"You could if I were with you," Caleb says, and when I start to object, he takes my hand and laces his fingers through mine, a habit of ours from childhood. "Not just for company, but presenting together. So you wouldn't be alone onstage."

Maybe. Caleb makes me feel safe. And he's as good as—maybe better than—anyone at knowing when things get to be too much for me. But I'm not sure how to make this happen. The rules about intellectual contribution at Frontier are explicit. The only way he could be with me during my presentations is as a coauthor. He would have to answer questions about the part of the problem he solved, so the project would have to involve coding. I adore Caleb, and he's magic on a computer, but there's no way he can do Frontier-level mathematics.

"Let me think about it."

"Okay, but not for too long." He lets go of my hand and stands. "Humanities?"

I nod and follow.

I should spend humanities thinking about the overlap between coding and adinkras—the ludicrous discussions in these classes do not deserve my attention—but instead, I find myself thinking about Anita encouraging me to make friends. Leo surprised me in physics. His solution wasn't as clean as mine, but it explained the problem so well. Maybe Anita's right and there are other people worth knowing.

In the cafeteria, I pick up a grilled cheese sandwich and an apple and sit with Bex and Caleb. Because Caleb isn't seeing anyone, the fourth chair at our table is empty, so I shouldn't be as surprised as I am when Leo asks me if the seat is taken.

I look up at him, a little panicked. Something about the way he's looking at me is shutting down the language centers in my brain. I turn to Bex and Caleb for help. When new people come to our table, they're usually not hoping to sit with me.

Leo's hesitant smile is not making it any easier for me to find my words.

"Seems like the question is harder than I thought," he says.

"Go ahead," Bex says, looking between me and Caleb, who, strangely, seems as frozen as I am. "Leo, right?"

"Yeah. And thanks." Leo gestures toward the rest of the cafeteria. "I haven't really settled in anywhere. It's hard when everyone knows each other."

I'm instantly sympathetic. Bex adopted me pretty fast, but if I hadn't had Caleb my first month here, I don't know what I would have done.

"You came from Newton South?" Bex asks, and I am so grateful to her for keeping the conversation going that I vow to get cookies whenever she asks instead of complaining that it's interrupting my work.

"Newton South" is what we call the other private school run by the Newton trustees. It officially goes by the ridiculous name Knights of Pythagoras and remains an all-male academy. This is a continual source of outrage for Bex, although she has no desire to set foot in Louisiana, where it's located.

Leo nods.

"And how do we compare?"

"Favorably," he says with a glance at me. *What does that mean?*

Sarah-Kate Quinn, one of Bex's soccer teammates, passes by, and Bex holds her hand behind her head for Sarah-Kate to slap. Sarah-Kate pauses and nods at Leo. Then she says, "Evie, Caleb," looking at each of us. Her voice has a touch of acid when she says our names, and Leo raises his eyebrows.

Bex explains. "Caleb and Sarah-Kate dated last year."

"Three months of constant shouting," Sarah-Kate says.

Caleb brushes his blond hair out of his eyes and looks up at her. "Not *constant* shouting," he says softly. There's something in the way he talks to her that makes me feel very young. As if there is a whole world out there that I know nothing about.

Sarah-Kate smiles at him. "I may remember a moment or two when we were otherwise occupied," she says before going to sit down at her own table.

"Caleb has gone out with every girl in our year," Bex says.

"Present company excluded," Caleb adds. And then after a moment, "And Callie and Alexa."

"They're together," Bex says for Leo's sake.

"That record sounds worse than it is," Caleb continues. "Nine girls in three years isn't unreasonable. Especially if you consider that Margot only lasted two days."

Two days too many, as far as I'm concerned. Margot has no trouble keeping up in classes but spends her free time talking about cat videos, unboxing channels on YouTube, and the best places to get bubble tea. I don't enjoy it.

And no matter how much time goes by, Caleb will always be someone who thought it was a good idea to date Margot. It does not speak well of him.

Looking at me, Caleb says, "Cut me some slack. I was fourteen."

"That's no excuse."

Leo, in what I assume is an attempt to change the subject, says, "Sarah-Kate seems chill. Why were you always shouting?"

Both Caleb and Bex look at me quickly and then away. I study my plate.

"Evie and Caleb grew up together, and now they've got this whole courtly love thing going on," Bex says, gesturing between us. She found the Arthurian legends of our Brit lit class last year to be hilariously descriptive of Caleb and me. "Sarah-Kate couldn't accept the sacred and non-carnal nature of their relationship."

Caleb rolls his eyes but doesn't disagree. Neither do I. It's as good a description as any for this thing between us.

When lunch is over, Leo says he has a question about physics and offers to walk me to math. He asks about one of the equations in my solution in a way that makes it clear he understands what I did. Which makes him unlike almost everyone else in our class. When we get to math, I'm sorry to see him go.

Surprising.

I take my seat next to David, who says, "I voted for your paper today. Leo was right. It was beautiful. You know you'll never make him happy, right? You just keep doing the work."

He isn't talking about Leo. David, one of eight Black kids at Newton, knows something about the weight of other people's expectations. He told me that on his first day here, Dean Santori asked if he was in the wrong building. I'm not surprised he's noticed the way Dr. Lewis treats me. David's more Caleb's friend than mine, but because we both major in math and minor in physics, we've spent a lot of time together over the years.

Yanaan, the third math major and the only other girl in the class, throws her bag onto the ground and slides into the chair on the other side of David. He looks at her a moment and then picks up her ponytail to examine the end.

"Did you set your hair on fire again?" he asks with a smile.

"Yes," she admits. "I didn't even notice until I smelled it."

Chemistry labs seem dangerous. One time Bex inhaled something that nearly singed off all her nose hairs. It makes me glad I chose physics.

The three of us open our notebooks and focus on Dr. Biesta, a mathematician from the university who just started working with the seniors. So far, I like her. She is soft-spoken, but because there are only nine of us in the class, it hardly matters. She sets problems and leaves us alone to do them. Our instructor last year saw teaching as more of a performance, scrawling elaborate proofs across the board while we copied them down. Once he got going, I think he would have continued on through the end of class even if we had all walked away. Dr. Biesta teaches as if she knows other people are in the room.

Today, she writes a theorem on the board, asks us to prove it, and moves around, quietly offering guidance. By the end of the period, I'm not worried about being able to finish before tomorrow, even though I have to study for physics, so when the six math minors leave for another class, I put my schoolwork away and pull out my adinkras.

S. James Gates Jr. used adinkras to describe relationships between quantum particles. I want to use the model he developed to do something similar, focused on helium-3 atoms.

I am talking my ideas over with Dr. Biesta when Dean Santori comes in. He looks around, seeming surprised to find himself in a mostly empty room. Then he clears his throat and says, "I thought I'd check in on what we're working on for Frontier this year. These are our math majors?"

"Our seniors, yes," Dr. Biesta says.

"Hmm," Dean Santori says, looking at us. David was a finalist last year. This means he's already won a scholarship, so he's ineligible.

"Don't look at me," Yanaan says. "I do chemistry, not physics."

Dean Santori's eyes slide over me and back to Dr. Biesta. "I guess I'll come back in a bit and check with the juniors?"

So I don't have to worry about him pushing me to enter, then.

CALEB

AS SOON AS OUR CODING LAB ENDS, LEO LEAVES for soccer, promising to return after dinner. Sometime tonight I need to study for physics (although, unlike Dr. Lewis, I have no objection to a career in engineering), but first I need to clear my head.

Working with Leo on the midterm project seemed like such a good idea. He's fluent in C++, pretty cheerful, and didn't have a partner, but when I asked him, I didn't know about his obsession with Evie, and I've since discovered that having a shared interest does not do as much for team bonding as you might hope.

Today, his frequent distracted smiles left me desperate for a long, slow run outside Newton's walls. I head out into the residential neighborhoods, not worrying about where I'm going or how long it will take.

Evie's interest in Leo is definitely messing with my head. Because in what universe does it make sense that she would choose someone else?

I am her best friend. And I love her. And I almost kissed her fourteen times. I keep a mental list of almost-kisses, and these are my favorites:

#1. We were thirteen, playing hide-and-seek with my brothers. I caged her in with my hands against the wall of our garage and probably would have done it if she hadn't ducked under my arm and run.

#4. A year later, I held her during a panic attack until she stopped shaking and crying. I wanted to kiss every one of those tears off her face.

#7. That winter, we tumbled out of a sled. If I close my eyes, I can still see Evie laughing in the snow.

#11. She was sixteen; my birthday was still a few weeks away. We spent the day at the county fair shuddering at over-fed pigs, eating funnel cakes, and quietly mocking a magic show. In some ways, you could count our ride on the Ferris wheel at twilight seven separate times.

#12. On my sixteenth birthday, I took her for our first independent car ride. She actually did kiss me on the cheek when she said good night, but I almost turned my head.

#13. Still sixteen. (It was a rough summer.) The night before we went back to Newton, she fell asleep curled up next to me while we were watching television. I texted her mother to say she'd be staying at our house, and when I covered her with a blanket, she blinked up at me sleepily and sighed. I went upstairs.

So Leo can take his secret smiles and go to hell.

I am winding my way back to school when I see a dark-haired girl in a Newton uniform up ahead. Bex.

When I come up behind her, she turns, yelps, and swats my arm. "Don't run up behind women on the street, you idiot."

"Sorry," I say, slowing to a walk. "What are you doing?"

"I had a meeting with my action group. We're trying to get the city to ban plastic grocery bags."

I grin. Bex loves her little projects. She shoves me with her shoulder.

"Don't smile at me in that patronizing way. Someday, when your children look out into the ocean and see nothing but a mountain of plastic, you're going to wish you came to these meetings with me."

"My children will live in the Midwest. They'll never see the ocean."

We walk in silence for a little while. Then she says, "What's your plan with Leo?"

I trip over the curb but don't bother to pretend I don't know what she's talking about.

"Same as always. Watch the show. Eat popcorn. Be there to clear away the rubble."

"What's wrong with you?"

I raise my eyebrows.

"You are in love with her," Bex says. "As far as I can tell, you have always been in love with her. And yet you've spent three years dating every single girl at Newton who is not Evie. And now you're just going to sit back and not say anything while she takes up with some blue-eyed, floppy-haired, soccer-playing stamp collector?"

"Well, when you put it that way, it just sounds stupid," I say. But I smile, because Bex is so great. Once, Ernest Rutherford said that all of science was either physics or stamp collecting, making the latter an arcane insult among science folk. It's totally how I'm going to think of Leo from now on.

We're back at Newton, and I climb up on one of the concrete dragons before pulling Bex up after me. "Look, as soon as Evie figures out he wants more than the answers to physics problems, she'll be done with him. That's how this works."

"Maybe," Bex says, although she doesn't look convinced. Her doubt sends a spike of fear straight to my stomach. "But why didn't you ever try for more?"

"I did," I say. "In the great let's-have-a-campfire-and-risk-a-decade-of-friendship-because-I-can't-stop-thinking-about-your-mouth debacle."

Bex looks shocked. I guess Evie didn't tell her. I'm not surprised, because we both pretend it never happened. But since Bex is pushing me, I tell her now.

The summer after our freshman year, my parents took my youngest brother to a swim meet in northern Wisconsin, and for the first time ever, they let my brother Nolan and me stay home alone. He, Evie, and I made a fire in the pit out back. We roasted marshmallows, told ghost stories, and solved logic puzzles. And then Nolan went in, leaving me alone with the girl of my dreams. At this point, Evie and I had nine almost-kisses between us, but she'd never given a single sign that she recognized even one of those moments of possibility. I decided to be more direct.

Blaming the shifting winds and the smoke, I moved out of my chair and sat next to her on the blanket, so close I could see the summer freckles coming out on her nose and cheeks. Evie started to scoot back, but I grabbed her hand.

Her eyes flew to mine, confused but not yet suspicious. "Caleb?"

Her lips, barely parted as she tried to figure out what I was doing, claimed all of my attention. Summoning my courage, I cupped her cheek. "Kiss me, Evie?" In my head, it was done. Number ten seemed like the perfect time to trade our almosts for the real thing.

But she pushed me back—not just reluctant but alarmed.

"No, Caleb. This isn't what I want. Not with anyone, but especially not with you."

"Especially not with me?" I reeled back, unable to make sense of what she was saying. I'd known she might not be ready, but it had never crossed my mind that it was me in particular she objected to.

She stood. "You're my friend. I don't want to be afraid that you're going to try to do . . . *this* . . . whenever we're together." Her tone made it clear that her feelings about *this* were very different from mine.

Trying to mitigate the damage, I held out my hand. "Evie, don't go. I'm sorry. Forget I said anything. It was a whim, that's all."

She looked stricken. "A whim? You'd risk our friendship for a whim?"

And she went home while I watched the fire die out.

The next day, when I texted her, she told me she was "busy." It was a week before she spoke to me again, a month before she was willing to be alone with me, three months before I could touch her without her regarding me suspiciously, and half a year before I was sure we were back to normal. Since then, I have been a machine. In my own mind, there have been a few more almosts, but I have never let her think—even for a moment—that I want to be anything other than her closest friend. And as long as I do that, she chooses me. Which is good.

Because during our time apart, I learned that while I *want* to kiss Evie, I *need* her in my life. Without her, my world is ordinary.

Following her, I learned to succeed at a place like Newton—which matters to me more than I ever would have guessed before we came. Protecting her, I learned to be brave.

I can't imagine who I'd be without her. And fortunately, I don't have to.

As long as I keep my lips off hers.

Bex pats me on the leg when I finish. "I know you don't want to hear this," she says. "But I think it's time to cowboy up and try again."

EVIE

NEWTON REQUIRES THAT WE PARTICIPATE IN AT least one athletic activity. I chose yoga my first year only because it seemed least likely to produce sweat or heavy breathing, but I like it now, and I have to admit the meditation helps my anxiety. Plus, the pre-breakfast start time keeps everyone pretty quiet during class, which I enjoy. Silent is my preferred state for most people.

Molly leads us through breathing meditations and sun salutations before moving on to inversions, backbends, and planks. By the time we're done, I feel ready for the physics midterm and centered in my body in a way that makes having a panic attack seem unlikely. Not that tests have ever been a trigger. I feel at home behind a desk working equations, no matter the stakes.

Even so, Caleb almost entirely shatters my calm during

breakfast by peppering me with questions and asking me to check the problems he worked through last night. He recites equations under his breath as we walk from the cafeteria to class but goes silent when we see Leo in the seat next to mine. Caleb's usual place.

"Do you want—" I start, gesturing to the empty chairs in the back.

"No, it's fine." Caleb takes the desk behind mine.

When I look over at Leo, he raises his eyebrows. "Ready?"

"We'll see." Bex taught me not to say "yes" to questions like this. Apparently, people don't like it when you tell the truth.

Dr. Lewis passes out the exams without ceremony, saying we have forty-five minutes. The first page, all multiple-choice questions, is easy. When Leo and I flip the page at the same time, we look at each other and smile. I don't know about him, but I'm used to working much more quickly than the people around me. It's unusual but not unpleasant to have someone match my pace.

The second page is trickier—a few short-answer questions and some scenarios we have to write equations for. I am looking over my answers when Leo turns the page, so I do the same, glancing over to see him grinning. The third and fourth pages are all single-step problems, and I work through them quickly but without artistry. I take a minute to check my equations before flipping to the last page. Leo does the same a couple of seconds afterward.

This last problem is complex, but similar to what we did for homework the day before. I think about it for a moment and decide that instead of using my solution strategy, I will use Leo's, even though it takes longer. I sketch out and label the diagrams, put in the accompanying equations, and write a brief explanation.

Leo and I turn toward each other at the same time, and when our eyes meet, we flip our tests facedown on our desks. I check the clock: a little more than fifteen minutes left. Given how quickly I worked through some of those problems, it wouldn't hurt to look them over.

Leo leans back in his chair and crosses his arms over his chest. Something about this pose makes me want to keep peeking at him. He obviously does not intend to look at his test again, so I sit back too, watching Dr. Lewis's countdown clock. My entire body tingles with adrenaline from the test and something else I don't quite understand.

When there are two minutes left, my hand moves toward my pencil, and I sense Leo turn his head toward me. I give him a wide-eyed, innocent look as I pick up my pencil and twirl it through my fingers as if that was what I intended to do all along.

When Dr. Lewis collects our papers, Leo says, "Thanks."

"For what?"

"The most fun I've ever had taking a midterm."

From behind me, Caleb says, "You're both out of your

minds. You finished in half an hour, and you didn't even check your answers."

"It was twenty-seven minutes," I say, "and I checked it as I went."

"I was trained not to make mistakes," Leo says. "At Knights, our keyboards didn't have delete keys."

It takes me a second to realize he's joking. I like it.

Dr. Lewis uses the last five minutes of class to say that we're beginning a unit on theoretical physics next. "This requires a certain flexibility of the mind. It is the heart of physics, and it demands more than an ability to execute equations," he says, barely flicking a glance in my direction.

"Like some trained monkey," Caleb whispers in my ear, and I laugh. Dr. Lewis glares at us, and Leo frowns.

"There won't be any problem sets for the weekend, but be ready to talk in some depth about the articles."

"See you at lunch again?" Leo asks before leaving. I nod.

Caleb and I wander toward the lounge, and I half listen to his postmortem on the exam. Before we head in, I stop and look up at him.

"I'm not going to humanities today," I say.

"What?"

"Our midterms aren't until next week. Missing a class won't kill me."

Caleb sticks out his hand. "Hi, I'm Caleb Covic. And you are?"

"Will you tell Abbie and Mr. Stein I'm not feeling well?"

I feel bad about the lie, but I'm giddy, and I can't sit through those two endless, discussion-based classes. I want to draw and daydream and work on my adinkras. Caleb studies my face.

"You do *not* look ill," he says. "You look like we could hook you up to a generator and power the city."

"Please?" I say. Knowing this will convince him, I add, "I want to work on the Frontier problem."

He nods, saying with a hint of sarcasm, "I assume I'll see you at lunch?"

On my whiteboard, I work on an adinkra. Physicists have always privileged equations in their representations, so it's a little bit of a risk to put a geometric model at the center of a Frontier paper, but I have this instinct I've always trusted pushing me forward. And I see what Caleb can do for me. I can't play with the model on the board, but on a computer we could rotate it and fold it. This will not only make the work more interesting, but it will give him a legitimate reason to write with me.

Bex and Caleb are already sitting at our table when I come into the cafeteria. They lean back in their chairs and glare, looking so much like angry parents that I want to laugh. After getting my lunch, I sit across from Bex, who says, "You're skipping class now, Evie?"

Leo approaches. "Evie's skipping class?" He sits next to me.

I turn to Bex. "It was only humanities. It doesn't count."

"She's never missed a class before," Bex says to Leo.

"And she sped through that test," Caleb says. Like he's tattling.

"Don't talk about me like I'm not here. And I assure you that even having done that test in thirty minutes—"

"Twenty-seven," Leo says with a smile.

"Yes," I agree. "Twenty-seven. My score will wipe the floor with yours, so relax, and someone tell me what I missed in English."

Bex looks at the table and mumbles.

"Sorry?" I say.

She sighs. "We found all the times Shakespeare used the words *dream* and *moon* and talked about what they meant."

"*A Midsummer Night's Dream* has to be the most inane series of words ever strung together and assigned in an English class," I say.

"Yes," Caleb says, looking at me, "because a beautiful girl could never fall in love with an ass."

I'm trying to figure out where he's going with this when Bex shoves him before drawing him into a quiet conversation.

Leo says, "They're pretty protective, aren't they?"

"Yes. I love them, but sometimes I have to remind Bex and Caleb that they're not the boss of me." I pick up my knife and work on cutting my apple into slices so I can dip them into peanut butter—my lunch of choice more often than not. "Do you have people you miss from Knights?"

"A few."

"What was it like?"

"Small. Or at least it felt that way. I guess it has more students than Newton, but because it starts in kindergarten, there's a lot fewer people in each grade." He pauses. "And no girls."

"Disappointing."

"Very," he says. "It could get a little grim. It was out on the edge of this town in the middle of nowhere, and in the fall, they'd burn back the sugarcane fields. The smoke would hang over the ground. I always imagine that's what hell looks like. And it was much more competitive than here, so it was hard to have friends."

I try to imagine an environment more competitive than Newton and fail. Every semester, our class is ranked from one to forty. I've always been in the top five, although because of my humanities scores, I'm never any higher up than third. I once used a differential equation to answer an exam question about the plot of *Pride and Prejudice* (initially a stable system, thrown into disequilibrium by the introduction of something new before achieving a new rest state). This did not go over well.

I ask Leo more about Knights, finding out what he liked (physics, Cajun food, and photography) and what he didn't (morning assemblies, shared rooms, and humidity). Before

I'm ready, the bell rings, and Leo and Caleb leave for coding while Bex and I walk toward the math hallway.

Just before Bex leaves, she says, "You like him, don't you? This Leo McGill?"

"Yes," I say, deciding. "He's my new friend."

CALEB

HERE'S THE THING. I FOLLOWED EVIE INTO ALL the best things in my life—coding and gifted programs and even baseball, which I started because she said it was the sport with the most interesting math. If she asked, I would burn forests, wreck cars, or take Newton apart brick by brick.

But Evie doesn't want destruction. She wants Leo. I know—and thank God for it—that the first person you date isn't the last. But I'm worried.

As long as Evie wasn't into anyone, I could tell myself that one day—when she was ready—she would wake up and see what I meant to her. (Imagining this moment is a hobby of mine. My favorite setting is rainstorms.)

But now she is ready, and she wants someone else. And not just anyone else, but someone perfect for her—quiet and mathy and a little on the outside.

I don't know what to do. Bex thinks I should declare myself, but I already told Evie what I want, and she said she wasn't interested. What good would bringing it up again do?

All of this is making it pretty tough to focus on my coding project, which is due Tuesday. Leo and I are a long way from finished, so we're spending all of our free time in the lab. I can concentrate only because I know he's not with her.

By Friday evening, we're a little bleary-eyed, and the program acts up. We spend thirty minutes scanning code and running diagnostics, but we don't have the time for this. I need Evie. She has an eye for detail that's unmatched, and she's better than anyone at finding my mistakes.

Leo loves this plan.

When she opens the door a few minutes later, we turn toward her. She's self-conscious, and something in me is soothed when she looks to me for reassurance. But as soon as I give her a quick smile, her eyes slide back to Leo, who is out of uniform and wearing one of those obnoxious coder T-shirts (THERE ARE 10 KINDS OF PEOPLE IN THE WORLD: THOSE WHO UNDERSTAND BINARY AND THOSE WHO DON'T). From the way her eyes linger on his chest, Evie's clearly more impressed with it than I am.

She drags her gaze back to me, and I swear I can see the effort it takes. "What do you need?" she asks.

"Can you take a look at this? It's for that browser we're working on. There's got to be a mistake, but we can't find it."

She takes my seat. "Prima donna." Evie says I can't find my own errors because I consider proofreading beneath me. There's some truth to this.

Eyes on the screen, she throws off her hoodie and grabs a pencil to wrap her hair around, and I'm caught. By the way she looks with her hands in her hair, but also by that fierce intensity she radiates whenever she tackles a problem. I will never get tired of watching her mind work on my code.

"Got it," she says, and breaks the spell. Probably a good thing, since I don't think either Leo or I have taken a breath in the last two minutes.

I look over her shoulder.

"There was an extra character at the end of a line. Again." She glares up at me. "Next time I'm not coming unless you check for this first."

I give my best little-kid grin. "Sorry."

Slowly, her expression softens into a smile.

Studying us, Leo says, "Are you sure you're not . . ."

"We're just friends," I answer. Because I want to say it before she does.

It's not nearly enough, but I'm grateful when Evie threads her fingers through mine, and says, "There's nothing 'just' about us."

She lets go of my hand and turns back to the screen, scrolling down as her eyes scan the code. "What is this?" she says, pointing to a couple of lines.

"Error-correcting code. It finds the redundant bits."

"Right. So it's related to Shannon code?"

"Yeah." I have no idea what she's thinking about.

She turns to the screen again, lost in thought while Leo and I exchange puzzled looks. "Can you print this for me?" she asks.

"Sure," I say. "What's up?"

"I think I have an idea for Frontier, but I need you to talk me through how you go from this to binary. How much time do you have this weekend?"

"As much as you need," I say, thrilled.

"I'm going to let Mr. Mitchum know we're ready to run this thing again," Leo says. He slams the door behind him.

Amateur.

EVIE

THE NEXT MORNING DURING YOGA, I SEE MY WAY through the mathematics of my Frontier problem. After I shower and change, I get to work, although I lose a little momentum when Caleb texts to say their browser had a total collapse so he can't meet with me until tomorrow. I try not to panic. We have two weeks.

Because I need references on Clifford algebras and maybe topology to finish, I head to the university library, where I can get my books and grab a sandwich in the café.

Coming down the library steps with my tower of books, I'm surprised to see Leo pointing a camera up into the trees. He's so still. I know I have that ability to focus, but it's pretty much only around math.

When Leo finally lowers the camera, he spots me, and

he's so obviously happy, I'm not even embarrassed that he caught me watching him.

"Carry your books?" he says with an ironic little smile.

"You have all that." I gesture with my head toward the camera around his neck and the backpack slung over his shoulders.

"My hands are free."

After he carefully puts his camera into a case and stuffs it into his backpack, I let him take half the books, watching his hands as he adjusts his grip. Something about the way Leo's been looking at me is making me notice all these little parts of bodies I never thought about before—wrists and collarbones and shoulders. It's very odd.

He looks down at the top book. "*Counterexamples in Topology*? I thought math was combinatorics this semester."

I raise my eyebrows. Usually kids who aren't in math don't pay much attention to what we do.

"I asked about it when I was enrolling," he explains. "I was trying to decide whether to do coding or math as my minor." He gives me a sideways look. "Sadly, I think I made the wrong decision." Does he mean because of me? I need Bex.

"This is for a side project," I say, sticking to familiar ground.

"Frontier?"

I nod and then ask, "Will you submit something?"

"I'm doing some work with manifolds." Those are 3-D models you can use to describe the shapes of potential universes, among other things. He tells me more about the problem he's outlined. Broadly, it's a good topic for Frontier, hitting that sweet spot between mathematics and physics that they like, but nothing he describes sounds particularly original. Maybe he's holding back? If he is, I can't blame him, since when he asks me to tell him about what I'm working on, I do the same.

"What were you doing with the camera?" I ask, wondering if it's somehow related.

"Just taking pictures. Photography's a hobby. I'm still getting used to the light here, though. It's so different from Louisiana."

His mention of Louisiana reminds me of something I've been wondering about. "How come you don't have much of an accent? Or is that rude to ask? I don't always . . ." I stop talking, since I can't seem to finish a sentence.

He laughs. "It's fine. My mom grew up in Ohio, so that's mostly how I talk. I like *y'all*, though. It's useful."

"I like the way you say it," I tell him, and he smiles in a way that makes me feel like I admitted something more.

We're back at Newton now, and we pause on the second-floor landing of the dorm so he can return my books.

"Thanks for this," I say. "I probably wouldn't have made it back without your help."

"I thought you kept Caleb around for heavy lifting."

"He's multipurpose. But we don't spend all of our time together."

"Good to know," Leo says with a mysterious smile before going through the door.

Back in my room, I text Bex to come find me, but she says she needs another couple of hours in the lab. Bio and chem have their practicals on Monday.

By the time she gets to me, I'm lost in my own work. When she sees my books, piles of papers, and the new notes across my whiteboard, she recognizes that I am in what she calls a "mathematics fugue state" and will not be able to attend to anything else until I work through it. Because she is the best friend in the world, she brings me dinner (grilled cheese) in violation of the rules and leaves without saying three words.

It is late Saturday when I wind down. I have the equations and a sketch of the model. Tomorrow, I'll get Caleb working on the program.

I text Bex: *Do you have time for me in the morning?*

She responds: *Sure, although I still have homework. How about the bookstore?*

Perfect.

After breakfast, we take our backpacks and head downtown. We're early enough to get a table by an outlet and make camp.

"So," she says, drawing pictures in the top of her latte with a straw, "what's up?"

I'm not quite sure how to start this conversation. Because Bex's parents don't let her date, and because I am . . . well . . . the way I am, this is new ground.

Eventually, Bex, who's used to helping me out, says, "Is this about Leo?"

"Anita told me I should make more friends. Besides you and Caleb. I thought that's what I was doing, but I think Leo might want something else."

"Yes," Bex says. "He does. What about you?"

I sip my tea and think about her question. Bex waits. This is one of the reasons we can be friends.

Although I've never spent much time thinking about it, I always vaguely assumed that one day I would meet someone. Like, when I was in college or graduate school, and then I'd do all the things people do—fall in love, get married, have children. But I never thought there was any point to doing anything with boys until I was ready for all of that.

And the one time it came up—which I try never to think about—I'd been a little put off by the whole idea. Kissing seemed strange, and honestly, a little unsanitary. I didn't want anyone's saliva—even Caleb's—anywhere near my mouth. But Leo is making me wonder if there might be something to this whole kissing thing.

"Maybe," I say.

"You know you don't have to pay by the word when you talk, right?"

"I'm not totally sure what I want. But maybe I should give this a try? Almost everyone else seems to like it." As soon as I say this, I feel bad for Bex, and I reach for her hand.

She waves me off. "Don't worry about me. My situation is unique. But, Evie, there're two questions here. One, should you start dating? And two, should it be Leo?"

"Who else would it be?" I say, surprised.

Bex gives me a look. I recognize it because it's the same expression Dr. Lewis gets every time he looks at Blake Winters's homework.

"You mean Caleb." I shake my head. "No."

"Why not?"

"What's the longest two people at Newton have ever dated?"

Bex thinks about this. "I think Sasha and Christopher have been together for almost two years."

"And what's the longest Caleb and a girl have ever dated?"

"Three months?"

"And that's an outlier," I say. "Caleb and I have been friends for twelve years, and I need him around for at least twelve more. I like Leo. But I can afford to lose him."

"I don't know if you're thinking about this the right way."

"I can't risk Caleb. I wouldn't even know how to be Evie

without him." I think of the only poem I ever read in an English class and loved, maybe because of the math metaphor. "His firmness makes my circle just."

Bex wrinkles her nose. "What does that mean?"

"Like a compass. He's my center. Home. It's from a poem," I finish apologetically.

"You're sure?"

"It's not just that I don't want to mess up what Caleb and I are. I've known him since kindergarten. It would be pretty weird to kiss him." I consider telling Bex about the terrifying campfire night but decide I don't want to get into all that. "Leo is mysterious. In a good way. And when he looks at me, I go a little fluttery inside."

"Because of his spinning top diagrams?" Bex asks.

"You mock me, but they were gorgeous."

"Are you sure you're thinking about his diagrams and not his shoulders?"

I consider that for a minute. "It could be both," I acknowledge.

When we get back to Newton, we stop at our mailboxes, and Bex pulls out a thick package. She tells me it's a guide to med schools that her parents sent her. Looking at the heavy book, I say, "Don't they understand about the internet?"

"They're just excited. The whole idea of me being a doctor has really brought them around on this science academy thing. They get nervous when I talk about climate change, but saving babies makes sense to them."

I can't totally read Bex's face, but her voice sounds a little sad.

"That's what you want too, right?"

Bex smiles. "Sometimes it's really hard to know what you want."

I can't argue with her there.

CALEB

LEO THROWS A TANTRUM WHEN I LEAVE HIM amid the wreckage of our code on Sunday afternoon, but I remind him of the many hours I've spent in the lab while he's been at soccer. I know it's not me taking a break that he objects to, only what I'm doing. But that doesn't mean I care.

Evie and I walk over to the public library. It's a little farther than the one on the university campus, but the first floor has a sunny atrium where we like to sit, and I'm happy for an excuse to browse the science fiction section.

When Evie starts talking, I get overwhelmed, thinking there is no way I can contribute to her project. My head swims as she describes matrices and Clifford algebras and square-derived adinkras. She can tell she's losing me, so she puts aside the equations and pulls out colorful diagrams of what look like cartoon spaceships. Then she says the magic words: "I want to assign binary addresses to all the dots."

And now we are speaking my language: information processing and bits and code. Yes, I tell her, I can make models of this. Yes, you will be able to rotate them, fold them, and look at them from any angle. And then, as I'm starting to sketch out my ideas with a pencil in her notebook, I see where she's going, and I understand why she was so excited when she saw our code the other day.

Shocked, I look at her. "When we fold these up, match the symmetries, and reassign the addresses, the code will change."

She nods.

"You think it's going to show error-correcting code."

"I do."

I'm pretty sure she's right. "But how can that be? This"—I pick up her notebook—"is a mathematical description of the particles in an atom?"

She nods again.

"But how could error-correcting code be in the equations that model an atom? That would suggest that . . ."

". . . computer code is written into the building blocks of the universe."

I look at her. "We live in the Matrix."

"Don't be ridiculous. There are lots of other explanations."

"Name one."

"We live in the universe and therefore have an intuitive

understanding of the code it's written in, which we replicate with our computers."

"Humph," I say. Her explanation is more plausible but not as much fun.

Evie's phone buzzes. She looks down and sighs. "It's my mother. I'd better take it." She goes out front while I open my laptop and map out ideas for a program that will do what she needs.

When Evie comes back, her eyes are flat. Surprise, surprise. It's a mystery to me how someone so concerned with Evie's mental health can't see what she does to her. Evie won't want to talk about the call, so I propose a distraction.

"Let's play Can You Help Me Find?"

She gives her head a little shake. "I don't have trouble asking for library books anymore."

"Maybe it's time to level up."

Can You Help Me Find? is a game invented by one of Evie's doctors as a form of exposure therapy. She was supposed to go to libraries and ask people to help her find books.

Because she hated doing it, I turned it into a competitive sport. I'd give her something exceedingly ordinary, like *The Book Thief*, and in return she'd force me to ask for *Understanding Puberty: A Boy's Guide*.

I still always won, but we haven't played in years.

Now I look at the catalog on my phone, find a candidate that will be a little more challenging, and push it across to her.

She grins. "Two up, two down?"

I nod. The number of times you can play is limited by the number of people on staff. They get ornery if you bother them too often. There are two librarians down here and two upstairs in children's and young adult. We'll each ask one person on each floor.

Evie takes a deep breath and says, "Give me your phone. I'll never remember all of that." The rules are that you must ask for the title by the full name, and you can offer no explanations about why you want it. She heads off to the front desk. Three minutes later, she's back, tossing *High Performance Beauty: Makeup & Skin Care for Dance, Cheer, Show Choir, Pageants & Ice Skating* on the table.

"Please," she says. "I've had ten years of therapy." She types on her laptop, scrawls something on a piece of paper, and slides it across to me.

I open it and roll my eyes, but I don't get the true mastery of what Evie's done until I see the librarian at the reference desk. Evie's already taken the guy at the front desk, so this seventy-year-old volunteer is my only option. She's wearing a CRAZY CAT LADY sweatshirt, cat earrings, and—I swear to God—a headband with little jeweled cat ears. She is delighted when I ask her to help me find *Why Cats Paint: A Theory of Feline Aesthetics*. It's a long fifteen minutes later when I drop the book on the table in front of Evie.

She smiles up at me. "You found it."

"You are officially in trouble," I say. Playing with Evie is tricky, though. I don't want to do anything to shake her confidence, but she looks lit up from her victory over *High Performance Beauty*. I turn my phone around.

"Caleb!" she says, but I don't back down. She can do this.

"Fine." Evie marches up the stairs. When she comes down a few minutes later, her face is flushed. She drops *My Teen Pregnancy* in front of me without comment.

Then she turns to her computer and spends a frightening amount of time searching. She writes the title down, and as she passes it over, she says, "I asked the librarian in the red shirt."

I take the paper from her and bound up the stairs, opening it on the way. It's *Boy's Guide to Girls: 30 Pointers You Won't Get from Your Parents or Friends*. It could be worse, and who knows, maybe I'll learn something. From the landing, I look into the nonfiction section, where I see the librarian Evie said she talked to, so I turn toward fiction, and there at the desk is Lissa Halverson.

Lissa is a nineteen-year-old, blond-haired, green-eyed elementary education major who occasionally works in the children's section on weekends. I've been flirting with her on and off for the last year. It hasn't gone anywhere, in part because of Evie, who is almost always with me when I'm here, and in part because Lissa knows I'm still in high school. She's told me more than once to let her know if I end up on the campus here next year.

Lissa looks up from what she's reading and says, "Hey, Caleb." I can do this. I remind myself that I don't care about

Lissa Halverson. I never have to come back to this library. Evie cannot scare me.

But the words will not come out of my mouth.

"Are you looking for Evie? I saw her up here a little while ago. I called her name, but I don't think she saw me."

"Oh, I think she did," I say quietly.

"Well, can I help you with something?" She puts her hand on my arm. I think briefly about cheating. I could find the book and bring it down, but that's such a spirit-of-the-game foul.

"No, thanks," I say in defeat.

I'm two steps away when Lissa says, "Did you drop this?" She's holding the slip of paper. It must have fallen out of my hand.

I say, "Ah! No! I mean, yes," and snatch it back.

Lissa does not ask me to look her up next year.

Back downstairs, I chuck the balled-up paper at Evie's laptop. "You are evil, Evie Beckham."

Her expression is aggressively innocent. "Was it checked out?"

I'm caught by the laughter in her eyes, and I hold her gaze as I sink into my chair. Maybe Bex is right. Maybe I should do something.

"How are you feeling about Frontier?" I ask, thinking I'll work up to it.

"Okay. Better now that you're involved. I might actually make it to the conference this year."

I take her hand, exactly as I have hundreds of times before. She's entirely comfortable with this. "I'd have no chance at all without you." I drop my voice to a pitch other girls seem to enjoy. "We're good for each other, Eves." Watching her carefully, I brush my thumb along the inside of her wrist, trying to see if there's anything there without spooking her.

Oblivious, she smiles. "Anita says sometimes friends grow apart when they get older, but I told her that wouldn't happen with us."

I look into her eyes, searching for any kind of encouragement, but there's nothing. So I say, "Of course not," and drop her hand.

EVIE

THE NEXT DAY, CALEB'S NOT AT BREAKFAST, AND he's not in physics either. When I text to check in, he tells me he was up late coding and slept in. I can't remember this ever happening before. Maybe I'm a bad influence on him?

Leo asks if I made any progress on Frontier over the weekend.

"We did," I say. "How about you?"

"Not so much. We found a hydra, so we had to spend all our free time this weekend rebuilding the program."

I already know the outline of this story from Caleb, but he didn't share the details. "What's a hydra?"

"A bug—every time you fix it, two new ones appear. Essentially makes the program useless."

I wince. "One of the many reasons I don't like coding. In math, problems sit quietly while you solve them."

Leo grins. "But where's the fun in that?" My stomach flips.

Dr. Lewis turns on the projector and says, "We're going to start with Bostrom's 2003 essay. It's pretty different from what you're used to in this class, so why don't you take a few minutes to refamiliarize yourselves with it?"

I did not enjoy the essay, but I am plenty familiar, and another five minutes of review is not going to make me like it any better.

"You're not impressed?" Leo says, looking at my face as I flip pages.

"There's not a single bit of proof in here. Not an equation or a model or an empirical observation. It's a fairy tale."

"But an interesting one."

"Maybe," I concede. "But I don't want to read it in my physics class."

Dr. Lewis, who should know better, attempts to call me out for my lack of attention: "Ms. Beckham, please feel free to continue gazing at Mr. McGill, but could you also summarize Bostrom's arguments for the simulation?"

This is an entirely new level of hostility from Dr. Lewis. I can't stop my cheeks from warming, but in defiance, I answer without looking down at the essay or turning away from Leo. "Bostrom argued that at least one of the following statements must be true. One: No civilization can survive long enough to create realistic simulations of universes populated with intelligent life. Or two: Some civilizations do survive that long but choose not to run simulations of living beings because of ethical concerns. Or three: Our universe is, most likely, a simulation, because if simulations exist, it figures that there would be many more simulated universes than real ones."

Leo raises his eyebrows and mouths, "And while gazing."

"And in your opinion, Ms. Beckham, which of those statements is true?"

I turn back toward the front of the room, so irritated by the essay that I'm not even self-conscious. "The first. Artificial intelligence, okay. Maybe some machine-based consciousness. But the entire architecture of the universe, including the self-aware beings who populate it? That's incredibly unlikely."

"And do you agree, Mr. McGill?"

"No."

I look back at Leo.

"And what evidence would you offer Ms. Beckham?"

"I'm sure Evie would say that given the incredible complexity of simulating a universe, we would expect some gaps, things that wouldn't make sense to the self-conscious inhabitants of the simulation."

I fold my arms over my chest. "I would."

"And could you point her toward any such gaps?" Dr. Lewis asks.

He grins. "Well, we can only find about five percent of our universe. That's a pretty big gap."

My mouth falls open. "Dark energy. That's your evidence that we're living in a computer simulation?"

"And dark matter."

I peer at him, trying to figure out if he means what he's saying. "That's ridiculous."

"Uh-oh," Dr. Lewis says with a sigh. "Trouble in paradise." The class laughs, and Dr. Lewis moves on to torment other students.

At the end of class, he passes back our exams, putting them facedown on our desks. Leo and I turn ours over at the same time. We both got perfect scores. After looking at our own tests, we trade papers without comment. Flipping through his, I see that he lost two points on the fourth page because of a careless error but got them back as extra credit on the fifth page, where he used my solution to solve the last problem. Next to this, Dr. Lewis wrote, "Simple and clear!" I can't help rolling my eyes.

Leo smiles at this and says, "I concede defeat."

∞ ∞ ∞ ∞ ∞ ∞ ∞ ∞ ∞ ∞ ∞

When I meet Caleb in the lounge, I ask if he's okay.

"Sure. Just couldn't face physics this morning. You have every right to mock me for missing class, but please let me have your notes anyway. I'd hate to flunk out at this point."

"You'll be fine. We talked about that inane essay that argues that we're all living in a computer simulation."

"I loved that piece," Caleb says.

"That's because it makes coders into gods."

"We don't need an essay for that."

Our social science class this semester is religion and ethics, which I'm finding even more unpleasant than the usual humanities classes. This is largely because the teacher, Abbie, thinks it's her special mission to unlock our right brains. She dresses in flowing skirts and scarves, calls us by our first names, insists we do the same with her, and occasionally steps out of her ugly sandals to wander around the classroom barefoot. Our first assignment was a collage. It was upsetting.

Since I didn't grow up in a religious home, I am encountering a lot of religious stories for the first time and finding them pretty troubling. Bex seems alternately amused and disturbed by my ignorance.

Today, Abbie's long blond hair is down around her shoulders. In her floor-length pink dress, she looks like an aging wood fairy. She surprises me by looking down at her grade book and saying, "Evelyn, I don't think you've said more than three words all semester."

I look up at her and freeze.

My mouth goes dry, and an all-too-familiar heaviness settles in my chest.

It's been a long time since I've felt this level of discomfort about speaking in a class. I never enjoy the conversations after gallery walks in physics, but I'm not swamped by physical sensations the way I am now. My heart rate goes up, and my breathing becomes shallower. It's not a full-on panic attack, but it's headed in that direction.

I close my eyes and count my breaths, willing my pulse to slow as I practiced in so many CBT sessions. I slide my hands between my legs. If you can get them warm, you can trick your brain into thinking it hasn't engaged the flight response.

Psychology is its own kind of magic.

Caleb leaps in to fill the space while I get myself together.

"Abbie, there seems to be a disturbing amount of human sacrifice in the Bible," he says. "Maybe you could talk about that."

Hearing his voice—even saying the words *human sacrifice*—calms me.

"Yes, yes," she says. "But first I want to hear from Evelyn. Is there a reason you don't participate?"

In my head, I say the things I've practiced: *It doesn't matter that I don't know. The danger isn't real. This is Newton. My classmates are not looking for reasons to attack.*

My heartbeat slows.

When I can speak, I say, "Religion is not so much my thing, 'Abbie.'" My voice is quiet, and I can hear myself putting her name in quotation marks. It didn't bother me at all when Anita asked me to call her by her first name—it seemed right in a relationship so intimate—but Abbie's decision to do it at Newton, where the convention is so much the opposite, feels like an affectation.

"Too improbable?" she asks.

"No, that's not it," I say, grateful that she's led me back to firmer ground. *Improbable* is a word I've thought about. "I believe that if we know how fast a quantum particle is going, we can't know where it is. I believe that how we *will* observe particles in the future changes what they are now. And I am willing to believe we live in eleven or thirteen or twenty-six dimensions coiled together like little balls of string. As much as I might wish otherwise, the universe is full of improbable things."

Caleb coughs into his hand and says, "Simulation," and everyone who was in physics laughs.

"Then why don't you engage in the class?" Abbie persists, ignoring the laughter. I think about all the stories we've been reading, and look over at Bex, remembering her uncharacteristically fragile expression when she showed me that ring from her parents.

"It's not so much that I find religion improbable. It's more that I don't get this God. He makes all these rules about eating lobsters and wearing clothes made out of different fabrics, but He's completely lax about parents sacrificing their children. And I don't like that part where He drowns everyone on the planet and celebrates with a rainbow. That's not nice."

This is pretty much the most I've ever said in a class other than physics or math. Caleb gives me an encouraging smile, and I know he's thinking that if I can do this, I can do Frontier. On the other hand, Bex looks like she's expecting a lightning strike to take me out. Abbie watches me silently for a moment. Then she gives a little laugh.

"Well, if nothing else, I guess you've done the reading," she says, making a little tick in her book.

My comments launch a swirl of discussion. Abbie focuses on two topics: the impossibility of humanity understanding God's grand plan, and the redemptive role of Jesus in the Christian faith. I go back to being silent. I'm not interested in any plan I'm not allowed to understand, and I have no problem with Jesus. It's unreasonable to hold children responsible for the behavior of their parents.

CALEB

AFTER SCHOOL, WHEN THE THREE OF US MEET IN the lounge to start on homework, Bex turns to Evie and says, "You know the rainbow isn't celebrating the genocide, right? It's His promise not to do it again."

Evie shrugs. "I'm not all that impressed by the distinction."

"It's a parable. It's not like it was real," Bex says. She's irritated with Evie, which almost never happens. "The geological record proves there was never a worldwide flood."

"I know," Evie responds, obviously surprised Bex would think she didn't. "But that doesn't make the story any less horrible. Children would have died, Bex."

Bex looks at Evie for a long moment, then shakes her head. "I guess you're right. It's just that I remember reading all those Noah's Ark picture books as a child. The story felt hopeful then."

"All the animals get partnered up," I say. "That's hopeful."

"Unless you're the unicorn," Bex says.

Evie looks back and forth between us a bit, decides she doesn't want to know, and pulls out her physics article. She spends the next half hour trying to read, but mostly she stares off into space and twirls her hair around her finger. Bex and I watch her and exchange a look. Evie doesn't notice.

"Trouble concentrating?" I say.

With a sympathetic look at me, Bex says, "Leo asked Evie to go to his soccer game tonight."

I manage to smile. "I'm not surprised," I say to Evie. "Leo's about five minutes from grabbing a Sharpie and writing 'Mine' across your forehead."

Evie opens her eyes wide. "Really?"

Despite everything, I laugh. "Not literally, Eves. I just meant he wants to make this thing between you public so everyone else will back off." By everyone else, I mean me, but I keep this to myself. "When you told him you were going to spend the weekend working with me on Frontier, he—"

Freaking. Leo. Freaking. McGill. I can't believe I didn't figure this out earlier, but I didn't think he was this diabolical. (Or this good.) Leo went full-on Anonymous on our coding midterm: He wrote a bug into our browser so I'd be tied up in the lab all weekend instead of with Evie.

"Caleb?" Bex asks. "Is everything okay?"

I shake my head, brushing aside the question. I throw

my French book into my bag. "I have to go. What are you two going to do?"

"Dinner. And then the game," Bex says. She looks worried.

I smile reassuringly. I can do this. If I love Evie for real—and I think I do—then I need to get out of her way so she can go get what she wants.

"I'll meet you when it's time to walk over," I say. "Grab me something to eat?"

"Sure," Evie says, her mind elsewhere.

∞ ∞ ∞ ∞ ∞ ∞ ∞ ∞ ∞ ∞ ∞ ∞

When I go up to the lab to review our old files, I see that I'm right. Leo introduced that hydra Friday night because he didn't want me spending all that time with Evie. I'm sympathetic to a point. What I can't forgive is not making a new backup before he did it. We had to rewrite three days of code, and we're still behind.

When I meet Bex and Evie at the front door, Evie's wearing a pale blue shirt, a short jean skirt, and her boots. She's carrying her white jacket and a pink scarf, and her hair is down and sprinkled throughout with little pastel butterflies, which are so silly and unlike her, I know they must have come from Bex. It's . . . adorable.

I give Bex a half-playful anguished look, and she squeezes my hand. Newton soccer games are played at the university's practice stadium, a good mile walk. Bex plays in the same place in the spring, and Evie and I have been there a ton to watch her. When we arrive, it's not quite dark, but the lights are on.

I reach for Evie's hand to lead her up the bleachers, which are all on one side of the field.

"I am perfectly capable of climbing bleachers on my own," she says.

"And I am perfectly capable of acting like a gentleman." I pull her up the next step, focusing on the feel of her hand in mine and trying not to think about how this easy contact between us will change if she and Leo get serious. There was always an odd renegotiation between us whenever I dated someone. My girlfriends generally did not enjoy seeing me hold someone else's hand. I can't imagine Leo will feel differently about Evie.

We sit on the far end, and Leo looks up at Evie from the field, where he's doing those odd bounces soccer players do to warm up. Evie waves, and he smiles.

After kickoff, the ball shoots toward the other team's goal, and Leo moves up to half field with the other defenders. Bex becomes absorbed in the game, occasionally hollering at the players. I've never seen her on the sidelines, and her intensity is a little frightening.

When the ball gets booted back down to our end of the field, Leo traps it and kicks it to Caden, who breaks away from the kid defending him and scores almost immediately. The other team—a school from somewhere I've never heard of—is outmatched, and most of the action is happening in front of their goal, leaving Leo with little to do. Even so, he's looking up at Evie more often than is probably wise.

To torment him, I put my arm around her shoulders while I explain the finer points of the game, which I mostly make up. The offside rules in soccer are particularly mysterious to me, but it makes no difference to Evie, who doesn't care at all about sports. I could probably switch over to the rules of Quidditch without her noticing.

She turns toward me to ask a question, bringing her face temptingly close. I can't help but think about how easy it would be to close the gap between us. But I don't.

Instead, I think: *Almost-kiss number fifteen.*

EVIE

AFTER THE GAME, I MEET LEO ON THE SIDELINES.

"Thanks for coming," he says.

"Congratulations on the win."

"Not much for me to do today." He glances up at where Caleb and Bex are still sitting and says, "Which was just as well." Leo's eyes roam over the butterflies Bex put in my hair. "You look cute. Can you wait while I get cleaned up? We could go get something to eat? I missed dinner."

"Okay," I say. This must be a real date. I wasn't sure when Leo asked me to come, despite everything Bex said. "Bex and Caleb will stay with me until you're ready."

"I'll hurry." He takes two steps away and then comes back. "Actually, can we try something first? So then we can relax and enjoy the night?"

"What do you have in mind?"

He smiles before lowering his mouth toward mine.

Oh.

Do I want this?

Maybe.

I definitely don't *not* want it.

He stops, his mouth inches from mine. "Is this okay?"

I nod, at a loss for words. I hadn't expected this to happen quite so fast. Or in front of so many people.

Then he kisses me, and perhaps more remarkably, I kiss him back, my lips moving in response to his, as if answering a question. This is not something you have to learn to do, I realize. The knowledge lies dormant until it's needed.

Leo pulls back and looks into my eyes. "Was that okay?"

"I think I liked it." I can hear the surprise in my voice.

He laughs. "I'm glad. Ten minutes." He runs off toward the field house.

The stands have mostly cleared by now, but Caleb and Bex are still there. I wish they hadn't seen that.

Caleb whispers in Bex's ear, and I feel a flash of . . . I don't know—wrongness, I guess. I remember the hurt on his face when I pushed him away all that time ago. But surely he understands why it has to be like this. It's like Bex says: We are sacred and non-carnal.

I should go talk to them, but I'm embarrassed, and I don't know what to say, so I turn back to the now-empty field, wondering about what's coming next. I'm about to go out to eat with someone I've kissed. How does that work?

After a few minutes, I hear Bex and Caleb come up behind me. Bex touches me on the shoulder, and I turn toward her.

"You all right over here?"

I nod. Then I look at Caleb, a little nervous. "Are we okay?"

He smiles. "Always." And I have to wipe away the tears that spring up in response.

Then Leo's out of the field house and moving back toward us. Bex hugs me and whispers in my ear, "Come see me when you get home. I want to hear all about it."

Caleb stuffs his hands in his pockets as he turns, saying, "Night, Eves. Don't do anything I wouldn't do."

"That's a few more degrees of freedom than I need."

They go, and it's incredibly strange to see them leaving together, Caleb's head bending toward Bex as he listens to her. A pang of loss and a fluttery sense of happiness tumble around inside of me, and I don't understand how my body can hold two such opposing feelings at the same time.

Emotions are nothing like mathematics. You don't put positive and negative feelings together and end up with some neutral middle. Instead, it's like occupying two different places on the number line simultaneously, which makes feelings more like quantum physics, I guess.

Leo puts his hand on my back and suggests walking over to a diner on the other end of campus. I agree, eager to put aside my confusion.

An older waitress seats us in a booth in the back corner of the restaurant, saying, "Aren't you just too cute" in a tone

I find intolerable. I take off my jacket and rest my hands on the sticky table, trying not to think about what Bex might see under a microscope if I brought a sample back. Without opening the menu, Leo asks for French toast and orange juice. I say, "Hot chocolate" when she turns to me.

There's a moment of awkward silence, and then Leo says, "Should we get the name, rank, and serial number stuff out of the way?"

When I give him a confused look, he adds, "Middle name, birthday, favorite color—all those things it's embarrassing not to know after you've kissed someone."

I blush, and his blue eyes crinkle at the corners.

"Evelyn Jane, April second, turquoise." I wonder how many times he's done this, but I'm not quite brave enough to ask.

"Evelyn Jane," he repeats slowly. "It suits you. You're not really frivolous enough to be an Evie."

Leo says this like it's a compliment, but I'm not opposed to frivolity.

Then he says, "Leo Henry, December thirtieth, and lately partial to any color that's not blue, black, or gray."

"I always think December birthdays are sad. You get all your presents at once."

His eyes flick away from mine, and something flashes across his face too fast for me to decipher, but he says only, "I guess."

I wait for him to say more. When he doesn't, I fold my

hands together and look down, anxious about explaining this but feeling like it's necessary.

"If we're going to . . . if you're going to be around me . . . you should know that I can't always figure out what people mean if they don't put it into words." I glance up. "So I know something just happened, but you're going to have to tell me what."

"Feels like a dark turn for a first date." He sighs. "When I was little, I lived with just my mom, and she had some problems. Then I was in the foster system some. It wasn't until middle school that my foster mom, Kate, adopted me and things got more stable. There were a lot of years when there weren't many presents."

"How long were you at Knights?"

"I started in ninth grade. It was okay. A lot of new kids came for high school. It was harder coming here."

"Why did you?" I ask.

"More classes, and they have a scholarship program where if you graduate from Newton, you can go to the university and live there for free as a resident assistant."

I nod. This is what Evan does.

The waitress appears, carrying a tray, and sets a giant mug of hot chocolate in front of me with an elegant mound of whipped cream covered in tiny chocolate curls.

"Wow."

I unwrap my spoon from the napkin and scoop up some of the whipped cream before closing my eyes to focus on the taste. The cream melts in my mouth first, only slightly sweet, followed by hits from the grated chocolate. Amazing. I open my eyes to tell Leo this is my new favorite restaurant and find him watching me, his fork poised above his plate, with a look that sends heat flooding through my entire body.

I look down at the table.

"I'm getting the idea that you're kind of new at this," Leo says.

"You could say that." And then something alarming occurs to me. "Wait. Are you saying that because I was bad at the kissing part?"

"No. You were amazing at the kissing part. But did it bother you that I did it in front of so many people? You seemed a little freaked out."

"I'm not sure how I felt about the audience," I say honestly, hoping I don't hurt his feelings. "Was it because you were trying to write on my forehead?"

Leo gives me a startled look. "Was I what?"

I explain Caleb's Sharpie comment.

"That's ridiculous."

"I thought so too."

"I wouldn't mar your face. Back of your hand is as far as it would have gone."

I giggle.

Leo studies me. "I'm having a hard time reconciling that laugh with the Evie the Ice Queen meme."

"There's a meme?"

"There may as well be. There are a lot of Evie Beckham crash-and-burn stories."

"Daniel Chao," I say darkly. When we were sophomores, Daniel asked me to go to the Spring Fling with him. Over and over again. My last refusal may have been rather loud. And also pretty public. People like to tell the story.

"That one was brutal, Evelyn Jane. Made me a little worried about tonight."

"You didn't need to be."

"No," he says. "I guess not."

As we walk home through the campus, he takes my hand in his, wrapping his fingers around mine instead of lacing them together the way Caleb does. It's different, but nice.

The night is clear and cold without being unpleasant, yet the campus is strangely quiet.

Searching for a topic of conversation, I remember physics this morning and ask, "Do you really think all this could be a simulation?"

"No. I just said that to irritate you."

"It worked. Bostrom isn't even a physicist. He's some philosopher who thinks he's clever. What about parallel universes?" This is the reading for tomorrow.

"Maybe. When the math leads you somewhere, I think you have to follow, even if it seems improbable."

"It's strange to think about, though. I don't feel like I'm one of millions of Evies."

"I'm not sure that's much of an argument. Do you feel

like you're hurtling around the sun at thousands of miles per hour?"

I look up at him. "Only when I'm with you."

"Cute."

We cross the street between the campus and the Newton grounds, going around back through the sculpture garden.

On the stairs leading to the back door, he stops one step below me and takes my hands again. "I find you strangely distracting."

"Strangely?" I ask, not liking the qualifier.

"Well, it's not like you've been trying to get my attention. Unlike some people I could name."

I narrow my eyes at him. Now that I've been watching, I've seen quite a few girls doing a lot of arm-touching and hair-tossing around Leo. "I considered it, but the strategies employed didn't seem to be getting the desired results."

"I promise that you would have found those strategies quite effective," he says. "I had no idea if you were interested, and I'd have found a little pencil-dropping or eyelash-fluttering reassuring."

So I bat my eyelashes. He grins and kisses me.

CALEB

ALL I CAN THINK IS THAT SHE HAD HER FIRST kiss, and it wasn't with me.

I'm lying on the floor, hands behind my head, trying to pull off rakish. My mood is more facedown, spread-eagled, but the lounge is jittery with talk of Evie and Leo, and tomorrow will be easier for all of us if I can keep from looking devastated tonight. Bex is doing her best to help me through this, but she can't make the audience go away.

It's hard to find places to be alone at Newton. Or rather, being alone is easy—we all have single rooms. But the tight security and constant surveillance make being alone with someone else tricky. This is a problem Sarah-Kate and I were unable to adequately solve last spring. And we put some shoulder into it.

So Bex and I have taken over a quiet corner of the lounge, and I'm letting my body show as much misery as I can get away with.

Bex, who is lying on the couch above me, props her head up on her hand and looks down. "I'm sorry, Caleb."

I turn my eyes toward her but don't speak.

"I know this is hard."

"Well, gravity is doing most of the work right now."

"Oh, you tragic clown," she says pityingly.

I study her face. "You're prettier than she is. Margot too. Objectively speaking."

"And are you objective?"

"God, no, Bex." I pull one of my arms out from under my head and drape it across my face. "There were these two trees in my backyard that grew all twisted around each other. One year, one got struck by lightning, and we had to cut it down. But when you look at the one that's still there, you can see all the spaces where that other tree is supposed to be. Its whole existence is a response. That's me and Evie."

"I've seen you twisted around plenty of other trees."

"Nice. Thank you for cheapening my romantic metaphor. I dated other girls because she wasn't interested, and I wanted to be sure how I felt." My eyes are still hidden under my arm, but I sense her raising her eyebrows at me, so I grin. "And it was fun."

"That's all this is for her. She loves you."

"Just not like that."

"Yes," Bex says. "Like that. But she doesn't know it yet."

I take my arm off my head and sit up so my face is even with hers. "What do you know?"

She lies back on the couch. "It's hard being friends with you both sometimes."

"Bex," I say, and there's enough desperation in my voice that she gives in.

"I asked her what the difference was between how she felt about Leo and how she felt about you. She said Leo's mysterious, and he makes her feel fluttery." She gives me a little look of apology.

After a few moments of silence, I say, "Don't make me ask."

"Caleb, she said you're home. That you make her circle just. Evie Beckham quoted poetry, for goodness' sake. Right now, she thinks this trembly, anxious feeling is exciting, but she'll figure it out. Deep down, she knows what she wants."

I think about this. "I could be mysterious."

"No. No. That's not what I'm saying. Give her some time. She's only just figuring out what it means to feel something like this."

"What if she never figures it out, Bex?" Saying this out loud feels dangerous. As if I'm giving the universe ideas.

Bex scrambles off the couch and wraps her arms around me.

"For what it's worth, I think she will."

I rest my head on hers. "I hope so."

ꝏ ꝏ ꝏ ꝏ ꝏ ꝏ ꝏ ꝏ ꝏ ꝏ ꝏ ꝏ

In the morning, I text Evie to ask if she'll check the corrections I made to my physics midterm. I'm desperate to know some things won't change. She tells me to meet her in the hallway, and when I get there, Leo's leaning against the wall, smiling down at her.

I hear him say, "Do you smell like this to everyone, or did you fry my circuits last night so now I confuse desire with French toast?"

She laughs, and I think, *Cinnamon and vanilla. That's what Evie smells like.* I hand her my test, doing my best not to think about what might have been involved in the circuit-frying.

Margot leans back against the wall next to Leo and across from me. To Evie, she says, "Nice pull. Does this mean you're turning Caleb loose?"

I look at her. "If you think we broke up because of Evie, you weren't paying attention." I didn't enjoy her cat video obsession any more than Evie did.

Evie looks up from my paper. "Caleb's all about catch and release. I wouldn't take it personally."

"It's all catch and release until the last one," I say. Leo gives me a look, which I ignore.

The bell rings. As we move toward the door, Evie hands me my test and says I'm missing a step in the last problem.

Dr. Lewis, who's writing on the board, looks at the four of us over his shoulder and says, "School bus late this morning, boys and girls?"

I work through the warm-up problem methodically while Leo and Evie race to the solution. Then Evie rolls a pencil off her desk toward Leo. He grins, clearly at some private joke, and then retrieves it for her before I can use it to put out both my eyes.

Dr. Lewis collects our papers and says, "Today, my friends, we put away the childish things of Newtonian physics and turn our attention toward the wonderful world of quantum weirdness. Can someone give me an example of what we might mean when we use this phrase?"

David calls out, "Heisenberg's uncertainty principle."

"Which is?"

"We can't know everything there is to know about a particle at any given time. Like, the more we know about how fast it's going, the less we know about where it is."

"Strange but true. Others? Mr. McGill?"

"Observer effects?"

"Example?"

"Delayed-choice experiments. If you're measuring the path of a photon and you change what you're measuring midflight, then you change what it was when it started. Essentially changing the past."

"No," someone says.

"This is why we call it weirdness," Dr. Lewis responds. "Anything else?"

"Isn't Schrödinger's cat observer effects too?" I ask.

"Yes, that's the famous one. Care to explain?"

"A cat's in a box with a poison that will be triggered by the decay of a radioactive particle. As long as no one observes it, the particle is both decayed and not decayed and the cat is both dead and alive. But as soon as someone looks in the box, goodbye, cat."

"Feeling pessimistic this morning, Mr. Covic? It could just as well be alive. The point is the particle is in superposition—both decayed and not—until observed," Dr. Lewis says. "Let's get one more example before we move on to the readings."

"Spooky action at a distance," Evie says.

"You know he was being—" Dr. Lewis starts.

"Sarcastic, yes," Evie cuts him off. The more arcane the topic, the more confident she is, and I am here for it. "Einstein may not have cared for it, but experiments show it's true. Two particles can get so entangled that their connection can never be undone. For the rest of their existence, however far apart they are, what happens to one will affect the other."

I study the back of her neck, looking at the stray curls that have escaped her bun. Entangled. Dr. Lewis hates it when we use physics concepts as social metaphors, but I'm captivated by this one. I like the idea of entanglement not as something that joins you together physically but as something that forever alters who you are and what you do.

For the rest of our existence, Evie.

"I know last night's readings seem a little out there, but that was true of most big ideas in physics at some point. Let's try some small-group conversations to see if you can make sense of the Many-Worlds Interpretation. And the dream team can stay together." He gestures to Leo, David, Evie, and me. "I want to hear what the rest of you are thinking."

Yippee. I'm on the dream team.

"The idea here," David says after we draw our desks together, "is that in the multiverse, there's a different universe for every possible decision—quantum or otherwise?"

"Sort of," Leo and Evie say at the same time. They grin at each other, delighted by their hive mind. Leo defers to Evie.

She says, "With Many-Worlds, particles don't come out of superposition because of observation. Both outcomes happen each time, but in different universes. Two cats: one dead, one alive. Every time a choice is made, the timeline branches off, creating a new universe, so the number of yous in the multiverse is increasing exponentially all the time."

"I hate that," I say.

"The mathematics is cleaner than the theory," she says. "And the good thing is you don't have to worry too much about your decisions, because you know that somewhere out there, another you is making the choice you're leaving on the table."

I gaze back at her, thinking that if this is true, in some other universe, another Caleb has gotten to kiss his Evie each of the fifteen times I decided not to. "Maybe it's not the worst theory ever," I say.

EVIE

IN THE BREAK BETWEEN PHYSICS AND HUMAN-
ities, I let Leo lead me into a deserted hallway instead of following Caleb into the lounge.

"What are we doing?" I ask, although I think I know.

"I'm still pretty new here. I thought you could give me
a tour."

I look around. I'm not actually sure where we are. "I think
this is world languages." I point vaguely in the direction of a
classroom. "Spanish?"

"French," he says with a smile. "Didn't you have to take a
language?"

"I did two years of Latin. There were only five of us, so we
met in the library. I took it because the instructor promised
we didn't have to talk."

Leo stops and gently backs me up against the wall. "Evie?"

"Yes?" I whisper.

"I promise you don't have to talk."

All in all, I like kissing more than I expected to. It's less slobbery than I imagined, and it makes me feel floaty. Also normal.

Given everything that's going on, I have a hard time tracking the conversations in both my humanities classes, although I don't think this is entirely my fault. In religion, the discussion seems to be about foods mentioned in the Bible (*why?*), while in English, the focus is on the symbolism of monsters and fairies (*why? why?*). I can hardly believe I have to take midterms on these subjects.

When Leo arrives at lunch, he tilts my chin up and kisses my nose by way of greeting. This is a little much, and I'm trying to figure out how to discourage it, but nicely, when Caleb says, "Could you two dial the cuteness back to a level no higher than hamsters eating popcorn?"

"We can try, but I'm not optimistic," Leo says, wrapping one of my curls around his finger. Gently, I take Leo's hand and pull it out of my hair. We don't need to do this here, in front of Bex and Caleb.

Leo looks between me and Caleb. "Evie said this was okay with you."

"It is," Caleb says with a look I can't make sense of.

Automatically, I turn to Bex.

"Amused," she says after a pause. I meet her eyes. Because no, it wasn't. I sometimes miss the subtleties in facial expressions, but I know what Caleb looks like when he's amused.

She shrugs, turns to Leo, and says, "Infatuated."

I look up at him, and he smiles. "Got that right."

∞ ∞ ∞ ∞ ∞ ∞ ∞ ∞ ∞ ∞ ∞

Leo has soccer in the afternoon, which makes it easy to slip away to see Anita without having to lie or provide explanations I don't want to give.

She begins by asking if I had any episodes this week, and I tell her about the way I froze in Abbie's class. "But I did my breathing exercises, and then I answered her question. It turned out fine."

"What was going on while you calmed down?"

"Caleb covered for me."

Anita nods as though she expected this. "What would you have done if he hadn't been there?"

"Waited, I guess. A little silence wouldn't have hurt anything."

Anita doesn't answer, but she sits back, so I think I've pleased her.

For the rest of the session, I talk about Leo, feeling like an ordinary teenage girl who's had her first kiss and gone out on a date. Take that, psychiatric industrial complex.

On the way home, Bex texts to ask if I want to do tea party night. I tell her I'll stop at the store and come to her room.

My freshman year, I sometimes got a little overwhelmed by all the people everywhere all the time and would hide in my room to eat every now and then. Bex turned this into an event by joining me with a china tea set and candles. I'm pretty comfortable at Newton now, but she and I still do this sometimes when we want to catch up alone.

Tea party night is all about finger food, so I buy cheese and crackers, little cups of hummus and peanut butter, celery sticks, strawberries, and mini cupcakes.

Bex's room is an odd mix of pink floral bedding, inspirational quotes, and prints of Surrealist artwork. But the thing I can never stop looking at is a giant, full-color graph of the projected rise in the earth's temperature. There's a yellow line showing when food supplies will grow scarce and a red line showing when life on the planet will become untenable. I'd have a nervous breakdown if this were the first thing I saw every morning, but Bex says it helps her focus.

Bex spreads a picnic blanket on the floor, sets out the teapot and plates, and puts on classical music. I arrange the food, and we curl up beside each other to eat.

Out of the blue, Bex asks, "Are you applying anywhere other than the University of Chicago?"

Surprised, I look at her. "Why would I? Do you think I won't get in?"

"Of course you'll get in. But you don't even want to look at anywhere else?"

"I really don't. I love their theoretical physics program. The campus is the right size. And I can cope with the people who go there. I can't be at one of those face-painter schools," I say with a little shudder. Caleb is thinking about Madison, but we went to a football game there once, and it scared the living daylights out of me. "And besides, you'll be there. Right?"

There's a little flash of panic, but I breathe through it.

"Sure," she says. "Although I'm having some second thoughts about my major. They have this great climate science program."

"Could you go to med school after that?"

"I could," she says slowly. "If I wanted to."

I study her face. "But you don't?"

"Evie, I think I picked medicine to make my parents happy."

I completely understand this. "That's why I stayed on my anxiety meds for so long. To make my mom happy. But I had to do what was right for me. Anita helped me see that."

"I don't want to disappoint them," Bex says. "Or have them think I'm siding with the enemy. They already worry about that because I'm here."

"It's scary," I say, thinking about Mom. "But sometimes you have to be brave." This advice is a lot easier to give than to follow.

After I leave Bex, I go up to the computer lab to see if Leo can afford to take a break. He's so focused on what he's doing that he doesn't notice me until I'm right next to him. When he finally looks up, I say, "I was thinking about a walk. Do you want to come?"

"I'd love to, but I'd better stay here. We're still behind, and it's pretty much my fault."

"Why? Caleb's the major. Shouldn't this be his show?"

"Remember the hydra?"

I nod. "But how was that your fault?"

"Because he wrote it into our midterm on purpose less than a week before it was due," Caleb says venomously, coming up behind me. "So take that face that launched a thousand bugs right back out of here. He can't think straight when you're around."

Leo grimaces at Caleb. "I never asked—how did you figure it out?"

"Yoda conditions. You may as well have signed your name." At my blank look, Caleb says, "Your boyfriend writes his code backwards." I start a little at the word *boyfriend*. Is that what Leo is now? After one date and a couple of kisses? I sort of thought there'd be a conversation first.

Leo opens his mouth to respond, but Caleb talks over him. "Do *not* say it's easier to debug that way, or I swear I will lose it." He turns to me. "And you. You need to leave before he decides to drag a magnet across our hard drive to impress you."

"I don't know what any of this has to do with me," I say, a little alarmed by Caleb's fury. This is not like him.

Both Leo and Caleb look at me in silence, and the solution clicks into place.

Focusing on Leo, I say, "You put the hydra into the program on purpose . . . because you didn't want Caleb working with me all weekend."

"In my defense, it wasn't so much the working I was worried about."

Caleb smacks him on the back of the head. "That's not a defense. *And* you didn't make a backup first. Three days of work gone." He points at me and says, "Leave!" Then he points at Leo and says, "Code!" before stalking off back to his computer.

I turn to go, thinking Caleb is a little bit marvelous when he's angry.

CALEB

BY WEDNESDAY AFTERNOON, MY ROUGHEST edges are smoothed out. Both humanities midterms are behind me, and despite Leo's stunt, we got the browser turned in on time, and it's good. Because of Dean Santori's Frontier lust, for the next three afternoons, Evie and I have one of Newton's coveted study rooms (Orwellian in name, because they are rarely used for studying).

In between my work on the browser and rereading Shakespeare, I've been writing Evie's program. I'm impatient to see if it will work. When I started this, it was only for her. A way of offering my presence on the Frontier stage so she'd feel confident enough to do what I know she's capable of: school a room full of geniuses.

But the more time I spend on this and the more I read about Frontier, the more a second reason circles around and around in my head. One I can't bring myself to say out loud: MIT. Where magnetic core memory was invented. Quarks discovered. Electronic encryption created. I want to be a part of it, and the wanting is a visceral thing.

This fall, I let myself apply there to keep the dream alive a little longer, but I try not to think about it, because I'm not sure I can get in. My test scores are good, but not rock star level like Evie's. Plus, my parents make too much money for me to be eligible for much financial aid but not enough that cost doesn't matter. They've already spent the equivalent of one college education on Newton, and I have two brothers coming up behind me. If they had to, they could manage the tuition, but I feel too guilty to ask. But if Evie and I make it to Frontier, admission won't be a problem. And if we finish in the top five, there is the scholarship.

The door opens, and Evie appears looking flushed and starry-eyed. I return my gaze to my laptop, trying not to think about why she looks like that. Running from the math hall, I tell myself.

"Let's see my program!" she says.

"How do you know it's done?"

"Because I know you, Caleb."

She's right, but I'm irritated by her certainty after everything Bex said about her finding Leo mysterious.

"You don't know everything about me."

"Bring it," she says.

"Favorite fictional character?"

"Marvin the Paranoid Android, but your favorite fictional scene is when Arthur eats all of that other guy's cookies."

"Biscuits."

"Whatever."

"First kiss?" It's petty, but I want to remind her that I was messing around with girls who aren't her long before she met Leo.

"Marissa Matson. You were in Ryland Shelman's basement, and she attacked you during a *Star Wars* marathon."

Sadly, Evie doesn't seem in any way bothered by this. "I never told you that's how it started."

"All those girls couldn't wait to tell me."

"If I had three wishes?"

She doesn't hesitate.

"Pitch a perfect game, write code for NASA, vacation home on the ocean."

I look at her mouth and think: *Missed one.*

I don't need the vacation home. (I'll be too busy at NASA!) But I can't tell her that, so she thinks she's won. And while I've totally failed to be mysterious, I don't hate that she knows me so well. I spin my laptop around and show her where to input the equations.

When she does, a model appears on the screen, exactly like the one she drew, only more precise. Evie checks it against the equations in her notebook. After a while, she looks up and whispers, "It's perfect. Can we fold it?"

I pull the computer back toward me and execute the

function I wrote to fold the diagram by matching pairs of identical dots. A couple of keystrokes, and this happens on the screen.

"And the binary addresses?" Evie says. I glare at her. It took hours of work to get this far, and I am not feeling the love. But I remind myself that while I've been working on this for days, Evie's been working on it for weeks. So I assign binary addresses to the matched pairs and add together the appropriate bits. And then there it is: error-correcting code blocks hidden in Evie's geometric representation of a helium atom. The hairs on my arms stand up.

I look up over my shoulder at Evie. "What does this mean?"

"Potentially, that there's binary code in everything if you know how to find it."

"And not just binary code, but Hamming code," I say, looking at the screen. "This mirrors the bits they embedded in those early digital transmissions. You have to admit it now: We totally live in the Matrix."

"We do not," she says, sitting next to me and taking my hand. "I know you thought you were only providing moral support on this, but I couldn't have finished the problem without you."

I pull her into a hug, burying my face in the cinnamon smell of her hair. "Evie, it's not just that I wouldn't have started the problem without you—I would never have come to Newton. I wouldn't even have known Frontier existed."

She sits back and thinks about this. "On the upside, you might still be dating Marissa Matson."

"That's not an upside."

We go back and take screenshots of the diagram at each stage of the process. Then she hands me her equations, and I give her my code, and we do our best to proofread each other's work. But the truth is we're both working too far beyond what the other can do to be helpful, and we give up after about an hour.

"Tomorrow, we'll check our own stuff. Work from the bottom up, line by line," she says. "It's not enough that the code works. It has to be clean."

"Hey," I say, offended.

"Sorry. But we need to be ready."

The submission deadline is Sunday.

∽ ∽ ∽ ∽ ∽ ∽ ∽ ∽ ∽ ∽ ∽ ∽

The next day, Evie comes into the room and puts a cup from Starbucks in front of me. I smell it. It's a cinnamon dolce latte—my favorite. She kisses the top of my head. "For my favorite coder."

Here's what I'm thinking: First, I love this smell. As far as I'm concerned, we're done—the combined aroma of cinnamon and coffee is so clearly the whole point of human evolution that it renders all other achievements superfluous. Second, I'm obviously happy that Evie got this for me. Aside from the drink, I like that when she was somewhere else, she was thinking about me. But third, Evie doesn't drink coffee, and she thinks the tea at Starbucks is contaminated with coffee essences, so she had no reason to be there unless she was with Leo. And finally, why is she kissing my hair?

Here's what I say: "Thanks."

She puts one hand on my shoulder, reaches out with the other, and says, "Does that need to—" When her finger brushes the screen, I slap it, even though it's Evie. I hate fingerprints.

"It's good," I say. "I went over it last night and again in labs."

"Okay. I need to check some of the matrices."

Because you skipped out of math lab to canoodle over coffee.

She trails her hand across my back as she moves to the other side of the table. I thought one of the things that would get to me about Evie dating Leo would be that we'd have so many more physical boundaries, but if anything, the opposite is true. It's as if these few days with Leo have expanded Evie's repertoire of touches, and she's trying them all out. I would have thought I'd love this, but it turns out it's like movie popcorn for dinner. Nice enough in the moment, but you're left wanting something more substantial.

For two hours, we work silently. I write about error-correcting code and explain the program. Evie completes the last check of her equations, which she's already transferred from her notebook into a Word document. When she sends them to me, I paste them into the paper. We can't work online because it messes with the formatting.

"Tonight, I'll write the lead-in," Evie says. "And tomorrow, we need to write about significance."

"What will we say?"

"Do you remember the fine-tuning problem?"

I shake my head, thinking she must mean a warm-up we did in physics.

"The constants in our universe—the amount of dark matter and dark energy, the strength of electromagnetic and nuclear forces, even the weight of protons—all have to be almost precisely what they are for conscious life to exist. If any of those things were the tiniest bit different, we wouldn't be here. And yet, here we are, in a universe perfectly suited for us. It's entirely improbable."

"Okay. But what does that have to do with our paper?"

"Well, finding these codes could be a way of investigating fine-tuning. Figuring out how the parameters for the universe are set. We don't have to say we're doing it, only that this opens avenues worth exploring."

"You can write that?" I ask.

"Sure. And I want to talk about the unreasonable effectiveness of mathematics."

"Like, why math is so good at describing the world?"

"Exactly. Doesn't it seem a little uncanny that mathematicians keep predicting things that experimental physicists find, sometimes decades before they do? But if the whole world is written in binary, then maybe that's not so weird."

"And can I talk about the simulation?"

She grins. "If you must."

On Friday, Evie's in the study room when I get there, her fingers flying across her keyboard. Normally, she does not put words together this quickly, but she's been thinking about this for so long. I've already written about the simulation and gone over as much of her lead-in as I can make sense of. The repetition of the phrase "Clifford algebra fiber bundles" made my brain turn off.

So I kick back on the couch with my earbuds in, waiting for her to finish. It's a rare treat to watch her without having to force my face not to reveal anything other than the friendly affection I show in public. If Bex could see me, she'd label it longing. It's never been this bad before, but I'm starting to realize there's a pretty big difference between the sentences "Evie doesn't date" and "Evie doesn't date *me*."

After about half an hour, Evie sends me the most recent version of the paper. While I go through it, she packs up her things and then sits cross-legged on the couch, facing me. I make only a few edits. When I'm done, I ask, "What now?"

She says, "I think we should leave it alone tomorrow and then do a couple of reads on Sunday with fresh eyes before we submit."

"It's good, isn't it?"

She nods. Evie has never been one for false modesty. "It'll get in. Then we can worry about the conference."

I take her hand. "I'll help you this time."

"I know." We sit like that for a while.

Then she pulls her hand back, saying, "I have to go."

"Big plans?"

She gives me a bashful smile. "Planetarium."

This is a ridiculously clichéd date for Newton students, and most of us are over it by the time we're juniors. When I asked Sarah-Kate last year, she said, "I refuse to be the ninth girl you put your arm around in those reclining seats," which endeared her to me. But Leo is new, and Evie has never gone—it would have been too weird for us to do it together—so it makes sense for them. I'm not thrilled by the news, but the part of me that always has been and always will be her friend is happy she's joining in this Newton tradition.

"Well, have fun," I say, opening the door.

Blake, Lucas, and Mason are waiting. Mason's holding a box of gaming crap, so I'm guessing Dean Santori hasn't commandeered the rooms for anyone else for Frontier. I'm still holding the door when Blake says, "Evie, sweetie. Tired of McGill already? Or did he sign on knowing he'd have to share with Caleb?"

Without thinking, I shove him hard, my hands smacking both of his shoulders. He staggers back a little. Satisfying, but not enough.

"Caleb," Evie says, but I don't look away from Blake, who is regaining his footing.

"It's not as much fun when *she's* the one with someone else, is it?" Blake says with a little smirk. "Evie, how about a side-by-side comparison? How does Leo stack up against the infamous Caleb Covic?"

I imagine punching him, and the motion feels familiar because it's so much like a pitch. The coiling of energy in the windup and lovely release of the follow-through. Only, instead of putting all that energy into a baseball, I could slam it into Blake's head. But when I pull back my arm, Evie steps in front of me and puts her hands on my chest, using all her weight to hold me back. My right arm is still half-raised, but my left closes around her.

Looking over her shoulder at my face, Blake must see that I am truly about to lose it, because he lifts his hands in a placating gesture. "Chill. It was a joke." He backs away, and Lucas grabs him by the shirt to pull him around me and push him into the study room.

Before going in himself, Lucas gives me a little smack on the arm and says, "We good?" I nod.

Once we're alone, I become excruciatingly aware of the way Evie is pressed all the way up against me, her hands on my shoulders, still trying to hold me in place. I let her go. When she doesn't move, I gently take her shoulders and remove her.

She steps back, and it destroys me that she's looking at me like she doesn't know who I am.

"I'm okay," I say.

"Are you sure?"

I nod.

"You know Blake. And Mason," she says.

I do. But knowing someone's an ass doesn't make you enjoy him any more.

"I'm fine. Go ahead. I'll see you tomorrow," I tell her.

She grabs my wrist, squeezes briefly, and leaves.

Once she's gone, I text David and Dev to ask if they want to see a movie. I'm in the mood to watch things explode.

EVIE

BACK ON THE THIRD FLOOR, I MAKE MY WAY through the sea of girls going in and out of each other's rooms, doing makeup and borrowing clothes for Friday night activities. I have never been a part of this scene, so it's easy enough to push through without meeting anyone's eyes. Bex is going to a movie with her soccer friends. She won't be looking for me.

Safely hidden in my room, I put on music to block out the noise and lie down. Once I'm calm, I let myself consider what just happened. I stepped in front of Caleb because I was afraid—afraid he'd get hurt or that he'd hurt someone else. But when I laid my head on his chest and he pressed his hand against my back, I felt something else. Something new.

I don't like this confusion being mixed up with Caleb. It feels dangerous and unfamiliar and reminds me of that time by the campfire. As if I could lose him to this weird boy-girl stuff. But I won't let that happen.

Leo is for flutters and confusion and whims and good-byes. Caleb is my friend, and he is forever.

Locking all of this away—I don't even want to talk to Anita about it—I get ready for Leo, putting on mascara and lip gloss and throwing a clingy purple sweaterdress over my leggings.

When I meet Leo in the lobby, his eyes go big. "Wow," he says.

"You like the dress?"

"I do." He puts his hands in his pockets and rocks back on his heels. "Makes me wish I could be your derivative."

"My derivative?" I say, confused.

"So I could lie tangent to your curves."

"That's terrible," I say. "Do those sorts of lines ever work?"

Leo puts his hand on my back. "You tell me."

After eating meals with Leo for two weeks, I'm pretty sure he's a vegetarian, which is the inspiration for my dinner plans tonight. When he confirms that he is, I say, "You're in for a treat."

On the way, I ask how he came to vegetarianism.

"Did you know that eighteen percent—" he begins.

I finish his sentence: "Of greenhouse gases are produced by livestock?"

"You too?" he asks.

I shake my head. "Bex. I try because of her. It's either

comply or spend meals listening to scary statistics. I can't quite commit, though. Because bacon."

When we get to our destination—a tiny restaurant a few blocks off the main street with only six tables—I tell him to close his eyes before leading him in and positioning him in front of the menu board.

It's a list of sixteen different kinds of macaroni and cheese, the most magical of all foods (except chocolate, obviously).

"Why didn't I know about this?" he asks.

"Because you've only been here for two months, and you're in physics and coding, so you spend all your time with boys, who—no offense—mostly cannot appreciate the wonder that is macaroni and cheese. Caleb hates coming here."

"Bex hasn't bullied him into being a vegetarian too?"

"No. His strategy is to eat fast so she doesn't notice."

Leo orders three different kinds, even though I tell him he'll never be able to eat it all. I ask for the same thing I always get—a combination of sharp white cheddar and sundried tomatoes.

Over dinner, he says, "I know we can't talk about the details, but how are things going for you Frontier-wise?"

"I think we're done, but we'll go through it all again on Sunday before we submit. How about you?"

"Getting there. I'm going to have to put some hours in this weekend, though. Have you and Caleb worked together before?"

"No." I think about how to put this. "I submitted something last year on my own, but I didn't present."

"It didn't get in?" He shrugs. "Neither did mine. They say papers almost never do your first time."

"No, my paper got accepted, but I didn't go." It would be easier to let him think I didn't get in, but I have too much pride.

"Did you get sick?"

I shake my head. I'm not ready to let him in on the full craziness that is Evie, but I don't want to entirely make something up.

"I got stage fright," I finally say. This is close enough to the truth, but it sounds ordinary. Sweet, even.

"Really?" Leo makes a strange face.

"I don't like being in front of people. I think I'll be able to do it with Caleb, though."

He smiles. "You're so sure the work will be good enough to get you onstage."

"That's the part I'm good at."

When we leave the restaurant after dinner, we find the temperature has dropped, and my sweaterdress, which was more than adequate on the walk over, is no longer keeping me warm.

Leo insists I take his jacket. "It's my own fault. I was going to suggest you get yours when we left, but I got distracted by that dress."

"Thanks." I like hearing Leo say these sorts of things almost as much as I like kissing him. I feel this strange sort of power when he does it. I'm starting to get why Bex dresses in so many different ways. It's like you're a different person each time.

"Maybe you could wear it again sometime, and I could take pictures? I could use some help figuring out this Midwestern light." From the tone of his voice, I'm guessing the light is not his primary concern, but I don't mind.

The planetarium shows a campy adaptation of an Asimov story in which humanity evolves into a bodiless hive mind and then merges with its conscious technology. The story makes almost no sense, but it doesn't matter, because Leo's arm is around me and my head is on his shoulder. He's drawing little patterns on my arm with his fingers, and I'm paying more attention to that than the show.

When we leave the theater, Leo pulls me out of the stream of people heading for the doors and into a narrow corridor that runs along the back of the theater. One side is cinder block and the other mostly windows. About halfway along, the windows curve out to form a circular seating area that's also glassed in. Leo pulls me into it. There's just enough light that I can see his face.

He points up. "The roof is glass too. On clear nights, they give night sky talks here."

He pulls me down onto the bench.

"How did you even know this was here?" I ask.

"Because I'm in coding and physics, so I spend all my time with boys."

I give him a confused look, because that doesn't answer the question.

He smiles. "They may be ignorant about macaroni and cheese, but their knowledge of quiet spots on campus is comprehensive."

When he kisses me, I slide my hands into his wonderful, messy hair, enjoying the feel of it between my fingers. I like how my brain stops when I'm kissing him. In that way, it's kind of like yoga.

We abandon the room when we hear voices down the hall, but before we emerge from the corridor and into the lobby, Leo leans back against the wall and pulls me in for one last kiss. Suddenly a spider drops down from somewhere above, skittering along the wall, shockingly close to my hand on Leo's arm, and I leap back, starting to hyperventilate and shudder at once.

Unreasoning terror churns through me. All my strategies for calming myself are gone, lost when this eight-legged creature leapt out of nowhere. It's awful, with its bulbous body and thick legs. What if it had crawled onto my hand? My arm? A violent twitch runs through me.

Leo turns toward me, confused and then alarmed. I'm backed all the way up against the windows, my eyes fixed on the spider, breaths fast and shallow. I need to cup my hands over my mouth to catch the CO_2, but I can't make myself do anything except press back as far away as I can.

Finally, seeming to grasp the situation, Leo looks from

me to the spider, knocks it to the floor with his hand, and steps on it. It's not until he moves his foot and I see its squashed body that some sort of executive function returns and I can draw a breath in through my nose, hold it for three heartbeats, and exhale. Repeat. In another minute, I meet Leo's eyes. He looks terrified.

Instead of reaching for me, he points toward the lobby, which, because the next show has started, is empty except for a single employee at the ticket counter, who seems unconcerned. I nod and follow him to a bench by the door, where I go through my brain-fooling routine. Candy in my mouth to keep it from drying out, hands under my legs to warm them up, breaths slow and steady. *Stand down, nervous system. Everything's fine.*

I sit on one side of the bench, and Leo sits on the other, turned toward me. Maybe I'm imagining it, but it seems like he's being careful not to touch me. I'm tempted to say that crazy isn't communicable, but it feels too soon for humor.

"You want to tell me what that was about?" he says.

I suspect *Not really* will not be an acceptable answer.

"I have some issues with anxiety. Spiders are one of my triggers."

"Issues," he says carefully.

"The big thing is social anxiety disorder, although I've been seeing therapists for years, and it's mostly under control. There are some extra bonus phobias that go along with it that are harder to shake."

"You're seeing a psychiatrist?" Something a little ugly flashes across his face before he manages to chase it away. I can't name the emotion exactly, but I know what's happening behind it: the instinctive horror surrounding mental illness and then the recitation of politically correct talking points. *It's a disease, like diabetes. I wouldn't blame her for needing insulin.* This is why I don't tell people.

"A psychologist, but yes. Tuesday afternoons."

He nods. "What else besides spiders?"

I tell him the big ones. He nods again.

I'm working really hard not to lose it. While I didn't expect this to be easy, I am not prepared for the intensity of his reaction.

He runs one of his hands through his hair and says quietly, "This is why you didn't present at Frontier last year."

Despite my best efforts, tears fill my eyes and spill over onto my cheeks. "Oh, Evie," he says. He pulls me toward him, one arm around my shoulders. We sit like that for a long time.

Without letting me go, he speaks softly in my ear. "I told you my mom had problems, but I didn't tell you what they were. I grew up with my mom talking to voices that weren't there, hiding me in closets from monsters, even moving so that whoever she thought was chasing her couldn't find us."

"That must have been awful."

"It was," he says. "And when you . . . reacted to the spider the way you did, it brought back some memories I wasn't prepared for. But it's not really about you. Does that make sense?"

"I guess so." I'm not sure if it's better or worse that Leo has this up-close experience with mental illness. I'm a little worried that what happened with his mother will make him think my problems are worse than they are, and I get enough of that from my mom.

Leo takes my hand and pulls me upright. "We need to head back."

We wind our way through campus back to Newton. Leo asks question after question about my phobias. I don't know if he's really that interested or if he's trying to show he's not afraid.

Once he's exhausted the topic, he says, "I told you about my mom, but you never talk about your parents."

"My father is a mathematician, and my mother is a psychologist who studies mathematicians who aren't quite right."

"So you're, like, their perfect child."

I snort. "No, that's Caleb."

"Why?"

"They'd never say it out loud, but they'd love an extro-verted, well-adjusted coder-athlete. Although I'm not sure how they thought that was an option considering the gene pool they were working with."

"They must be proud of you, though."

"Maybe. But they both see my mathematics as a threat. Because of my mother's work, she sees everything I do—even the good stuff—as further evidence of mental illness, and it's probably terrible to say this, but I think my father might envy me. He doesn't have much of an imagination."

"Yikes," Leo says.

"Yeah. But I feel bad complaining. It's nothing like what you must have gone through."

"No point in playing misery Olympics."

When we get back to Newton, Leo leads me to a bench in the statue garden, pulling me onto his lap when I shiver.

"I'm so sorry. I feel like I failed my first big boyfriend test tonight," he says.

"It wasn't a test," I say. "It was more of a pop quiz."

"Still, I'd like to make it up to you. I really do have to bury myself in Frontier this weekend, but ready or not, I'll be free five p.m. Sunday. Want to meet for dinner and hot chocolate? Maybe a photo shoot?"

"I'd like that."

"Good. And I'll grovel some more."

"Does that mean you're planning to apologize again, or is it code for something else?"

"A little of both?" he says before kissing me lightly on the lips.

I go to bed feeling better than I would have thought possible an hour ago, but even so, I can't quite wipe from my mind the way Leo looked at me when I told him.

CALEB

I WAKE UP SATURDAY MORNING SICK TO MY stomach. After a few minutes, I remember it's not because of late-night fast food but my encounter with Blake. Instead of breakfast in the cafeteria, I head out for a muffin and coffee.

After I eat, I force myself to think about why I'm hiding at a coffee shop. If it had just been Blake being a jerk, I'd be over it, but I shoved him because he got a little too close to the truth: This is hard, and I hate sharing Evie. And I can't shake the thought that the reason she never fell for me is because I couldn't figure out what she needs, and somehow Leo has.

I want to get rid of all these complicated feelings and go back to the way things were before.

This gives me an idea, so I pull out my phone and text her: *Evie and Caleb Day of Fun. 10:00. Bring your bus pass.*

It's a risk, but when I went by Leo's room this morning, he appeared to be holed up, working on Frontier. His DO NOT DISTURB sign had none of the geek whimsy typical at Newton—"If anyone asks where I am, I've left the country"—but was emphatically straightforward—"Bother me and I will end you." So I'm guessing he and Evie don't have plans.

This is confirmed two minutes later when Evie texts me back a red balloon.

My dad is the originator of the Evie and Caleb Day of Fun, which was a reward for the first punch I ever threw. There have only been two, both in defense of Evie.

Evie and I were in the same class in kindergarten and first grade. In kindergarten, she would not speak to anyone but me, including the teacher. I know it's wrong, but I'm still flattered by this. By the end of first grade, she was answering questions when called on and would speak quietly to a couple of girls, so the adults (I blame Evie's mother, but it could just as easily have been the school) decided to separate us so she didn't become too dependent on me.

She never complained, and I didn't know how bad it had gotten until I opened her backpack one afternoon looking for something—I don't remember what—and saw it was filled with Cocoa Puffs cereal. The meaning of this was not clear to seven-year-old me, but I knew it wasn't good. Evie refused to explain.

The next day, I discovered that after her second panic attack of the year, Jon Smagorinsky had started calling her

Cuckoo for Cocoa Puffs. This was eventually shortened to Cocoa, which was what everyone in her class was calling her, even the teacher, who was an idiot and thought it was an adorable nickname.

At recess, I expressed my displeasure to Jon Smagorinsky with a pretty good punch, making up with emotion what it lacked in form. The teasing stopped, and on the day I was suspended, Dad (using the dimples and charm I inherited from him) convinced Evie's mother to pull her out of school too, and Day of Fun was born. We went to the zoo. Dad bought us balloons.

When I meet Evie in the lobby, she's wearing her winter jacket and looks ready for anything.

"This is such a good idea," she says, and there's absolutely no awkwardness. Relief sweeps over me. We're okay. I can make it through Leo if we can keep being what we are.

We've never had a Day of Fun at Newton, although we still do it in the summer sometimes. (See the trip to the county fair and the temptation of the twilight Ferris wheel ride, but I don't intend for this to be that kind of day.)

On the bus down to the science museum, we speak in British accents. Evie's really good at this because of her father. As always happens, someone sitting nearby asks where we're from and what we're doing here. For some reason, speaking in an accent gives Evie confidence, so she answers, saying she wants to go to "uni" in America because her mother won't allow her to date outside the aristocracy.

She tells the woman that she broke her engagement to the man her mother wanted her to marry because he was blackmailing her. I think she's ripping off an episode of *Downton Abbey*, which we binge-watched last summer. Evie knows I will never speak to her again if she reveals that fact to anyone.

The woman looks questioningly at me.

"He's my cousin," Evie tells her as the bus stops in front of the science museum.

I give Evie an incredulous look. "I am not."

"He wants to marry me to keep the ancestral home in the family," Evie stage-whispers to the woman, who glares at me until I get off the bus.

After the bus pulls away, Evie gives me a little smile and says, "Sorry."

"I don't ever want to hear you say another Shakespeare play is ridiculous."

The museum is quiet, and we start in the light room, which is Evie's favorite. We make fractals with the different-colored pegs on the wall-sized light board and take pictures of our shadows before moving on to the sound exhibit. There's a piano here. It's out of tune, and getting sound out of the keys is a workout, but Newton is not so big on the fine arts, and I miss playing, so I lead a sing-along to the *Sponge-Bob SquarePants* theme song.

Finally, we go to the bubble room. Evie tries to talk to kids about the surface areas of different-shaped bubble wands, but they are uninterested, so instead I blow bubbles across the room and she, hands soaked in soapy water, catches them on her fingers. The children are more impressed with this and demand to be shown the secret.

We leave the museum for a late lunch and walk to the Pie Shoppe. Both of us get grilled cheese with tomato and bacon because Bex isn't here to police us. I also order a slice of apple pie. Evie says she doesn't want any and then eats half of mine. I don't complain. Instead, I get a piece of cherry after we finish. When I offer her a bite, she says without irony, "No, I told you I don't want any." I smile and eat my emergency backup pie, wondering if the authors of *Boy's Guide to Girls* included this tip. Maybe I should write my own manual.

On the bus ride home, I nudge her leg. "Can we talk about yesterday?"

She makes a face. "Since when do you need to ask to talk about something?"

"Sorry I lost it."

"He was awful. If I didn't think you'd get in trouble for it, I would have let you hit him."

I grin. "Three months until baseball practice."

"At some point, someone's going to wonder why your pitches go wild only when Mason and Blake are at the plate."

I suspect our coach has already decided to look the other way regarding this sort of thing, because he knows there are some infractions I'm better at policing than he is. But none of that is my point here.

"I'm afraid I may have made it worse. If anyone bothers you, tell me."

"What do you mean?" She looks baffled, and I'm relieved to know she hasn't been hiding anything.

"Well, me Hulking out and you clinging to me like the heroine on the cover of a romance novel is not going to do much to reduce gossip about us."

She blushes in a gorgeous and honestly pretty intriguing way, but I've vowed not to go down that path today, even mentally.

"There's gossip about us?" she asks.

Sometimes I literally wonder if Evie inhabits a slightly different dimension.

"Ever since we were freshmen," I say. "Plus, you dating someone else has made a lot of guys think they have a chance with you. You're trending on the second floor. So tell me if you need help."

She nods.

"And you can tell Leo," I add, although I don't want to.

"I guess," she says with a little shrug.

Interesting.

"Did something happen last night?" I ask lightly.

"We had a lovely dinner at that macaroni and cheese place," she says pointedly. I will never understand why anyone would organize a whole restaurant around a side dish. "And then we went to the planetarium, and I saw a spider and had a panic attack." Her voice is flat.

"Oh, Eves. I'm sorry." I take her hand. "What happened?"

"He killed it. I recovered. We agreed to go out again on Sunday."

"But?"

"The way he looked at me . . . it was awful. Like being at home again."

I have three equally strong feelings all at once. First, I want to kill Leo for making her feel, even for a second, like something is wrong with her. Second, I am deeply grateful to Newton for offering her a place to start over, where her anxieties are largely unknown and her mathematical genius is appealing instead of another thing to mock. And finally—and I'm not proud of this one—I'm relieved to learn that Leo is not the perfect boyfriend.

"So, what now?" I ask.

"I don't know. He's sorry. He says he's going to grovel more on Sunday."

"Let me know if I should ask him to play catch."

"Will do."

EVIE

CALEB AND I SUBMIT OUR PAPER TO FRONTIER at 3:00 p.m. on Sunday, two hours ahead of the deadline. Leo gets his in at 4:53. He and I go back to the diner that evening, where he apologizes again for his reaction at the planetarium. I apologize for flipping out, he watches me eat whipped cream, and we go back to Newton to make out in the statue garden.

Over the next two weeks, I talk to Anita about spiders and Frontier, look at videos of spiders for homework (exposure therapy is the worst), let Leo take pictures of me all over campus, do another tea party with Bex, and hang out with Caleb during morning breaks.

I also spend more and more of my evenings amid a large group in the center of the senior lounge. Now that Leo and I are together, both Caleb and Bex seem to want more people around when we study at night.

If you'd asked me a few months ago if I'd like this, I would have said absolutely not, but mostly I do enjoy being on the edges of the constant conversation, and I get to report to Anita that I made another friend. (She rejects my suggestion of a sticker chart to keep track. She says friends are supposed to be intrinsically motivating.)

Alexa, like Bex, majors in bio and minors in chem. She and I have never had a class together, so I don't know her well, but the first time she flopped down next to me on the couch, she looked over at the religion text I had open and must have read something on my face, because she said, "How much do we hate Abbie?"

"So much," I replied.

"Callie loves her," Alexa said.

"Bex too," I added. "She goes in early to spend time with her during the break. It's the worst thing I know about Bex."

"Why does she take off her shoes?" Alexa asked.

"Why did she make us do a collage?" I responded.

Since then, Alexa and I sit together on the couch working quietly while Leo, Caleb, Dev, and Callie do French and Bex and Sarah-Kate push through calculus homework, which I check for them.

Sometimes Leo hides behind his camera, taking pictures of everyone. I admire this as a socially acceptable strategy for getting a little distance, and I wish I'd thought of it when I was younger.

Other nights, Leo makes phone calls for Bex's environmental action group, since he was more easily persuaded than either Caleb or I of the importance of banning plastic bags. He's sitting on the floor doing this now while I read *Persepolis* for English.

I like the feel of his back pressed against my legs, and I'm thinking about running my fingers through his hair, but that isn't something I've ever done in public.

On the other end of the couch, Alexa curls a finger around Callie's ear, and Callie turns her head to kiss Alexa's palm. I look back at Leo, pick my hand up, and put it down again.

When I look over at Alexa again, she mouths, "Just do it."

So I slide my fingers into his hair. Leo puts the phone down and tilts his head back to grin at me. He's never pushed, really, but he's made it clear that he wishes I were more comfortable with visible displays of affection.

I go back to *Persepolis*, but I keep playing with Leo's hair until I look up to see Caleb watching me, an odd expression on his face.

This is why I don't do this. "What?"

"Nothing. You're just looking very much like a typical teenage girl over there, Eves."

Leo pauses mid-dial to grab my hand and hold it in place. "If you embarrass her into taking her hands off me, you and I are going to have words," he says to Caleb.

Then both Leo and Caleb check their email. I shake my head at them. We're supposed to hear about Frontier tomorrow, but Caleb and Leo are convinced that word might come early and have been obsessively checking their email all day. I'm not sure what Leo's chances are, but I wish Caleb would trust me. We'll be fine.

The next morning in humanities, we find our desks moved into groups. When Caleb sees that he and I have been put together with Yanaan and Blake, he grabs Blake's name card and tries to switch it to another group, but Abbie sees him and insists he leave it where it is.

Blake comes in and watches Caleb deliberate over where to place his card. It's clear he does not want to put Blake by either Yanaan or me, but he gives up and puts him by Yanaan. Blake smirks.

On our desks is an ethical dilemma to discuss: "A train is hurtling toward five people and will certainly kill them. If you flip a lever, it will jump to another track where it will kill only one person. What do you do?" We are supposed to talk about the morality of both choices from Greek and Judeo-Christian perspectives and record our thoughts before moving on to another dilemma.

Caleb writes, $5 > 1$ on a piece of paper and raises his hand for the next problem.

When Abbie comes over, Caleb says, "This one's just math."

"You've talked this through, and your whole group agrees?"

Yanaan, whom Abbie likes best of the four of us, says, "We found Caleb's proof convincing."

I can see this is one of those moments when Abbie regrets teaching at Newton. I'm happy to be a part of it. "You don't do a proof in ethics, you *reason*," she says, but she picks up our paper and replaces it with a second one. The dilemma here is the same, except that instead of a lever, the only option for saving the five people is to push a guy off a bridge and into the path of the train.

And people complain that math problems are unrealistic.

Blake shrugs. "It's exactly the same. Reduce it to a previously solved problem." He smiles at me. I ignore him.

"It's not the same," Yanaan says. "With the lever, both flipping it and not flipping are choices. Either way, there's going to be an accident you can't prevent. With the bridge, you're actively murdering someone. It's like harvesting the organs from a healthy person to save five sick people. The math is the same, but the ethics aren't."

Caleb smiles at her with real affection, and I'm reminded that Yanaan was his first girlfriend at Newton. Unbelievably, he broke up with her for Margot, which just goes to show about his attention span.

"What?" he says to me, a little alarmed, and I realize I've been glaring at him.

"Nothing. Give me the paper." I write, *5 accidental deaths < 1 murder*.

"Zeus would probably save all the hot girls on the

train," Blake says. He looks at Yanaan and me. "So you'd be safe."

Yanaan and I exchange looks that say, *Let's talk about how awful Blake is in math later*. Or at least that's what I'm saying with mine.

"Let me expand on that, Evie," Yanaan says, taking the paper from me. "I think we'll go with the whole 'Thou shalt not kill' thing here. That seems pretty straightforward."

When Abbie returns, she looks at our new paper and says, "Okay, so that's what the Bible says. But what about you? Would you push one man off a bridge to save five people?"

"No," Yanaan says. "Even to save others, you can't murder someone."

Abbie turns to me for a response, and I look right at Blake as I answer. "Honestly, I think it would depend on who the man on the bridge was."

Caleb, who has just taken a drink from his water bottle, spits all over me when he laughs.

My mind wanders while the biologists drag out the class discussion with a survival-of-the-fittest argument. But I'm snapped back into the room when Caleb, phone in hand, leaps out of his seat and says, "We did it!" before picking me up and spinning me around. The class erupts into applause while Abbie looks on, confused.

Caleb puts me down and holds out his phone so I can see the email. It starts with "Congratulations!" and even though

I'm not surprised, I'm pretty excited. And then scared. But not panicked. Progress.

Bex hugs us, and I hear Abbie ask, "What's Frontier?" In Bex's ear, I say, "This is why it is unacceptable that she teaches here."

Bex swats me on the arm. "You can complain about Abbie later. Go check on Leo."

I grab my bag and leave without saying anything to Abbie. I've just become one of Newton's chosen few, and for the next few weeks, rules do not apply to me. I cross the hall to the English classroom, but I don't even have a chance to be nervous for Leo, because I hear clapping as I approach the door. Leo looks up when I come in, and my face must give me away, because he leaps out of his seat and looks over at Mr. Stein. "Can we?" Mr. Stein nods and waves us off, saying, "Congratulations, Evie." He's been here for two decades and knows what a big deal this is.

"Anyone else?" Leo asks on the way out.

"I don't know. Maybe some of the juniors?"

"Come here," he says, pulling me toward him. "Congratulations." He kisses me softly.

Caleb comes out of Abbie's classroom, and we jump apart. Or more accurately, I jump, and Leo gives me an irritated look.

Caleb clears his throat and says, "Santori wants to see us in his office."

Chandran Sharma, a math major junior, is waiting when we arrive and gives us a big grin. Then Dean Santori tells us how proud he is, because this is the first time in twelve years that Newton will have three papers at Frontier. He is taking us out to dinner to celebrate. I look at Caleb, who gives me a little head shake to indicate that attendance is not optional.

My phone vibrates while Santori's talking. I have enough sense to let it be. But two of the three people who text me regularly are right next to me, and I just left Bex, so I'm puzzled.

I stop thinking about it soon enough, because the next words out of Santori's mouth are magic. "We want to give you the best chance of making it into the top five, so starting after Thanksgiving, you can use the humanities block to prepare for your presentations, and you'll be excused from finals."

I'm seriously tempted to hug Santori. Two weeks without humanities. No finals. He didn't do this last year. Then my phone buzzes again, reminding me of my worry.

When Santori dismisses the boys, he asks me to stay a minute. I turn to Caleb. "We'll wait outside," he says.

Caleb leaves the door open a crack when he goes out after Leo. I see Santori register this, and then he seems to decide it's a good idea. "How are you feeling about all this, Evelyn?"

"I'm doing all right." Frontier matters to Santori. It nearly killed him last year when I didn't show up. But I don't want to talk about my anxiety with him. It feels much too personal. "Presenting with Caleb will help."

"Good, good," he says. "Is there anything else we can do? I want to support you in any way we can. Obviously." Obviously. Frontier winners are marks of prestige for schools like Newton.

"I can't think of anything," I say.

"If you do, let me know."

Both Leo and Caleb look at me curiously when I step out of the office, but I shake my head, more interested in checking my phone.

The first message says: *Well done, Evelyn! A huge honor. You've been doing so much better. I know it will go well this time.* I hold the phone to my chest as if I can feel his arms around me. It's rare that I generate this kind of enthusiasm from Dad.

When I can't put it off any longer, I check the text from Mom: *Your father has been getting messages about Frontier from his colleagues. I'm not sure when you were planning to tell us about this. Frankly, I'm surprised you entered at all after last year. Especially without talking to us. We need to consider your health.*

I can't even figure out what I think about this before a text comes in from Caleb's mom: *Sit tight, Evie. We're working on this.*

I reach out and grab Caleb's wrist, pulling him back toward me. He's in the process of reading his texts. Without speaking, we exchange phones. I think Leo might say something, but I'm not really paying attention.

On Caleb's phone, his mother has written: *Beth is losing her $#%@ about Evie and Frontier.* Despite everything, I want to laugh, because it's so much like Monica to take the time to type symbols even at a moment like this, as if her seventeen-year-old son would be shocked by a swear word. The next message says: *Trying to talk her down. Tell Evie not to worry.*

We exchange phones again and stare at each other, crowds of students parting around us as we stand unmoving in the middle of the corridor.

"What's going on?" Leo asks, looking from one of us to the other.

"Wunderlochen," we say together.

CALEB

LEO OBVIOUSLY DOESN'T FEEL LIKE WE'VE answered his question, but selfishly, I want to hold the shared memory—as disastrous as it was—a few moments longer.

"Let's go get lunch," I say.

With Leo's hand on her back, Evie moves toward the cafeteria. While we're walking, I text Mom: *There is no way we're not going. The only question is how much deception will be involved.*

Her response: *Obvs.* I love my mom.

"So," Leo says when we're at the table with Bex. "Wunder-lochen?"

I look at Evie to see if she wants to start. She doesn't.

"When we were thirteen, we ran away together," I begin, even though this is actually the end. The dramatic start pleases me.

Bex looks shocked. "Why?"

"We were on the lam," I say, and smile a little.

"Fracking green Jell-O," Evie says quietly. I badly want to twist my fingers through hers, but she's across the table from me, so I can't.

Leo and Bex can't tell if they're supposed to laugh, and I don't think Evie and I know either. The whole thing was such a mix of the awful and the sublime.

In seventh grade, our gifted teacher recommended us both for a two-week math and science camp in north nowhere, Wisconsin. Wunderlochen was designed for computer geeks and math nerds, and while the brochures had pictures of swimming pools and horses, campers slept in the dorms of a small liberal arts college, not in the woods, so it seemed doable for Evie. The sample schedules were filled with one kind of awesomeness after another: classes in C++, science labs, robotics, and evening readings of *Hitchhiker's Guide* radio plays. We both badly wanted to go.

Three of our four parents were on our side, but Evie's mother insisted Evie wasn't ready, arguing that a bad experience could lead to an epic setback. But she couldn't hold out against the five of us, particularly when Evie's therapist said the experience could be good for her.

And for three days, it was. I wrote my first computer game. Evie constructed proofs on Geometer's Sketchpad. We played in the pool and rode horses, which, although it makes no sense at all, Evie found less terrifying than bicycles.

Then, on the fourth day, the math kids did some kind of problem-solving competition. When Evie got the highest score, the instructor, who thought he was funny, chided the group for letting a girl embarrass them. The details didn't come out until much later, but things got bad quickly: guys made comments on her looks, put hands on her body, and after the first panic attack, talked about her being crazy.

I'd been having so much fun that it took me too long to figure out what it meant that she suddenly refused to leave my side and switched from math to coding. It was only when she stopped speaking to everyone but me that I really started paying attention. It was about then that her tormentors discovered the power of the green Jell-O served daily in the cafeteria.

Evie calls this one of her phobias, although I think technically it's more of an aversion, but either way, she's always found the texture horrifying, and she shudders when she touches it. They discovered her reaction by accident and exploited it on purpose. She found Jell-O everywhere. In her bag, in her dorm room, on her computer, and finally dumped in her lap by Ethan Miller.

She and I were sitting on a bench, where I'd been trying to coax her into telling me what was going on. Before Evie had brushed herself clean, I leapt over the bench and landed the second punch of my life. By this time, I had been pitching for a couple of years, and this was a camp for kids who spent most of their time in front of screens. Plus, I was outrageously angry. When Evie pulled me off of him, Ethan was no longer fighting back.

Our decision-making in the aftermath was not stellar. Evie was terrified I'd be charged with something. (The damage looked much worse than it turned out to be.) I was scared she'd be left alone at camp if I was sent home, so we decided to run away for a few days and return right before our parents were scheduled to pick us up.

We packed our stuff, headed to the bus station on campus, and I bought tickets to a small town a few hours away with the emergency credit card my parents had given me. Our phones told us there was a campground there. We were a little hazy on how exactly the camping was going to work, but we were savvy enough to know that there was no way two thirteen-year-olds were checking into a hotel. Evie spent the bus ride curled up against my chest, which was where the sublime came in. After about two hours, she spoke for the first and only time, whispering, "Thank you" as she looked into my eyes.

That was the moment I fell.

All of our parents were waiting for us when we got off the bus, none of them happy. Even so, Dad sprang into action at Wunderlochen, suggesting that because Evie's abuse had not only been ignored but initiated by an adult at the camp, it would probably be best to treat this as a learning experience for everyone. I wrote a letter of apology to Ethan Miller (making myself feel better by spelling *Suck it* with the first letter of every sentence); he wrote one to Evie that didn't have any coded messages in it, as far as I could tell; and Evie stopped speaking, even to me, for three weeks. Our first almost-kiss against the garage happened at the end of that summer.

After that, whenever we wanted to do something her mother disapproved of, the other adults would make modest efforts to support us, but all she had to say was "Wunderlochen," and the conversation was over.

After I finish the story, Bex and Leo sit in silence for a few minutes. Then Bex asks Evie, "How did you convince her to let you come to Newton?"

"It wasn't hard. If I'd stayed home, I would have had to take math at the university. I wasn't ready for that. And Wunderlochen was horrible, but school at home wasn't all that great either. So she said that as long as Caleb came and I kept up with therapy, it would be okay to try it."

I turn toward her. "You never told me she wouldn't let you come unless I did." I'm not sure which surprises me more: that Evie kept a secret from me all this time, or that her mother trusts me. I always give in when she mentions Wunderlochen, because I feel like she blames me for not doing enough to protect Evie.

"I didn't want you to come only because of me," Evie says.

What I want to say back is this: *Of course I came to Newton because of you. I draw breath because of you.*

But I'm sitting across a table from her with Bex and Leo watching, so instead I say, "We are going to Frontier."

Because that's as close as I can get.

∞ ∞ ∞ ∞ ∞ ∞ ∞ ∞ ∞ ∞ ∞ ∞

There's radio silence from my parents the rest of the afternoon, and I resist the temptation to check in with Mom. She'll tell me when a decision has been made, and getting the play-by-play is only going to make me angry.

After labs, I go to the lounge and work half-heartedly on some French and coding, but mostly I spend my time accepting the congratulations of classmates and reading the detailed instructions that came in the email from Frontier.

The conference is December 28–29 in Chicago. We got lucky on this. Because Chicago is the midpoint between home and Newton, Evie and I travel through there all the time. This will be so much easier for her than getting on a plane and going somewhere unfamiliar.

The letter asks us to register for an online forum. There's some emotional language about building community among the next generation of outstanding mathematicians and physicists, but they obviously don't trust our esprit de corps, because while we're invited to make home pages introducing ourselves, we're also asked to choose anonymous screen names and told to leave out all identifying details. I assume this is to prevent preconference sabotage and is a response to some atrocity committed in a previous year.

There's a standard template with a place for a hangman game using your favorite math or physics quote, a "Get to know me!" section where you can answer already-selected questions, and a space for your favorite joke. I'm thinking about smart-ass responses to all of these when Leo asks Evie if she's going to do a profile. She says she will if he does.

"Are you going to tell me your screen name?" he asks.

"No," she says, outraged. "That's cheating."

"I guess if it's true love, I'll find you."

Do I want to punch him in the face for saying the words *true love* to Evie?

Absolutely. But I also want to hug him.

Because I love this idea.

This forum will give me a chance to talk to Evie without the weight of all our history. Not the boy next door. Not her best friend. Just some guy she might like for who he is.

And I have to admit, I'm curious about myself too. How much of what I feel for Evie is bound up in liking who I am when I look out for her? Will it feel the same when she's a girl I'm chatting up online? I kind of can't wait to find out.

If I want her to find me, the screen name is most impor-tant. I can't count on her clicking on all 132 profiles. There are two ways to go here: famous dead mathematician or fictional character. Evie loves very few books, but she's read those few so many times the cracked spines are held together with rubber bands. *The Phantom Tollbooth* is the most obscure of her favorites, so I pick "Milo" as my alias. She's all about the Princess of Pure Reason and the Mathemagician, but I'm not feeling them for my own alter ego.

The rest is easy. For my hangman quote, I choose "We are a university, not a bathhouse." David Hilbert said this in 1915 to argue that Emmy Noether should be allowed to join the faculty of the University of Göttingen even though she was a woman. Noether, who wrote a theorem that straddles mathematics and physics, is a hero of Evie's.

For my favorite book, I say *Our Mathematical Universe* by Max Tegmark, a physicist who, as far as I know, was Evie's only crush before Leo. She claims she's only interested in his ideas, but that's a lie. Little cartoon birds circle her head when she watches his TED Talks. For my favorite physics concept, I say entanglement. And for my joke, I choose: "Schrödinger is pulled over for speeding. While inspecting the car, the police officer opens the trunk. He says to Schrödinger, 'Sir, do you know you have a dead cat back here?' Schrödinger replies, 'Well, I do now.'"

Then I give my homework some serious attention, occasionally checking the Frontier site. I'm visited by "Higgs Boson," "Dark Matter," and "Arthur Dent." Each guesses a single letter for hangman. Then "Tesseract" pops in, and instead of guessing a letter, she fills in the whole quote. I look over at Evie. She's smiling at her screen.

Hello, there.

Her screen name pops up in my IM box in the corner, and I invite her into a private chat room.

Tesseract: So you're a David Hilbert fan?

Milo: I like Hilbert space as much as the next guy, but I'm more of an Emmy Noether fan.

Tesseract: Because?

Milo: I've seen what it's like for STEM girls now. A hundred years ago, I can't even imagine. Although I probably don't need to tell you . . .

Tesseract: Because I know the quote?

Milo: Because no boy in this world or any other would choose Tesseract as a screen name.

Tesseract: Just when I thought you were a feminist! It's a mathematical object. Very gender-neutral.

Milo: Sorry, no. I'm going to go to the studio audience on this one. Ask any male in your vicinity right now.

I glance up at Evie, who's looking around the room, considering it.

Tesseract: All the boys here agree with me.

Milo: Liar.

Tesseract: Is this your first time at Frontier?

Milo: Yeah. You?

Tesseract: Yes. Are you nervous?

Milo: A little. I'm worried I'll do well enough to end up onstage and then I'll make a computational error in front of everyone. Make me feel better by telling me your biggest fear.

Tesseract: That I'll have to go onstage at all.

Milo: Isn't that kind of the point?

Tesseract: Doesn't make it any less scary.

Milo: Do you know the difference between an introverted mathematician and an extroverted mathematician?

Tesseract: One's imaginary?

Milo: So quick! But no. An introverted mathematician looks at her shoes while she talks to you.

Tesseract: And an extroverted mathematician?

Milo: Looks at *your* shoes.

Tesseract: Ha. *Her* shoes?

Milo: For my girl Emmy. Did I regain my feminist street cred?

Tesseract: Jury's still out. I have to go and talk to my shoes now. See you on here tomorrow?

Milo: I'll be here.

Tesseract: It was nice to meet you, Milo. You're not what I expected from the Frontier competition.

Online Evie is fun.

And I think she likes me.

EVIE

I CLOSE MY LAPTOP, FEELING PLEASED. I CAN make friends in real life and online. My social skills are excellent.

"Are you going to change out of your uniforms for dinner tonight?" I ask Caleb and Leo.

They both look at me vaguely, clearly not having thought at all about what they are supposed to wear to the dinner we're going to in twenty minutes. Boys.

Bex says, "Yes, change." She picks up her bag to come upstairs with me and then points at Leo and Caleb. "That goes for you two as well."

Caleb salutes. Leo says, "Yes, ma'am," and I smile. I like it when his voice turns Southern.

Upstairs, Bex tells me to wear my sweaterdress again.

I say, "Really? For dinner with Dean Santori?"

She rolls her eyes. "For dinner with Caleb and Leo."

"I eat dinner with Caleb and Leo every day," I say.

"You're going somewhere nice. Enjoy it."

When I come into the lobby, Leo grins at my dress. He's put on slacks and a slightly metallic purple button-down that makes his eyes look even more blue than usual. When he reaches for my hand on the way to the car, I let him take it even though Dean Santori is there.

The restaurant is dark and candlelit, and I don't know if it's the setting, or my earlier conversation with Milo, or talking about Wunderlochen today, but I'm having one of those moments where I'm very conscious of being the only girl.

Chandran, Leo, and Caleb talk easily with Dean Santori about their sports and their classes this semester. (We're not supposed to talk about our Frontier projects with mathematicians or physicists before the convention—and even though he didn't finish his doctoral degree, Dean Santori counts.) I drink my Diet Coke.

Over salads, Dean Santori tells us that Newton will organize the hotel rooms for the conference but that we should plan to travel there on our own since it will take place over the break. My discomfort provides me with an unexpected inspiration.

"Dean Santori," I say, and I don't have to fake the hesitancy in my voice. "Do you know how many girls were invited to Frontier this year?"

He gives me an uncomfortable look, as if I'm about

to stand up and accuse him of being sexist in front of the whole restaurant.

"I don't know, Evelyn. But experience would suggest not very many, which makes it an even bigger honor for you."

I always love this argument. It's such an honor to represent not just myself and Newton but also my entire gender. No pressure, though.

Caleb's hand fumbles for mine under the table, but rather than clasp it, I give it a quick squeeze and let go, telling him I've got this. He sits back and looks at me curiously.

"Yes, but you know those environments can be uncomfortable for girls. I would feel safer, and probably do a better job, if Rebeca de Silva could come and stay with me."

"Of course," he says quickly. "I don't see why that would be a problem. I should have thought of it myself."

"Do you think you could ask her parents? You know how they are."

He does. "It's the least I can do. Over the years, the reverend and I have reached an understanding. I think he'd be happy to help with this."

I offer him a sincere smile and say, "Thank you."

Caleb and I will have to practice our talk. But now I've done everything I can to guarantee my success. I'm sure my parents will come, but honestly, they're as likely to make things worse as they are to help. Last year, Mom's continual assessing looks and Dad's constant quizzing helped put me over the edge.

As Dean Santori's dropping us off back at Newton, Leo says, "We missed curfew. Our keycards won't work."

"They will tonight. I had Mrs. Anders reset them for weekend hours before we left."

Leo turns to me, smiling, and I'm glad I brought my coat.

Chandran heads inside immediately. Caleb says, "You two are staying out?"

Leo lets me answer. "I think so," I say. "See you in the morning?"

"Good night, Eves. Leo."

I watch him head into the building, thinking he looks a little sad, but then Leo pulls on my hand.

"River trail?" he asks. I'm surprised. And honestly a little disappointed. It's a beautiful night for kissing in the statue garden.

Once we're on the path, he says, "Can I ask you something?"

"Sure."

"Why did you stop talking after Wunderlochen?"

I have to think about the answer for a little while. I've never really considered why. In therapy at the time, all the focus was on getting me to speak again.

Finally, I say, "What happened there was awful. I'd been teased before—kind of a lot, really, growing up. But I never felt as threatened as I did there. When I got back, I couldn't deal with anyone else's thoughts or feelings. I needed to rebuild from the inside out."

"When you're upset, you still withdraw. Even now," he says. "Sometimes I feel like Caleb's the only one who knows what's going on in there. You two have this whole secret language of looks and touches, but I need words to know what you're thinking."

He looks so uncertain that I make an effort to name the amorphous dark thoughts swirling around in my brain.

"I was quiet tonight because I'm worried about Frontier and my mother. I don't know how much trouble she'll create for me. And . . ." I stop, because this part is harder to say out loud. "And I'm scared she could be right. Even if I manage to get there this time, there's a nonzero chance I'll have a complete breakdown in front of hundreds of people."

Leo's smart enough not to say that everything will be fine—that's a promise he can't make—but he stops walking and wraps his arms around me. I lean my head on his chest and enjoy the feeling of being taken care of.

Back in my room, I think about Caleb's bowed shoulders and text him: *Everything okay?*

He responds: *Check your email.*

There's a message from Mom telling me they'll be here in three days to celebrate Thanksgiving with us and discuss the Frontier situation.

I call Caleb.

When he answers, I say, "Why? Why? Why? Why? Why? I thought old people understood how phones work. Why do they need to come?"

"They made reservations at the U-Club. For all of us."

"Joel and Nolan too?"

"No. The lucky bastards are going to my grandparents'. How come you're back so early? I thought you and Leo were taking advantage of the late curfew."

Instead of answering, I say, "Leo! He's staying for Thanksgiving. He's going to expect to come."

Maybe it's early to meet my family, but I know after our conversation tonight that there's no way Leo is going to be happy about me going out with Caleb—even if it's with all four of our parents—and leaving him to eat at the dorm. And if it were an ordinary meal, I might not object. But I don't know if I have it in me to manage Leo's emotions as well as my own while dealing with my mother on the rampage. It's too much.

"Maybe they won't want to talk about Frontier in front of him?" Caleb says.

"How does that help? That just means we'll have to meet again the next day!"

"You want to get up early tomorrow? Go out for breakfast and strategize?"

I know what he's after. "You're just looking for an excuse to get that milkshake you call coffee."

"That's a fringe benefit," he says. "Whatever happens, we're in this together, Eves."

"Even if we have to make a run for it?"

"Especially then."

CALEB

ONCE WE'RE AT A TABLE AND I'M HAPPILY SPOON-
ing up my breakfast whipped cream, I say, "So, what are
you thinking?"

"I'm going to hard-line it," she says. "No excuses. No
explanations. The more I think about it, the angrier I am that
this committee is being assembled to decide what I'm capable of."

I suddenly feel defensive of my own parents. That's not
how they see this. "My mom and dad . . ."

She shrugs irritably. "I know. They want to help. But
still. I've been working with Anita for eight months now.
I'm not the same person I was last year. And you'll be with
me this time."

"I will," I agree. "What did you decide about Leo and
Thanksgiving?"

"I'm going to text my mother now. Tell her I have a plus-one."

I'm interested to see how this will go. After she sends the text, we eat silently for a while, keeping an eye on her phone.

When the message comes in, Evie says, "Humph," and then, "She wants to know what you think of him."

"Tell her I think he's dreamy."

Evie looks at me, unamused. I pull out my phone and start typing.

"What are you saying?" she asks suspiciously.

"That I admire his tattoos."

"Caleb."

"That he's a nice guy, a perfect gentleman, and in no way likely to tarnish the fragile flower that is their only daughter." Then I put the phone down to look at her. "He's not, right?"

"I'm not sure I understand your metaphor," she responds. "Which should not in any way be taken as a request for further explanation."

We look at each other for a few long moments before she blushes and drops her eyes. I suspect she understands my metaphor just fine.

Evie's phone chimes again. She looks up at me. "She's looking forward to meeting him, now that he has the Caleb Covic seal of approval. Do you ever get tired of being held responsible for my mental health?"

"No."

And then I get a real smile, and she reaches her hand across the table to clasp mine.

"We should go back. I forgot about Bex. I should tell her my plan before Dean Santori calls her parents."

We grab our cups and head out. On the way, Evie looks up at me and asks, "Have you been on that Frontier site at all?"

"Some. I haven't had a lot of time," I say. I don't want to lie, but I'm allowing myself to be evasive. This is, after all, the rule from Frontier: no identifying details. "Why?"

"Just wondering."

When we get back, Evie goes off to talk to Bex while I grab my backpack from my room and head to physics. Dr. Lewis looks up when I come in and says, "Mr. Covic, I hear congratulations are in order."

"Yes, sir," I say, smiling and taking my seat. I pull out my laptop, hoping we don't do a gallery walk today. Between the dinner last night and breakfast this morning, I half-assed my way through my homework and don't really want it on public display.

The bell rings as Evie walks in, backpack over her shoulder and cup of tea in her hand.

"Well, if it isn't our Frontier princess," Dr. Lewis says. "Better luck this year, I hope."

My rage is instant, but I swallow it, because saying something will only make things worse. Dr. Lewis has always been sarcastic, but lately he's turned cruel, at least with Evie.

When I meet her eyes to see if she's okay, she tilts her head to show she's not overly bothered. And something about her casual confidence lets me see it: Dr. Lewis is jealous.

Evie's going to do things in physics that he can't even imagine. This is why she never panics here, no matter what he does. She owns this space, and she doesn't need me to protect her.

Leo looks at Evie as she sets down her cup, then glances back at the matching one in front of me. I make no effort to hide my smile.

As we're doing the warm-up problems, Leo says quietly to Evie, "If I'd known you were going to Starbucks, I would have asked you to get me something."

"Sorry," she says. "I was dealing with my mother."

I smile again, because when she goes without me, I get coffee without having to ask.

∞ ∞ ∞ ∞ ∞ ∞ ∞ ∞ ∞ ∞ ∞ ∞

During coding, I sit in the corner and use my laptop so my screen is less visible, and instead of working on my final project, I explore Tesseract's home page.

Evie says her favorite physics concept is Many-Worlds and her favorite book is *A Wrinkle in Time*—sadly clichéd for a math and science girl, but since it's Evie, I forgive her. She does better with her hangman quote, unsurprisingly from Tegmark, but she turned it into a riddle. Someone has filled in the *e*'s, *r*'s, and *a*'s. I do the rest: "Food, rearranged?" and then type the answer: "People."

She must get a notification when it happens, because suddenly she's here.

Tesseract: Tell the truth. Did you use the internet to solve the riddle?

Milo: You underestimate me. I've seen the talk.

Tesseract: And what did you think?

Milo: Consciousness as a mathematical pattern? Maybe, but what's it doing for me?

Tesseract: Oh. You're one of those.

Milo: *raising my eyebrows*

Tesseract: All knowledge must be useful.

I can practically hear her rolling her eyes.

Milo: A physicist and an engineer are lost in a hot-air balloon. They see a guy on the ground and call out, "Where are we?" The man answers, "You're in a hot-air balloon!" The engineer turns to the physicist and says, "Must be a mathematician. His answer's correct, but it's useless."

Tesseract: Cute. But don't you think there's something magical in it—this idea that mathematics doesn't describe the world, but that it *is* the world? That it's us? You, me, and everyone we know—bio-friendly mathematical structures bending toward and away from each other our whole lives.

Milo: Are you secretly a poet who hacked into the site?

Tesseract: Is there a poet anywhere who could hack into anything?

Milo: Touché. Personally, I lean more toward the hacking than the poetry.

Tesseract: You'd think someone who went to *The Phantom Tollbooth* for his screen name would be less practical.

Milo: Can I tell you a secret?

Tesseract: Please.

Milo: I only chose the screen name to meet girls.

Tesseract: Practical indeed.

Leo sits down next to me, and I feel a little guilty for flirting with his girlfriend right in front of him, so I sign off.

Milo: I'm in class so I have to go. Can I bend toward you tomorrow?

Tesseract: Theoretically, you already are.

I look at Leo over my laptop. "Let me guess. Just for kicks, you've written a Hindenburg bug into your final project, and you want me to help pick up the pieces?"

He shakes his head. "How worried should I be about Beckham family Thanksgiving?" He's clearly pretty nervous, so I tell him the truth.

"For you, it's probably going to be fine. Her father will like you because you got into Frontier, and her mother will like you because you're evidence that Evie is normal."

"And your parents?" he asks, obviously trying to make sense of their role in all this.

"They won't like you, because they think she should be dating me."

He gives me a tight smile. "So that's a family trait, then?"

"Either way, we're not going anywhere. If you stick around, you'll have to get used to all of us."

He looks at me in silence for a few moments. "Then I guess we'd better come to an agreement on a stuffing recipe."

"No apples or cranberries. I won't compromise on that one."

"Agreed. Fruit in stuffing is an abomination."

I really don't want to like him. But I do.

EVIE

AT THERAPY, I TELL ANITA ABOUT FRONTIER AND Mom's reaction, and we spend some time rehearsing for my Thanksgiving conversation.

When we finish, she says, "I'm going to write a prescription for something short-term. You should fill it before you go to Frontier."

"You can do that?" I thought I had to go to the doctor for this.

"Now that you're seventeen, I can. And you know it's not a failure if you need it, right?"

"I do."

"And you know you don't have to take it just because you have it?"

"I'm in charge," I say. We worked on this for a long time.

"And if you need me, you'll get in touch?"

"I'm not afraid to ask for help."

Anita smiles. "Then, Evie, I think it's time we talk about a plan for terminating our sessions."

"You don't want to see me anymore?" I feel tears prick my eyes. "I don't want to start over with someone else."

"I'm not saying you should start over. I'm saying you don't need this every week. Therapy doesn't have to be a way of life. It's been a month since your last panic attack. There was an even longer stretch before that one, and you know what to do when they happen."

"But . . . my social anxiety disorder?"

"It's not interfering with your life. You speak in class. You're making new friends. You have a boyfriend. You're about to go talk on a stage in front of hundreds of people."

"But I'm nervous."

I'm not sure why I'm arguing. I like Anita, but I don't want to be in therapy forever. This just feels so sudden.

"And it's appropriate to be nervous. But it hasn't even crossed your mind not to do it."

"No," I say, snapped out of the moment. "I'm doing it."

She nods. "Exactly."

"But what about Leo? I'm not sure that's going as well as it could. Sometimes it feels like a lot of work."

"First of all, Evie, I'm not kicking you out the door at the end of our session today. I just want you to start thinking about this so we can make a plan together. We can talk about Leo next week if you like, but big picture? You're seventeen.

You're going to have some stuff to figure out about boys, but you don't need a therapist for that."

And then time is up. I leave in a bit of a daze. Anita thinks I'm fine. She has a medical degree and has been treating people for decades, and she knows every little thing about me, and she thinks I'm fine. Tears drip off my face and onto the ground.

A woman walking past looks over at me. "Are you okay, sweetheart?" she asks. "Do you need help?"

I give her a big smile. "No," I say. "I'm fine."

Upstairs in my room, I wash my face and lie down with a cool washcloth over my eyes for a while before dinner. The idea of ending therapy, which has been part of my life for so long, feels too big to share with anyone, and especially too big to share with everyone. I want to hold it close for a while.

I'm quiet through dinner and during the first hour or so in the lounge. Leo doesn't push, either because he assumes I'm worried about my parents or because he's absorbed in his own work. We're all a little behind.

However, it becomes clear he's not happy with me when he, Caleb, and I move to a table to work through the particle-in-a-box problems Dr. Lewis gave us for homework. The three of us—in recognition of our Frontier-certified abilities—got a few extra to do.

Leo contributes almost nothing to the conversation about the problems and answers direct questions in as few words as possible. Caleb is irritated because he doesn't really understand what we're doing. Then I get irritated because nothing I say or do seems to get through to him and because Leo will not help, even though he's much better at explaining than I am. And because all of this is ruining the reflective mood I've had since leaving Anita's.

I'm standing behind Caleb with one hand on his shoulder, reaching around him to draw a diagram in his notebook, when Leo looks up at us from across the table and says in a biting voice, "Maybe you want to leave some daylight between the two of you, Evie? I don't think he's going to learn it by osmosis."

Under my hand, I feel Caleb's shoulders tense, but he sits back. "I don't know. At this point I have more hope for that than whatever the hell she's drawing here."

Leo glares at Caleb and says, "If you'd pay attention in class instead of relying on her to run a remedial physics lab for you every day, you'd be done by now."

Alexa looks up at me from across the room. "You okay?" she mouths.

I nod. I'm furious, but I am not going to have this fight in front of half the senior class. I do take my hand off Caleb's shoulder and go back to my seat. I turn so I'm facing Caleb with my back to Leo. "You're still thinking about it like a baseball," I say. "You've got to think in terms of the wave function."

Caleb puts both of his hands in his hair, but before he

can say anything, Bex, who has been sitting on the couch behind us, throws down her pencil and says, "Why? Why bother with any of this? Why have a huge fight about it? What possible difference could it make here in the real world?"

All three of us look over at her, surprised. It is not like Bex to throw accelerant on an argument.

"Bex?" I ask, unable to figure out the source of her anger. It seems entirely unrelated to what's going on.

"In biology and chemistry, people want to cure cancer and end hunger and figure out some way to power the planet that doesn't leave it uninhabitable for our grandchildren, and you're arguing about a particle that we need to spend billions of dollars to even be able to see," she says. "I can't listen to it anymore."

"I don't think that's actually what we're arguing about," Caleb says.

I stare at him, incredulous.

Bex throws her stuff in her bag and leaves. I look between Leo and Caleb.

"Evie, I'm sorry," Leo says. "Go after her. I'll help him."

I smile a little. And then I kiss him on the cheek. "Thank you." He pulls me back down and kisses me long and hard on the mouth. When he breaks away, I'm a little dizzy. "You'll tell me what that was all about later?"

"You can figure out what it was about. And now I'm over it. Go."

I hurry after Bex.

She opens her door when I knock, looking a little weepy. We sit together on her bed, backs against the wall.

"I know I'm not great at this stuff. But I'm guessing you're not angry about quantum physics."

"I wanted to wait to tell you this until after Frontier, but I think I'm feeling guilty, and it made me blow up."

"What's going on?" I ask, unable to imagine what Bex would have to feel guilty about.

She takes a deep breath. "I don't want to go to the University of Chicago."

I turn my whole body, folding my legs, so I can look at her. "Why?"

"I don't want to be a doctor, Evie." She gestures toward the scary climate change graph on her wall. "That's the work I want to do. I'm not going to be happy otherwise. And all this little *whatever* that everyone studies here just makes me angry."

I want to object to her calling the fundamental laws of the universe "little whatever," but I'm more worried about where she wants to go to school.

"You can't study climate science at U of C?"

"I could," she says. "But look at this." She hands me a brochure for the Lamont-Doherty Earth Observatory at Columbia University. I have to admit it seems amazing. As I look at the pictures of oceans and laboratories and forests, I wait for panic to rise within me at the thought of going to school without Bex. It's there. But it's manageable. Maybe Anita is right. Maybe I'm better.

"When did you decide this?"

"After our tea party. I realized I was looking at medicine because of my parents. They see it as a calling, so it makes them happy." She takes my hand. "And I was thinking about University of Chicago because of you."

I smile, although I feel sad. Bex needs to do what's right for her. But that doesn't mean I won't miss her. "Have you told your parents?"

She shakes her head. "I'm working up to it. Or maybe I'll steam open the envelopes and replace 'University of Chicago' with 'Columbia' on the tuition checks."

"As long as you have a plan," I say. "Maybe they'll be happy? You'll be closer to them." Bex's family lives in D.C.

She sighs. "No. Me being a pediatrician would've been something they could tell their friends. They were going to take me on mission work. That's not going to happen with their daughter the climate scientist."

I squeeze her hand. "When I told Anita that my mom wanted me to go back on meds, she said, 'They're your parents, but they don't own you.'"

Bex nods but doesn't look convinced. "But you'll be okay? If I don't go?"

For her sake, I force another smile. "I will. We can do virtual tea parties, and we'll visit on breaks, and I'll text you all the time."

"Thanks for making this easy on me," she says, and wraps her arms around me. We sit like that for a long time, and then she says, "You know Leo's jealous of Caleb, right?"

"Yeah. I got that one."

Back in my own room, I text both Caleb and Leo to make sure everything is okay, being very careful not to mix up my texts. Both of them seem fine, but I'm still too edgy to sleep. I know what I want to do, but it feels like I'm betraying them both, so I resist. I do a little math, finish my reading for English, sort my laundry, and get ready for bed.

I lie down for about two minutes, and then I get back up and open my laptop.

Tesseract: You're here late.

Milo: I was hoping you'd be back.

Tesseract: I couldn't sleep.

Milo: Ah, so now I know what you think of me. Better than sleeping pills.

Tesseract: Better than Xanax, more like. Tell me one thing that no one IRL knows.

Milo: Why?

Tesseract: I don't know. There are all these people in your life who know all kinds of things about you. I want one little piece that they don't have. Is that selfish? Or weird?

Milo: No. I get it. Here's a good one: I want to go to MIT. Badly.

Tesseract: You and half the people coming to Frontier. Why is that a secret?

Milo: I don't know if I can get in. Or I didn't know until I got the Frontier invite.

Tesseract: Wouldn't people understand? Lots of people don't get into their first-choice schools.

Milo: Maybe. I guess my instinct is to hide how much I care about things. Especially if I think I might not get them. I hate the idea of people feeling sorry for me.

Tesseract: Is that how people would feel? That, by the way, is a more genuine question than it might seem.

Milo: I think so. I don't really do publicly sad, so people wouldn't know what to do with it.

Tesseract: That sounds lonely.

Milo: I never thought about it like that. But I guess it is, a little. Maybe it's why I like talking to you like this.

Tesseract: I like talking to you too. Are you going to tell people now? With Frontier, you'll almost certainly get in.

Milo: I think I'll keep it secret a while longer. I'm not sure if my parents can afford it. And it feels selfish to ask. I don't want to pressure them into it.

Tesseract: Well, I hear there's this scholarship . . .

Milo: There's a 5 percent chance of that.

Tesseract: Your mathematical model isn't complex enough. They're not pulling names out of a hat. Your chances could be much higher . . . or lower, I guess.

Milo: Ouch.

Tesseract: Well, what do I know? Adorable on-screen personas may not necessarily translate to mathematical genius.

Milo: I'm blushing.

Tesseract: Is this a bad time to tell you I have a boyfriend?

Milo: There is no good time to tell me you have a boyfriend. Does he know you tell strangers you meet online that they're adorable?

Tesseract: You're not a stranger.

Milo: I suspect he won't find that very comforting. What's one thing no one knows about you?

Tesseract: That's hard, because there's one person in my real life who knows almost everything about me.

Milo: The boyfriend?

Tesseract: Not exactly. This one's a Boy. Space. Friend.

Milo: And do they get along—the boyfriend and the BSF?

Tesseract: Of course. They're very mature.

Milo: Yes, I've noticed that's a common characteristic of teen-age boys, especially when they're around pretty girls.

Tesseract: Why do you think I'm pretty?

Milo: You have three boys orbiting you.

Tesseract: But only two know what I look like.

Milo: Stop fishing for compliments. Time's up. What's your secret?

Tesseract: I only have one secret from people IRL.

Milo: And that is?

Tesseract: You.

Milo: Sleep tight, Tess.

Tesseract: You too, Milo.

CALEB

I LIE AWAKE THINKING ABOUT TESS. WHO IS EVIE. Somehow, this is harder to keep track of than I predicted. Talking to her like this is definitely not making me want her less. Online, she is clever and playful and honest, and I can say what I think without worrying whether she's going to be hurt or weirded out if I flirt with her.

When she called me adorable, I briefly considered the possibility that it was not Evie at all but some shockingly similar science girl. But the thing is, I know it's her—not because of her quotes and her favorite book and her boy-space-friend, but because it feels like *Evie.* Like what we could be.

And if she's feeling anything similar on her side of the screen, she's going to figure out Leo's not the right one. Which is good for me and for Milo, if I can be patient.

At breakfast, I realize I also have to be careful.

Coming off our conversation last night, I give her a big smile when I walk into the cafeteria until her confused reaction makes me remember that our last interaction as Evie and Caleb was that fight in the lounge. I'm more contained the rest of the morning, although whenever I remember that I'm Evie's secret, my smile creeps back.

"You're in a surprisingly good mood," Evie says, looking over her computer. We're in the study room. Because most kids go home for Thanksgiving, we have no classes this afternoon. David's flight doesn't leave until late, so he agreed to help us start our Frontier poster, and we're waiting on him.

"Just glad about the break."

She gives me another confused look, and I don't blame her. With all our parents coming tomorrow, I'm not actually that excited.

When David comes in, he tells us that in the public poster session, the judges evaluate your ability to explain the concepts in your paper by asking you to talk about your poster. They're trying to make sure that the people whose names are on the paper are the people who did the work.

If you're chosen as one of the top five, you give a ten-minute talk onstage. At that point, though, you're just playing for pride. The size of the scholarship for all finalists is the same.

The honor code around Frontier is fierce and involves all kinds of rules. No one but the authors can see a paper before it's submitted, although you can talk through concepts with teachers. Once you're accepted, you can get feedback on your paper from peers, but not from anyone who has earned a degree in mathematics or physics. You are also not supposed to be in contact with anyone else in your Frontier cohort, except anonymously on the site.

I suspect this is part of what's putting a strain on Leo and Evie. It's got to be hard not to talk about the most important thing in your life with the person you're dating, especially when that person happens to be one of the few people in the world who also knows what a big deal this is.

David says he wants to finish reading our paper before he gives us advice on the poster, so Evie and I pretend to work as we IM back and forth as Milo and Tess.

Milo: Do you think they'll ask us random physics questions in the poster round?

Tesseract: No, why would they do that?

Milo: I don't know. To cull the herd?

Tesseract: I'm not sure what that means, but I don't think the plan is to be deliberately cruel. I really think they want to find the best work. Have you heard something else?

Milo: No. But I want to study if I need to. I don't want to let my partner down, and I feel like I'm the weak link.

Tesseract: It's hard being responsible for someone else.

Milo: For this, definitely. It's so important, and I'm not as confident as I could be. Usually I don't mind people depending on me, though. Typical oldest child, I guess.

Tesseract: Really? You seem more like the goofy youngest.

Milo: I can't decide if that's an insult or a compliment.

Tesseract: Are you kidding? All the reliability of the oldest wrapped up in the fun package of the youngest? It's a selling point.

Milo: Are you buying?

Then, just to cause trouble, I say, "What are you working on, Eves?"

She looks up, caught. It's a good thing I already know her secret, because if I didn't, there's no way I'd let her keep it.

"English?"

"Why? We don't have humanities anymore." I'm a terrible person.

"Umm, I had some makeup work. What are you doing?"

I've already thought of an answer. "I'm talking to Nolan. They got out yesterday, so they're already at my grandparents'." This is true, and I did text him, so I'm not exactly lying.

As Milo, I send her a message.

Milo: Still there, or did I scare you away?

Flustered, she looks at her screen. Evie's having a hard time keeping up with all her suitors. She signs off.

David puts down the paper and looks at her, saying, "Jesus, Evie. This isn't a Frontier paper. It's a dissertation."

"It's good?" I ask.

He looks at me, openmouthed. "Do you understand what you submitted?"

Evie leaps in, sensitive to anyone questioning my intellect. "He did all the programming, David. I did the math."

David looks at her. "You know what that means."

She nods, but I have no idea what they're talking about. David looks over at me. "She can't freeze up when they're talking to her during the poster session. No offense, Caleb, but there's no way you can explain this, and if she can't, they're going to assume that someone did it for you. You could get disqualified. And you don't want the reputation that goes with that."

I shake my head a little. "But aren't math people notoriously bad at talking to strangers? Won't they just think she's nervous?"

Both David and Evie look at me a little sadly. "He can't help that everything's easy for him," Evie says.

"Hey!"

"Evie is a girl," David says.

"Yes. I have noticed," I answer. Evie scowls.

"What that means is that some of the judges will not believe she is capable of doing the work in this paper. They will assume that you are the brains of the operation, and when they discover that you are not—again, no offense—they will look for another explanation that fits their assumptions, and it will not be that Evie is an introvert."

I look from one of them to the other, not wanting to believe this is true.

"You've met Dr. Lewis, right?" David adds.

"Okay," I say. "So she needs to be ready."

I spend the rest of the afternoon doing an initial design of the poster while David circles parts of the paper they're most likely to ask about. Evie practices talking these through, but the real test will be whether she can do it with strangers.

As we're packing up before dinner, Evie puts her hand on David's forearm. "Have you seen Leo's paper?"

David looks at her and says, "Evie," warningly.

"You don't have to tell me anything. I just wondered if it was good."

"It wouldn't have gotten in if it wasn't good," David says.

She looks at him for a while, and I'm surprised to see that they know each other well enough to carry on a silent conversation. Maybe it's some kind of secret math language.

I open the door to the study room to find Leo and, strangely, Sarah-Kate. He watches David and Evie, who are standing close together, her hand still on his arm. Evie blushes, and David winces. I may not have caught everything that passed between them, but it's pretty clear David isn't nearly as impressed with Leo's paper as he is with ours. He gives an awkward little wave and heads off.

Surprised, Leo looks at me. I think he's trying to figure out how he should respond to the David-Evie thing by reading my reaction. I give him a shrug. I'm trying to figure out what the hell he's doing with Sarah-Kate.

Sarah-Kate claps her hands. "Field trip!" she says. "My parents came to do Thanksgiving with me tomorrow, so I have a car tonight."

"What are you thinking?"

She grins. "Skee-Ball?"

"You're on."

The strange thing about the evening is how easy it is. When Sarah-Kate and I were dating, she was consistently awful to Evie, which is the major reason we broke up. And for the last two weeks, it's been a little tense whenever Evie, Leo, and I are all together. But tonight we forget all that and simply become cute teenagers double-dating at the Chuck E. Cheese's.

Evie's right that if I had one wish, it would be to pitch a perfect game, but I know that's a dream only magic could make possible. However, a perfect Skee-Ball game is within my grasp.

The result of my commitment is that Sarah-Kate occasionally beats me, since I aim only for the hundred-point holes in the corners while she sends her balls consistently up the center.

"Oh, that's got to hurt," she says when she outscores me for the third time. "Losing to a girl who plays a sport where she's not even allowed to use her hands."

Sometime later—I could finance my MIT education myself with what I've put into this machine tonight—I put nine balls in a row exactly where they need to be. I hold the tenth in my hand and look at Sarah-Kate, prolonging the excitement. She reaches up to kiss my cheek, saying, "For luck."

I roll the last ball and miss.

When she says, "Maybe we'd better try the lips next time," I'm surprised to find myself interested. I don't understand why the depth of what I feel for Evie doesn't wash away this more mild affection for Sarah-Kate. But it doesn't. I have feelings for them both. And maybe that's how it is for Evie too with me and Leo. Only, what if she never sees how much better she and I could be? Or worse yet, what if that casual warmth is all she wants? Maybe that's why she pushed me away. Not because she didn't feel anything, but because she didn't want to feel too much.

"Should we order?" Sarah-Kate asks, and I pull my mind back to the present.

Leo and Evie are moving around, racing ducks with water guns, playing video games, and moving baskets to catch falling plastic apples. I can tell from Leo's face that he is truly horrified by her lack of hand-eye coordination. Watching her in this place, I honestly can't help wondering how she moves through the world without injuring herself.

Over a dinner of regrettable pizza (although even the worst pizza I've ever had was pretty good), I tell Leo and Sarah-Kate that Evie has only one arcade talent.

"Supporting the economy? Making small children feel competent?" Leo asks, and Evie shoves him with her shoulder.

"Gambling," I say.

Evie is freakishly good at those games where you press a button to make the light stop moving around the circle at just the right time. I have no idea why. I don't know if something in her math brain is able to calculate where the light is going to be or if she is merely ridiculously lucky, but she has always been able to coax wild numbers of tickets out of those machines.

We go over to try now, and Leo and Sarah-Kate watch, amazed, as ribbons of seventy-five, a hundred, and two hundred tickets spill out of the machine. Then she hits the jackpot: 750. Sarah-Kate gathers them up in her arms and takes them to the prize counter, trading them, along with our Skee-Ball winnings, for a tiara for Evie, a headband with stars on antennae for herself, and tattoos for me and Leo (baseball and soccer, respectively).

Then Sarah-Kate gets a wet napkin and presses the tattoo to my cheek, holding it there and looking into my eyes while she counts. When she pulls the backing off, she says, "Perfect."

It would be easier for all of us if I fell back into this thing with Sarah-Kate, but I can't make myself do it. Something's changed for me. Dating other people doesn't even seem fun anymore.

Back at Newton, as we're getting out of the car, Leo whispers to Evie, "You want to prep for Frontier? I bet the study room's open." I don't hear her response, but the accompanying giggle suggests it's a yes.

After saying good night (chastely) to Sarah-Kate, I go back to my room and open my laptop, but there's no sign of Tess by the time I go to bed two hours later.

In contrast to the night before, our mood in the morning is grim. Sarah-Kate leaves early to spend the day with her parents; the few students who have been entirely abandoned by their families start a gaming tournament in the media room; and Leo, Evie, and I mark time in the senior lounge. Our parents are traveling together, so we've agreed to meet them at the restaurant at one o'clock.

Mom texts me at noon: *Almost there. I think it's going to be ugly.*

I do not share this with Evie. I can tell from her face that she's not expecting anything different. On the walk over, she is pretty far gone inside herself. She gets like this when she's stressed, and you have to let her be. Leo's trying to give her space, but he's obviously anxious about meeting her family and occasionally reaches out for her hand or tries to start conversations for reassurance, but she doesn't have any to give. Dealing with her mother takes all of Evie's emotional resources.

All four of our parents are waiting in the lobby when we arrive, and despite the tension of the morning, I'm genuinely happy to see Mom and Dad. I'll always be grateful for the opportunities Newton opened for me, but leaving them when I was fourteen was hard.

Evie introduces Leo to her parents, and I can feel Mom not look at me when she calls him her boyfriend. We don't have the kind of relationship where we have heart-to-hearts about this sort of thing, but she has eyes.

Evie's father shakes Leo's hand and says, "Congratulations on Frontier," and her mother gives him a *Don't start* look.

We're seated at a table that looks out over an open area of campus. In the summer, it's beautiful and green, but at the end of November, the landscape is gray and barren.

The meal is a buffet, so we serve ourselves. When we're seated, we talk about the food: what's good, what's similar to our favorites at home, what's unacceptably innovative. Then Beth says, "So, Leo, tell us how you and Evie met."

Leo smiles at her and says, "Our eyes met across a crowded physics classroom."

Evie turns to her father. "He had the most beautiful solution to a spinning top problem."

Her father looks interested, but Evie's mother breaks in. "So you're a math major too." She says this as if she's taking his medical history, and Evie glares.

"No, physics, and I do coding with Caleb. But physics and math are pretty interchangeable at this level."

"Speaking of physics and math," Evie says.

Here we go.

"I know you're concerned about Frontier, but I've talked to Anita, and we agree that going is the right decision for me. So that's what I'm doing."

I'm proud of her. She didn't say it as a question, and although I'd like to take her hand, she doesn't need it. Leo looks at his plate, wishing, I'm sure, that a portal would open and take him anywhere not here.

Evie's mom clears her throat. "You've made a lot of

progress, Evie, but you're not thinking this through. Think about what happened last year. Something this stressful—"

"Beth." Evie's dad cuts her off. "You heard her say she's spoken to her therapist. She wants to do it. I don't think you understand what a big deal this is. We have to let her go." He looks from me to Leo to my parents, but Beth doesn't give anyone else a chance to speak.

"Liam, they took her out of the airport in a wheelchair last year. She was hysterical. And do you remember two years ago when we found her curled up in the corner of that store sobbing? And when she was thirteen and we let her go away because *you* thought she could handle it, and when she came home, she stopped speaking for a month? So no. I don't have to let her do anything, especially go somewhere that almost broke her less than twelve months ago."

I hate this picture she's painting of Evie. Yes, all of that happened. But she's left out so much. I want to say: *Do you remember when she built that cardboard boat and won a hundred dollars because hers stayed afloat longer than anyone else's, even all the adults'? Do you remember when she planned a scavenger hunt across the city for Joel's tenth birthday that had thirty-nine clues because those were his favorite books? Or when she sat up all night with me when our dog died because she was the only person I would cry in front of?* It's not that I think these things would sway her mother, but I want Evie to remember who she is.

Lost in thought, I miss some of the conversation.

Her father is saying, "The math doesn't cause this. Most of us are terribly normal."

"Most of you aren't like her," her mother answers. "Maybe you're willing to risk this because you resent her. Then you don't have to feel bad about not having her gift. But the math isn't worth it. Not to Evie. Not to me."

Evie's father opens his mouth to respond, but before he can, Evie, who, like the rest of us, has been watching in horrified silence, stands and heads for the door. I follow, turning as I leave to say, "Fix them" to my own parents.

This is not really fair. Mom's a hand surgeon, and Dad's an ER doc. I don't think any of this falls into their areas of expertise.

In the hall, I grab Evie's jacket and mine from the rack and turn toward the stairs. Leo is right behind me.

"No," I snarl at him, then stop. If I argue, he will stay with me. And whatever he is to Evie, he doesn't belong in this. "She's probably gone back to Newton. Why don't you check there?"

He looks a little dazed, which is good, because it keeps him from realizing I was about to head in the opposite direction.

"Should I take her jacket?" he asks, reaching for it.

I shake my head. "If she's going to Newton, she'll be back before you catch her. I'll keep it in case she's here somewhere."

After Leo leaves, I head for the stairs. There's a terrace on the fifth floor surrounding a pool that's open in the summer.

Despite all Evie's fears, heights have never bothered her. In fact, when she's stressed, she seeks them out. She says it isn't weird because high places are the opposite of the tight spaces she finds so terrifying.

When I open the door to the terrace, I see her right where I expect her to be, body pressed up against the barrier, hands gripping the railing, and hair blowing in the wind.

EVIE

THE DOOR OPENS BEHIND ME, AND I KNOW IT'S Caleb even before he says, "I don't have to remind you of the gravitational constant, right?"

He comes up behind me and holds open my jacket. I shrug into it.

"Is it wrong to dream of being an orphan?" I say.

"Not under the circumstances."

I love my parents, but I dread the lifetime of Thanksgivings stretching out before me where I'll constantly be evaluated for possible mental breakdowns.

Turning to Caleb, I say, "When we grow up, I want to spend every holiday with your family."

"I love that plan."

I lean my head against his shoulder and take deep CBT breaths, counting my heartbeats each time. "Where's Leo?"

I ask, even though I'm relieved he's not here. I don't want to explain my parents' behavior or talk about my past problems or hear about his feelings while I'm still making sense of mine.

"I told him you might be headed back to Newton and that he should check."

I look up at Caleb. "You knew I wouldn't be."

"I did." He's quiet. "Are you mad? Do you want him?" There's something vulnerable in Caleb's voice.

I find his hand and lace his fingers with mine. "No. I should probably text him soon. He'll be worried." But I don't move, and neither does Caleb. Being with him is so ridiculously easy. He is almost impossible to disappoint or make angry, and he's constantly reading everyone around him to make sure they're okay. I wonder if he's ever exhausted by this.

"You know she's wrong," he says after a little while.

"About which part?"

"That you can't handle it. That the mathematics isn't worth it. That a setback would break you. Maybe about your father too. I don't know."

"He is jealous sometimes. His work is incremental. He finds ways to do things that are more efficient. Sometimes more beautiful. But this thing you and I did together . . . it's more interesting than anything he'll ever do."

"What is it with her? Is it that disease, the one from *The Wizard of Oz*?"

I look at Caleb blankly.

"You know," he says, the corners of his mouth turning up. "That one about the munchkins?"

Grinning, I say, "You're trying to make me laugh."

He opens his eyes wide. "I have no idea what you're talking about. I'm trying to have a serious conversation about the appropriate diagnosis for your mother."

"It's not Munchausen by proxy. She doesn't want me to be sick. She's scared. For good reason, to be fair."

Because of everything she's seen me go through, Mom will never be able to see me as well, which makes me wonder about Leo. He can't be thrilled to have learned more of the gory details of his girlfriend's history of breakdowns.

"How do you do it?" I ask Caleb.

"What?"

"Treat me like I'm normal. You and Bex both do, but she's never seen me at my worst."

He folds his arms on the railing and bends down to rest his chin on them.

"I don't think I do see you as normal, Evie," he says, looking out over campus.

Hearing this hurts like a physical blow—far more than anything Mom said downstairs. Caleb's belief in me is my foundation.

"You are thunderstorms and supernovas and four-leaf clovers and jackpots. Normal would be a step down."

All of the upset I've been holding inside spills out, and I'm sobbing. Not crying, but hiccuping and gasping. His arms are around me, and I press into him, but I can't calm down, so I let myself cry until there are no more tears. Even then, I stay quiet for a long time. He never moves, making no demands, seeking no reassurance.

His jacket is sopping wet. "It's a good thing you dressed for the elements."

Only then does he put his hands on my face and force me to look at him. "Are you okay?"

I look into his eyes and say the truest thing I know. "If I am, it's because of you."

After studying my face for a while, he kisses my forehead and pulls an old paper napkin out of his pocket, which I use to wipe my face.

"What's our plan here?" he says.

I think about this for a minute. "I think you and your parents should go somewhere for dessert. They drove four hours to see you, and you haven't even gotten to talk. I'm going to make my dad sign the Frontier paperwork, and then I'll go back to Newton."

On the way downstairs, I text Leo, telling him that I'm going to have a conversation with my parents and I'll be back later. He texts me a heart. I don't know exactly what that means, but at least it's not a straightjacket.

Caleb's parents are sitting on a bench at the entrance of the restaurant. "Sorry about all of that," I say.

"No worries," Caleb's dad replies. "Last Thanksgiving, I pulled a carving fork out of someone's eye. This was nothing."

"They're still at the table," his mom says.

I kiss both of their cheeks. "See you in a couple of weeks."

"If you love me, you'll find somewhere that will feed me pie," Caleb says to them as I head into the restaurant.

Mom and Dad are sitting together at one end of the table, my purse in front of them. I sit down.

"I'm sorry I said all of that in front of Leo," Mom says. "He seems like a nice boy."

"He is a nice boy," I agree. "Nice enough that he'll probably overlook my history of crazy." Mom winces at the word, but I am beyond concern about appropriate language.

I turn to Dad. "There's a form I need signed for Frontier. Will you do it?"

"Evie!" Mom says. I don't blame her for being surprised. I don't know if I've ever done anything without her permission. "Your father says the first part of the conference is just talking one-on-one. That only five presenters end up onstage. If you think you're ready to go, I can live with that. As long as you don't end up in front of a big group."

"If we make the top five, I'm giving the talk."

"Can't Caleb do it?" Mom asks.

This makes me laugh. "No, he really can't. At least not alone."

"Well, you'll have to go back on your meds. It's the only way."

She's drowning in a mix of love and fear and the terrible

stories she reads as part of her work. I've been there, but it's not where I live anymore.

"No. I don't need them now."

"Maybe you need a change in dosage or a different kind?"

"Mom. No. I've got this. I need you to trust me."

It's so hard to say this when I don't 100 percent trust myself. I consider telling her that Anita said it's time to terminate, but I suspect this will scare her more than reassure, and I don't want to provoke a description of the many artists and mathematicians who rejected medication for the sake of creativity and then met horrible fates.

"Evie, with anxiety and depression—"

I cut her off. "I am not depressed. I have never been depressed." I am so tired of her making this bigger than it is.

"Anxiety and depression coincide."

"I am not a statistic. I am your actual human daughter. And I'm not dealing with this by pretending it's not there or getting my star signs done. A psychologist is treating me. And it's working. It would be nice if you could celebrate that instead of melting down."

"Of course I'm happy you're better. It's not about that."

"The CBT helps. And not getting teased helps." This is what Anita helped me see. Going to Frontier last year triggered a long-buried fear: that meeting new kids meant returning to the name-calling, and worse. It's continual work to remind myself all of that is behind me.

Mom hates hearing about this part. Because if the problem was only in my brain, she did all she could. But if part of the problem was school, she could have gotten me out earlier.

I pull the Frontier paperwork out of my purse and push it toward Dad. He signs it without looking at Mom.

"Evelyn," he says, "if I could make the leaps you do, I would take the anxiety as a fair price."

"Liam," Mom says, chiding.

"I don't know if the two are related," I tell him. "But if they are, you're right. It's worth it." This is maybe the most honest conversation Dad and I have ever had about this, and it feels like a small victory.

We linger at the table for a while before walking back across campus to Newton, and we talk of less fraught subjects, trying to reconnect before they leave. I suspect Mom is making some kind of plan, but I can't do anything about it until I know what it is.

I wait with them on the sidewalk in front of Newton until Caleb's parents arrive. They need to head back because Monica has surgery in the morning. It's a ridiculous amount of driving to do in one day, and I know all four of them did it because they love us.

Caleb puts his hand on my back as we watch them pull away.

"Did you get your pie?" I ask.

He jiggles the bag in his left hand. "Everything was closed, so we had to go to the grocery store, but the good news is I have leftovers. You want to find people inside? There's plenty."

I know he means Leo, but the truth is, I don't. I'm not quite ready to deal with anyone else. Caleb doesn't force me to say it.

"Study room?" he asks.

I nod, and we creep in the back way, looking around corners and listening for footsteps. I feel ridiculous, but I really don't want to talk to anyone. When we get to our room, Caleb pulls out the remains of three pies—pumpkin, apple, and cherry—and a handful of plastic forks. There's no point to pumpkin pie without whipped cream, so I pull the cherry one toward me.

As I lift the first bite to my mouth, I give Caleb sad eyes.

"What?" he says.

"I wish I had tea."

"Fine. Five minutes. But if a crowd follows me back, it's your own fault."

While he's gone, I'm tempted to pull out my phone and check if Milo's online, but I'm pretty sure he won't be, because he told me he'd be with family all day. I feel guilty even thinking about it. It's one thing to want to be with Caleb, who has known me since childhood, but it's something else entirely to choose this person I've never met over my boyfriend. I want to, though. Maybe I'm not cut out for dating.

Caleb opens the door carefully with two mugs in his hands. He puts the tea in front of me.

"You eluded pursuers?"

"The lounge is empty. It was sort of eerie."

We eat in silence, Caleb switching off between all three pies, which is pretty disgusting. I put my fork down.

"So how are things going with you and Leo?" he says into the silence.

"Why do you ask?"

"Eves. You're hiding in here with me, and you ate half a pie."

I sigh. I could blame this on Mom, but I think I might want to talk about Leo. Caleb knows a lot more about this stuff than either Bex or me.

"I don't know, Caleb. He's smart and sweet. I really do like him, and . . ." My voice trails off, and I feel my cheeks flush. I can tell Caleb almost anything, but not how it feels when Leo kisses me.

"I get the idea. What's the problem?"

I bite my lip, trying to decide if I'm going to say this out loud. To Caleb.

"Evie?" he says. "I'm dying here. What?"

"I might be feeling something for someone else?" I say it really fast, as if that will make it better. "Maybe."

He smirks. "You're certainly making up for lost time. Are you going to tell me who?"

I shake my head.

"Do I know him?"

I shake my head again.

"How did you meet someone not from Newton?"

I look up at the ceiling, surprised the answer isn't obvious. "You know the chat rooms on the Frontier site?" I ask.

He nods.

"Well . . ."

Grinning, Caleb says, "And you like him?"

"I really do," I admit. "Am I a horrible person?"

"No. No. You're allowed to talk to other boys. To have friends. Even if you have a boyfriend."

"But what if, hypothetically, I told the online boy that he was adorable?"

"Well, hypothetically, you might want to think about why you did that."

This thing with Milo is confusing. Despite the adorable slip, the connection I'm building with him feels more like what I have with Caleb than what I have with Leo. Maybe because I'm so honest with him.

Dating Leo has taught me that being romantically involved with someone requires hiding some parts of yourself. When I cried those ugly tears with Caleb, I wasn't worrying about how I looked, because I didn't have to think about whether he'd want to kiss me later. Probably I'm so comfortable with Milo because he's meant to be a friend, like Caleb.

I decide to test my theory. "Were you different with your girlfriends than you are with me?"

Caleb's eyes widen. "What do you mean?"

"Do you feel like they knew you as well as I do? That you could talk to them about anything?"

He shakes his head. "Of course not. I mean, they were all different. But Evie, none of them were you."

"What does that mean?" I need him to be clear. I want to understand this.

He laughs. "Well, for one, I'd never answer a question like this for anyone else. And for two, I'm a little more relaxed with you. Goofier, sometimes. And more honest about asking for help when I need it."

I draw in a shaky breath and squeeze his hand. I was right. He hides part of himself from the people he dates too. This makes sense, because I saw Caleb with those girls. He was always wrapping his arms around them and pulling them into corners and onto couches, but he never talked to them the way he talks to me. What we have is different.

So I don't need to feel guilty about Milo, who is so very easy to talk to. He's not a threat to Leo.

This should make me happy.

But for some reason, it doesn't.

CALEB

THE GOOD NEWS IS EVIE IS INTO MILO. THE BAD news is I am now jealous of myself.

After a few quiet minutes, Evie says she'd better find Leo. I stay in the study room, trying to figure out what the hell I am doing with my life. What I told Evie was true: I am more open with her than with anyone else in my life. But there are things Tess knows that Evie doesn't. I'm not sure what that means.

I toss the rest of the pies in the garbage and head out.

As I go by the lounge, I hear Evie's laugh, then her voice: "I don't want to talk anymore. Can we *forget* for a little while?" I don't slow down, and I don't look.

Going back to my tiny room seems more depressing than I can take, particularly since I suspect I won't be hearing from Tess anytime soon, but I also can't imagine joining the chaos in the media room. I go to the marble steps of the lobby, sit at the top, leaning back against a pillar, pull out my phone, and devote some attention to my fantasy baseball team (Not the 'Roids You're Looking For).

I don't notice Sarah-Kate until she sits down next to me, kisses my cheek, and says, "Happy Thanksgiving."

"Says you," I respond, putting away my phone.

"Oh, Caleb." She leans her head on my shoulder and takes my hand.

"Sarah-Kate," I say. "I'm not—"

She laughs, but not like she thinks anything is funny. "I am more aware than anyone else on the planet of what you are not." She puts her hand on my cheek and turns my face toward her, and I remember what it was like to kiss her.

"Do you want to take a break from the unrequited thing? Just for the night?"

I really do, but that doesn't seem fair to the girl in front of me.

"I'm not in a good place to start something."

"I don't want to start something." She looks up at the ceiling and smiles mischievously. "I just want a little epilogue."

"Why?"

"I'm bored. I like you. You know your way around a kiss."

"I don't suppose I could get you to write a reference letter to that effect?"

"You might be able to talk me into it," she says. "But I'll need to make sure your skills are up-to-date."

"Really?" I say.

She nods. "It's your lucky day."

When the front doors open a little later, I quickly take inventory of the situation. We've both lost our jackets, and Sarah-Kate's hair is a mess. I move to fix it, but she slaps my hand away and does it herself, so I scoot back and try to look unconcerned as Dev comes up the stairs.

He gives us an amused look. "If you're trying for discretion, maybe not the front lobby?" He turns down the main hall. In a few moments, we hear him say, "My eyes! I'm gone twenty-four hours, and the place turns into a brothel."

Sarah-Kate and I look at each other, and she giggles. I tuck her hair behind her ears, saying, "That was really nice."

"It was. You can count on that letter of reference. Top five percent of applicants for sure." She puts her hand on my cheek. "I don't think I should do it anymore, though. It would be too easy to fall for you again."

I take her hand and bring it to my mouth for a quick kiss. "I'm sorry it didn't work out between us."

"I can't imagine what Evie is thinking."

I pass her jacket to her, grab mine, and stand, reaching out a hand to pull her up. Once she's on her feet, I'm not sure if I should let go. The etiquette on what to do after you've made out with an ex-girlfriend who has told you that it's not going to happen again and that she knows you're in love with someone else is a little unclear.

Sarah-Kate laughs and pulls her hand away. "Now we go

back to how things were." But that's not so easy when I can still feel her lips on mine and see the aftermath of my hands in her hair.

I'm still figuring out what to say when Dev sticks his head out of the lounge. "If you're done with your tonsil check, come here. We're celebrating the true meaning of Thanksgiving with Risk: The Game of Global Domination."

I check with Sarah-Kate, and she nods, so we go in. Evie, Leo, and Dev are sitting around a table with the board in the middle, and when I meet Evie's eyes, I feel abruptly guilty, even though I know what she's been doing in here with Leo. Her gaze moves briefly to Sarah-Kate and then back to me, her face questioning.

I'm not sure how to communicate the state of things—even to Evie—with a look, especially with Sarah-Kate observing, so I give her a little wave and sit across the table.

Dev pulls cards and pieces out of the box and looks at all of us. "I assume you know how to play."

Evie says, "You'll have to remind me of the finer points." Leo picks up the cards and begins explaining them to her.

I interrupt. "I'm going to say this only once. If you let her, she will take you all in."

Next to me, Sarah-Kate says very quietly in my ear, "Speaking from experience, I assume?"

I grab the box of black armies at the same time Evie reaches for the green ones, and we grin at each other before beginning to count out our starter sets. Dev starts to check the rules to see how many you use for five players. Together, Evie and I say, "Twenty-five."

Dev and Leo look at us. "The finer points?" Dev says to Evie.

She smiles. "Sometimes I lose track of the Markov chains that govern the attack-defend rules and I have to rely on instinct."

"I think we have a game," Dev responds.

We pass out cards to distribute countries, and I end up with half of Australia, which is how I like it. Evie finds this strategy acceptable, if overly cautious. Leo's cards are distributed between Africa and South America, which he's mostly sharing with Dev and Evie, who also has a substantial presence in North America. Sarah-Kate is scattered all over the place.

We take turns placing our armies. Out of what I assume is some attempt at chivalry, Leo focuses on Africa, leaving South America for Evie. She is disgusted and whispers, "Africa! The limited rewards of Australia with none of the safety."

"There are three borders. It's the same as North America," he replies, gesturing toward the continent Evie's focusing on.

"But there are six invasion pathways. In North America, there are only three. And in Africa, you have to hold two territories for every bonus army you get."

Everyone else is watching them. "How many for North America?" he asks.

"One-point-eight."

"And Europe?" he says, amused.

"One-point-four."

"Do you know the ratios for each continent?"

"Of course! Do you not?" She seems as disturbed by this as he was by her lack of coordination last night.

He kisses her.

"Enough of that," Dev says. To reward him, I vow to postpone my attack on his lone armies in Asia.

Evie's North America strategy depends on her securing the continent early. I'm too far away to stop her, and Leo and Dev are fully occupied with sorting out South America and Africa. Sarah-Kate, who obviously doesn't have much experience with the game, decides on a go-for-broke strategy in Europe, which I don't have the heart to tell her is bound to fail.

At one point, Evie tries to give her advice. "When you're rolling multiple dice, you don't consider the probability of each independently. It's a Gaussian distribution. If you don't want to do the calculations each time, a good rule of thumb is not to attack unless you have twice as many armies as the defender."

Sarah-Kate looks like she might hiss at Evie, so I gently pat her leg to distract her. Four turns later, Dev wipes her out, and she goes upstairs, saying, "Good luck with that," in a tone that tells me she's talking about more than the game.

Evie took possession of North America a few turns ago and has been quietly reaping the benefits of her continent bonus. Dev, who was focused on driving Sarah-Kate out of Europe, is unprepared when Evie storms through South America.

Leo needs to attack right now, or she'll be unstoppable, but when he picks up the red dice, she blinks her big eyes at him and says, "Really? You'd go after your girlfriend?"

I snort, but he ignores me and chases Dev into Europe. A few turns later, Evie begins her conquest of Africa, giving Leo a small smile. All of that action has given me the opportunity to hold Asia for a turn or two and amass enough forces that I have a small chance of taking her down. We sweep toward the center of the board, destroying both Leo and Dev, and meet along a jagged border in Europe.

We both turn in the sets of cards we've been saving for this moment. I pick up the attack dice. "You ready to light this thing up?"

"It's all shock and awe now, Caleb."

Then we stop talking, communicating entirely in wry looks and grins. We've played this game so many times—with friends, with my brothers, with just us—that we know each other's styles well enough to anticipate not only where the other will attack but when they'll stop and start. We pass the dice back and forth without comment and count down armies on our fingers, not bothering to exchange the plastic pieces until each battle is over. It's almost like ballet.

In the end, Evie wins. I reach across the board and rumple her hair, saying, "Good game."

"That was a thing of beauty," Dev says.

"Yes," Leo agrees, but he's looking at her.

"Sorry I went all *Call of Duty* on you," she says.

He shakes his head. "Worth it. It's nice to see you smiling."

She lays her head on his shoulder and does not seem to have lost all respect for him despite his totally inadequate game play.

There is no justice in the world.

EVIE

CALEB AND DEV GO DOWNSTAIRS TO JOIN THE video game tournament, leaving Leo and me alone, but instead of pulling me close, Leo sits back and says, "So."

Reading him is getting easier. He wants talk about this afternoon, and he's not going to let me put it off any longer. "I'm sorry about everything with my parents today," I say.

Leo shakes his head. "Nothing to be sorry for. They love you. Your mom was worried?" His voice makes this a question.

"Everything she talked about did happen. You already know about Frontier and Wunderlochen. The rest . . . panic attacks."

Leo looks away. "Could she be right?"

"What do you mean?"

"That it's too big of a risk. That Frontier could retrigger your symptoms?"

Suppressing a flash of anger, I remind myself of how he grew up. It's no wonder he's scared.

"I can't promise it won't happen, but I think it's unlikely. Especially since I'll be with Caleb."

He nods. "He found you this afternoon."

"Yes." Leo means more than he's saying, but for now it seems best to keep my response simple.

"And you wanted him, not me?"

I look into his face, thinking about how best to respond. Lying is out. Not only is it unfair, but there's no way I'd get away with it. If I'd wanted him, I'd have used my phone to tell him where I was.

"I did." I think about my revelation in the study room about the differences between boyfriends and friends. "I don't want you to see me as broken. I like the way you look at me."

"How do I look at you?"

I drop my eyes. I'm embarrassed to say it out loud, but I do anyway. "Like I'm chocolate and you're hungry," I whisper.

He leans forward to kiss the corner of my mouth. "Sounds about right," he says. "But don't you think that's also how Caleb looks at you?"

"No," I say. "That's how Caleb looks at Sarah-Kate. At least tonight."

"Are you jealous?" Leo asks, his tone making it clear that I'd better not be.

"Why would I bother? In two weeks, it'll be someone else. And he and I will still be friends."

Leo takes both of my hands. "I get that Caleb's known you since kindergarten, and I can't expect you to trust me in the same way, but I wish you would try."

Leo had girlfriends before me in Louisiana, so I'm surprised he doesn't get this. "I don't think you want to be friends with me in the same way Caleb is." Pulling him toward me, I kiss him. His hands tighten on my waist. "This is not something I do with Caleb," I say, my lips still touching his.

"And I'm glad. But being emotionally and physically connected are not mutually exclusive."

Maybe not, but there are definitely boundaries that need to be observed. I'm not going to have an emotional breakdown in front of Leo any more than I'm going to make out with Caleb.

"Evie?" Leo says when I don't respond.

"Do you remember the night with the spider?"

"Of course," he says, sounding cautious.

"The way you looked at me then was not the way you look at someone you want to kiss."

"You can't keep holding that against me. I was surprised."

"Yes, but you've seen only a tiny part of my madness. If I let you all the way in, you may not like what you find."

We glare at each other for several long moments. Then he seems to will his body to relax. He nods to himself a few times and takes my hands again.

"I hear what you're saying, but you've got to hear me too. I need to be someone you talk to, not just someone you kiss. When you're upset, I want you to want me. I don't want to see you only after he's helped you recover."

"What are you asking me to do?" I say, afraid.

"Let me in a little. Tell me something small. Something about what it was like before you came to Newton."

I'm so relieved he's not asking me to spend less time with Caleb that I'm happy to comply. After a moment, I think of the perfect story, because it's more about how awful my classmates were than about me.

"Okay, here's one even Caleb doesn't know." Leo smiles. "In fifth grade, he started playing in this select baseball league, so he didn't ride the bus home anymore because he had all these practices. And whenever I got on the bus alone, everyone would flinch away from me. Squeeze toward the windows if I walked by or leap out of the seat squealing if I sat down with them. It started with the kids in my grade, but the younger ones figured out the game pretty fast."

I'm quiet for a minute, remembering. In some ways, I've never felt quite so crazy as I did during those walks down the bus aisle, because while there was cruelty in the faces of my classmates, there was also real fear.

"You never told anyone?"

"Just Anita. And when Caleb started riding the bus again, it stopped."

Leo puts his hands on either side of my face and says, "Thank you."

I nod, pleased he's no longer angry but also feeling done for the night. I'm used to doing therapy only once a week.

After I get cleaned up and settled in my room, I think about calling Bex, but she's not the one I want to check in with before bed.

When I log on to the Frontier site, Milo's waiting.

Tesseract: Happy Thanksgiving! Are you with family?

Milo: I was. I'm on my own now.

Tesseract: Me too.

Milo: I wish I were there. Or you here. I'm not picky.

I'm trying to figure out how to respond to this when he writes again.

Milo: Tess?

Tesseract: I don't want to stop talking to you, but I need to stay out of trouble.

Milo: What does that mean?

Tesseract: My boyfriend's been very understanding today, and I'm feeling guilty. Can we just be friends?

Milo: I don't think there are a lot of other options when we're only talking online. What happened today?

Tesseract: Honestly . . .

I pause, thinking about what to say. I could tell him anything, and he'd believe it. Maybe because that's the case, I tell the truth.

Tesseract: I have some problems with anxiety. It's under control now, but my family pretty much laid it all out there for him today, and so far, it hasn't scared him away.

Milo: Do you want to tell me more?

Tesseract: Not really. It's not so bad. Just enough to keep me from being entirely normal.

Milo: Normal's overrated.

Tesseract: Thanks. But that doesn't seem to be the modal response among boys. Or girls, for that matter.

Milo: What about your BSF?

Tesseract: He's good with me. Great, really. But he doesn't have a problem with normal. Judging from the girls he dates, I'd say he's a fan.

Milo: He's never shown any interest in you?

Tesseract: Once. A long time ago. For him, I think it was mostly that it had been a while since he'd kissed anyone, and I was the girl who happened to be sitting in front of him. His standard seems to be "physically present and willing."

There's a bit of a pause. This is one of the weird things about talking like this. You have no idea what's going on around the other person.

Milo: And were you willing?

Tesseract: No. The truth is, it took me a long time to see the point of kissing. When I was younger, it seemed like an odd way to spend time.

Milo: And now?

Tesseract: I've revised my opinion in light of new evidence.

Milo: The understanding boyfriend?

Tesseract: Understanding is only one of his admirable qualities.

Milo: I hate him.

Tesseract: You wouldn't if you met him. He's nice.

Milo: Is this wishful thinking, or is that faint praise?

Tesseract: Maybe some of each? He wants me to talk about my feelings all the time, but I keep going to my BSF. Or to you. That must mean something.

Milo: This is you staying out of trouble?

Tesseract: I'd better say good night.

As I'm going to sleep, I think about what Leo said about physical and emotional connections not being mutually exclusive, wondering if it's possible that he's right and I'm wrong. There is something both seductive and a little frightening in the possibility of being so totally *known*.

CALEB

OVER THE NEXT TWO WEEKS, THE ALMOST-KISS by the campfire plays on repeat in my mind.

This isn't what I want. Not with anyone. She wasn't ready. I figured that out a while ago. She said no to a lot of people before Leo.

But that next bit: *Especially not with you.*

Brutal. Thinking about it hurts, so I don't do it very often. But I assumed she meant she didn't want a relationship with me because we were friends, or because she wasn't attracted to me, or, in my worst moments, because I wasn't smart enough.

It never occurred to me that her "especially not with you" might have been because she thought I was only looking for a warm body. If I'd said more—made clear how I felt about her—would things have been different? Would she have wanted *me* to help her figure out the point of kissing?

All this time, I've been telling myself I took my shot.

But. She. Doesn't. Know.

Doesn't know that she is the North Star for every decision I've ever made. Doesn't know that being her friend is both everything and not nearly enough. Doesn't know how many times I've kissed her in my dreams and almost kissed her in real life.

But where does this get me? She's in the middle of a (mostly?) happy relationship. It is not the time for a dramatic gesture. I imagine the conversation. *It has recently been made clear to me that you think I wanted to kiss you because I was bored or something and not because you're the love of my life. So does this new information change anything for you?*

Oh, and also, that guy you seem to like so much online? He's me. So maybe factor that into your decision? Okay. Thanks. Bye.

I'm not nearly brave enough for that. If she heard everything I want to say and stayed with Leo anyway, it would destroy me.

So, after days of sitting in the study room with Evie and getting nowhere—except on our Frontier poster, which is now excellent—I decide I may as well go to the source.

Milo: Can I ask you something?

Tesseract: I love it when you ask me things.

Milo: I know you're very happy with the understanding boyfriend and all . . .

Tesseract: I'm pretty curious about where you're going with this.

Milo: What I was wondering is: Are there any circumstances under which you could imagine falling for your BSF?

Tesseract: Why are you asking me that?

Milo: I'm trying to figure out something in my own life. I need a girl's perspective.

Tesseract: Wait. Does this mean you have a girl-space-friend? And you're only telling me now?

Milo: Yeah . . . is that a problem for you?

Tesseract: No. I guess not. I'm just surprised.

Milo: So, back to my original question.

Tesseract: I don't know how to answer. The truth is that in some ways, I've already fallen for him. He's the most important person in my life. I tell him everything. It's just that we don't . . . I mean . . . he's not my boyfriend.

Milo: That's how I feel about this girl. But then, I also want to kiss her. A lot.

Tesseract: You do? Does she want that?

Milo: No. I mean, I don't think so. I haven't brought it up in a while, but she hasn't given me any sign that she's changed her mind. But I've realized that I might not have been as clear as I could have been about what I wanted. Maybe I should talk to her . . .

Tesseract: Maybe. But you don't want to ruin what you have. I don't have a ton of experience with this, but I think it's easier to find people to kiss than people you can really talk to. A friend like that can't be replaced. Trust me.

Milo: Well, I do have you to talk to now, so maybe . . .

Tesseract: Can I ask you something?

Milo: Can't wait.

Tesseract: You said you want to kiss her, but . . .

Milo: But?

Tesseract: But sometimes you make me feel like you want that with me too. I could be reading that wrong. I do that sometimes.

Milo: You're reading things fine. My situation is a little strange. But you can definitely want to kiss more than one person. Although it might mean different things with different people. And of course, just because you want to doesn't mean you should actually do it.

Tesseract: Wanting it doesn't make you a bad person though?

Milo: No, just a human one.

So now I know two things. First, Evie doesn't like thinking about Milo kissing someone else. And second, she is making a category error. Evie believes friends and boyfriends are disjoint sets. She's got me in one group and Leo in the other, and she's trying to figure out where Milo fits. Thinking about human beings in this orderly way would be all mathy and adorable if it weren't also messing with both of our lives.

She needs disconfirming data. Maybe if her best friend could get her to feel that little rush she expects from her boyfriend, she'd see that you can't classify people so neatly, and she'd be open to more possibilities.

Over the next few days, I try everything. Before answering her questions, I brush the hair out of my eyes and look up at her through my eyelashes. I give her my well-practiced lopsided grin, and I wear my closest-fitting T-shirts to our prep sessions.

One morning, Evie studies me a little too long, and I'm hopeful. But then she says, "It's freezing today. Go put on a sweatshirt or something."

Sigh.

That afternoon, I overhear Leo badgering Evie to tell him what she's thinking, and I realize he's doing the same thing I'm doing. Or the opposite, I guess. Leo wants Evie to see her boyfriend as a friend.

For the first time since he came into her life, I feel sorry for him. Because if she's holding back her thoughts, he's missing all the best stuff.

My sympathy diminishes significantly when I walk in on them in the laundry room that evening, and it vanishes entirely when Evie is fifteen minutes late to our second-to-last practice session.

"Where is she?" I ask Bex when she comes in with David.

They exchange a look.

"What?" I say.

Bex shrugs. "Leo. I'm sure she'll be here soon."

I push back from the table. "We have two days. Is he deliberately sabotaging us?"

"Get it together over there," Bex says. "He's not a supervillain."

David mumbles something.

I turn to him. "You want to share with the class?"

"If he were a supervillain, his paper would be better."

"What's your problem with him?" Bex asks David. She knows better than to ask me.

"I don't have a problem with him," David says. "He's plenty bright, and like I told Evie, if the paper wasn't good, it wouldn't have gotten in. But Evie's work is remarkable, and I hate that she might not make it to the top five because she could freeze up in front of the judges."

"Let's focus on that, then," Bex says. "What can we do to help?"

We all sit there, thinking. David has drilled Evie on the math until she can recite explanations in her sleep. She can tell you where every equation came from and provide the reasoning that led her to put them together. She can talk about dozens of connected problems and the mathematicians and physicists whose work she's building on. Bex has been working with her on eye contact and smiling, and when she talks to us, she looks good.

We've even done run-throughs of the ten-minute stage talk—even though I didn't want to because it felt jinxy—to be safe. But the challenge is talking to people she doesn't know.

"We've got to get out of this room," I say. "It's not the math she needs to practice. It's talking to strangers."

David jumps up. "Come with me."

He leads me down into a basement storage closet full of decorations for Spring Fling, Parents' Day, and other events.

After flipping through a bunch of plywood constructions, he pulls one out.

I laugh. "This is perfect."

We lug it upstairs. Leo is sitting on the table next to Bex, but Evie is still nowhere to be seen.

"Where's the star of our show?"

"Bathroom," says Bex. "What are we doing?"

"Field trip," I say.

"Can I come?" Leo asks.

I'm about to say no, but David says, "Sure." He looks at me. "Many hands, light work. And it's not like we'll be talking about your paper."

I shrug.

When Evie comes in, I hold up the stand for her. It's bright yellow, looks like a ticket booth, and says THE MATH GENIUS IS IN!

She takes one look at it, shakes her head, and says, "No, no, no, no."

"Oh yes, Evie. We're going to the union, and you are going to talk to strangers about math."

Leo looks from one of us to the other and says, "Are you sure?"

I raise my eyebrows at Evie. I know she can do this, but I need her to believe it.

She watches me for a while before giving in. "Okay. But I'm not carrying it."

At the union, we haul the stand up the steps and set it up in the common area. Evie insists that Bex sit with her. David, Leo, and I take up positions in three armchairs nearby.

The first people to stop are a couple of sorority girls who want help with their calculus homework. Evie talks them through it without apparent trouble, although I suspect Bex chides her afterward for letting her contempt show. Then a guy stops and asks her to multiply 1,456 by 834. "I'm not a calculator," she snaps. Another young woman asks her to check her homework, which Evie does courteously. And then a man who must be a professor stops by with a young girl.

He tells Evie that last night his daughter asked him about infinity but that he's a historian and isn't sure he got it right. Evie's whole face lights up, and she begins talking softly to the girl.

After they leave, it's quiet until an older man settles himself in the chair across from Evie.

"Math genius, hmm?" he says.

"Can I help you with something?" Evie asks. She drops her hand, probably to grab Bex. The three of us sit up, and David and I exchange a nervous look while Leo glares at us both.

"I don't suppose you could use Seifert–van Kampen's theorem to compute the fundamental group of the figure eight?"

Evie goes very still.

"Well, young woman? You can't very well bill yourself as a math genius and not answer basic questions."

I watch Evie inhale, and I count with her—one, two, three heartbeats, exhale. She does it again. And then she pulls out a piece of paper and starts writing and talking at the same time. The man continues to throw questions at her—some I recognize as algebra and real analysis, and some are indecipherable to me. But Evie is settled in. She's explaining and laughing and even asking a question or two of her own.

Looking over at David, I say, "This was a brilliant idea. Thank you."

He nods. "She's going to do fine."

When the math professor leaves, he slides a card over to Evie. She picks it up and smiles, her eyes bright.

A guy on the other side of the commons accidentally gets the full impact of her smile. He has slightly curly chin-length hair and is wearing dark green corduroy pants and a blazer with actual elbow patches. He's got a canvas messenger bag across his chest, which is covered with dozens of little buttons. They're too far away to read, but I'm guessing they say things like READ BANNED BOOKS and FREE TIBET. In his hand is a *Norton Anthology of Poetry* that must weigh ten pounds.

I turn to David. "Soulful poet just realized he has an urgent math question."

He sits down in front of Evie and asks her which math classes he should take next year. Evie extolls the virtues of various lines of mathematical inquiry. He asks which classes she is likely to be in. Bex looks at me and grins.

After a little more conversation, the guy pulls a green Sharpie out of his bag and hands it to Evie. She uncaps it to write on the back of his hand.

In the middle of this, Evie meets my eyes like she's asking for permission. I cross my arms and try to give her a stern look to indicate that she is supposed to be answering math questions, not picking up college boys, but I can't hide my grin. I like that she's playing. She got so used to being teased growing up that some part of her expects every person she meets to draw blood. Despite the evidence, she probably still doesn't believe this guy crossed the room to talk to her.

Leo, however, doesn't see it this way. He stands and says, "Did my girlfriend just give her number to that future fry cook? After checking with you to see if it was okay?"

He crosses to Evie. David says, "Soulful poet's got game."

I watch as Leo suggests that perhaps the poet's time with the math genius is over while Evie turns away from Leo's scowl to twinkle at me.

David throws a couple of M&M's into his mouth. "I don't know why anyone who goes to boarding school bothers with soap operas."

"I'm glad we can amuse."

"Least you can do. I'm not charging for my services."

The poet comes by our chairs, and seeing the anthology

in his hand makes me remember something from a long time ago. I call out, "Hey!" and he stops.

"Hi. I'm Caleb. Tech support for the math genius." I gesture to Evie.

He holds out his hand. "Hawthorne."

I can't help looking over my shoulder to smirk at David because of this guy's extremely appropriate name. "Can I ask you a poetry question?"

"Sure?"

"I have a line from a poem, but I don't know where it's from. Something about making a circle just?"

"Hmmm." He gets a thoughtful look, like Evie mulling over a tough proof. "Oh! I know. I think that's 'A Valediction: Forbidding Mourning' by John Donne. Some of his stuff is super religious, but a lot of it's pretty good. I probably have it here." He flips through the book and hands it to me.

My favorite British word is *gobsmacked*, and I'm grateful for it right now, because there is no other way to describe the experience of reading this poem while knowing it is what Evie thought of when Bex asked how she felt about me. The part about the circle is at the end, but it's a line in the middle that strikes me: "But we, by a love so much refined / That our selves know not what it is." This is how it has always been for Evie and me. Words continually fall short of describing what we are to each other. I'm amazed that Evie, with her distaste for poetry and metaphor, found her way to this description of us.

I hand the book back to Hawthorne and say, "Thanks," but I'm watching Evie, who is lit up and talking to Bex while Leo looks down at her.

"No problem," Hawthorne says, following my gaze. "What's the deal with the math genius and Abercrombie & Fitch over there? Are they together?"

"They are," I say. "But I think his days are numbered."

EVIE

AS I WAIT FOR CALEB IN THE STUDY ROOM, I CAN-not stop replaying yesterday. I talked to stranger after stranger, and I did not flinch. Well, maybe once with the math professor, but not for long.

My only regret is Leo. Yesterday made everything worse between us, and things weren't going all that well before that. Leo is increasingly insistent that I *talk* to him daily, and I'm spending more and more of my time racking my brain for stories to share. It's exhausting.

Caleb throws open the door. "Hello, girl genius!"

"Math genius, thank you very much. We prefer a gender-neutral stance in our answer booths."

He raises an eyebrow. "That was not the impression I got yesterday."

"Leo was really mad about that phone number thing," I confess. I'd been a little surprised by the extent of his anger.

"Well, as much as I hate to take his side . . ." Caleb says, his voice trailing off.

I shrug. "Hawthorne said he wanted to text me if he had another question about math classes."

This time, both eyebrows go up.

I fight to hide my smile. "It's not my fault he has that ridiculous name."

"Sweet Evie," Caleb says, "when you pick up a marker to write on a boy's skin, you are entering into a social contract that has nothing to do with course scheduling."

"That was more or less Leo's point." I don't add that when I appealed to Milo, he also sided with Leo, saying that exchanging numbers need not be an excuse for thinly veiled hand-holding. Milo suggested that this was further evidence that the understanding boyfriend needed to go, given that a) he was no longer so understanding, and b) I couldn't even stay interested in him when he was right in front of me.

I felt this was unduly harsh. Although possibly not untrue. The thing is, we haven't been together that long, and I don't want to give up too soon. I'm still learning how to be a girlfriend.

"And?" Caleb says, smiling.

"And what?" I ask.

"What else did your poetic friend want to know about math classes?"

"He wanted to go out for coffee tonight to talk more about it." After a few moments of silence in which Caleb watches me, I say, "I'm not going."

"What did you tell him?"

"I sent him a link for the university academic advisors."

"That's all?"

I nod.

Caleb laughs. "There's the ice queen we know and love. I hope you told Leo. It'll make him feel better."

"Really? I thought it would make him angry that Hawthorne texted me."

"You wrote your number on his hand. Of course he texted you. If you don't say anything, Leo will assume you're carrying on a secret flirtation."

"But I'm not," I say. Then I add, "Not with Hawthorne."

"Your friend from Frontier?"

I look away. "It's not exactly a flirtation. But it's not *not* a flirtation, either." At first, when Milo said he wanted to kiss some other girl, I was relieved. We were just friends for sure, so I could stop feeling guilty. But also, I was hurt. And that was confusing.

"Have you thought about what you're going to do? Will he want to meet when we go to Chicago?"

"I hope so. I think it's the only way I'll know if we're supposed to be friends or . . ."

"Or?"

"Or something more? And maybe—probably—I should tell Leo all this, but I don't want to break everything between us when maybe I'm just mixed up. Anita says that just because you feel a little spark of something with someone else, it doesn't mean you don't care about the person you're with or that the other person would be better for you. She says I shouldn't overreact, especially because I only just started to feel like this about anyone, and I do really like Leo, but that I should pay attention to what I'm feeling and probably write it down, and that the break will be a good time to get some clarity. And then I can decide what to do."

Caleb blinks. "Wow. That was kind of a lot."

"Sorry. I can't really talk about this with anyone else. Bex usually helps with this stuff, but . . ."

"Her experience is more theoretical?"

"Yes. Exactly." Plus, I haven't told Bex or Alexa about Milo. It feels like a lot to get into. "So what do you think?"

Caleb tilts his head, his eyes searching my face. "I think you should meet him. One way or the other, you'll know what to do after that."

"You think?"

"Yeah. I really do."

Caleb heads up to the computer lab to put the finishing touches on his final project for coding. I've already turned in my project for math, so I go to the lounge to wait for Bex to finish up with her calculus exam, but when I get there, she and Leo are already at a table.

I sit down by Leo and look across at Bex. "Caleb and I were just talking about Frontier. What are your plans? Will you come to my house first or meet us there?"

"Meet you there. I'll fly in early on the twenty-eighth. Caleb can get you there, right?"

"He can," I say. Not only will having him with me help, but taking the train will be a lot less stressful than flying. I've done it loads of times. "But you should come in the night before. Come to the big dinner with us."

Bex looks back and forth between Leo and me. "Should I?" she asks.

"Yes!" we both say.

"Do I need a special outfit?"

"It's not Comic Con," Leo says.

"No Princess Leia bikini then?" Bex responds.

"I didn't say that," Leo answers. "If that's how you're comfortable, no one would judge."

I look back and forth between them. Their emotions are so big that they're easy to read. He's happy—I'd just about forgotten what that looked like. And she's flattered.

They're flirting with each other! I don't know whether to be pleased that I figured this out or hurt that it's happening.

I have no idea what this means, and clearly, I can't ask Bex. Or Leo. I pull out my phone.

Milo is not on the site. I keep checking my phone as we walk to the cafeteria, and I leave it faceup next to me as I start on my chicken soup and salad. Bex is not allowed to mind, because the chicken pieces are very small and the lentil soup looked awful.

Bex asks Leo if he has plans over the break. He's starting to respond when Milo appears in our chat room.

Milo: Hey, Tess.

Tesseract: I think Bex is flirting with my boyfriend!

Milo: Bex?

Tesseract: I'm a little discombobulated. Can you pretend that's a pseudonym?

Milo: Um, no. I really can't. I need to get settled here, and then I'll be back.

I return to my soup and salad and contribute to Bex and Leo's conversation about Christmas trees. Although my family isn't religious, we always get one, usually on the day my parents' semester ends. Caleb comes in, gives me an odd look, sets his lunch down, and pulls out his phone. I look down at mine when Milo reappears.

Milo: So what's the problem?

Tesseract: I'm not totally sure. Maybe it's not a big deal.

I think about Hawthorne. I suppose I did flirt with him

a little, and it's not like I was ever going to do anything about it.

Milo: Do you trust your friend? Trust your boyfriend?

Tesseract: I do, but I don't understand what's going on.

Milo: Usually flirting is about possibility. Letting someone know what could be, even if you never act on it. It's like tossing a baseball . . . or no . . . like a soap bubble. Maybe the other person catches it, or maybe it pops—you're just putting it out there, and it's nice while it lasts.

Tesseract: Here's the thing . . .

Bex interrupts me at this point. She says, "You two have been glued to your phones lately. You're not texting each other, are you?"

"No!" we both say, and then our eyes meet across the table before I look quickly away.

"Why would you even think that?" I ask while Leo watches me.

Caleb says, "Nolan's having some freshman year drama. I'm trying to help." Leo and Bex turn to me.

"Okay. Full confession," I say. Caleb smirks at me, but I ignore him. "I'm on the Frontier site. I'm feeling a little obsessive about the conference, so I want to gather as much advice as I can."

I decide I don't have to feel guilty because everything I just said is true.

"Very sensible," Caleb says. I turn away before he decides to add anything else to the conversation.

"You're going to be fine, Evie," Leo says, taking my hand.

Okay, now I feel guilty. Again.

"I'm going to get ready for shopping. Save room for food court cookies," I say. Bex and I are looking for Frontier clothes after lunch.

"That sounds like a good idea," Leo says. "You need to relax."

I give Caleb and Bex a quick wave and dash upstairs so I can get back to my phone.

Tesseract: Sorry about that. The thing is, I think I should be more upset than I am. And I think the reason I'm not is because I've been flirting with other people too.

Milo: Anyone I know?

Tesseract: Now who's fishing for compliments?

Milo: It doesn't have to mean anything unless you want it to. With me or anyone else.

Tesseract: I'm having a hard time figuring out what I want lately. But thanks for talking me through it. What about you? How are things with your GSF?

Milo: Weird is probably the best descriptor at the moment.

Tesseract: Weird in a way that means you might want to see me in person at Frontier?

Milo: Weird in a way that means I definitely want to see you in person.

Tesseract: Good. Although I can't make any promises about what will happen after that.

Milo: That's okay. Neither can I.

∞ ∞ ∞ ∞ ∞ ∞ ∞ ∞ ∞ ∞ ∞

Bex and I take the bus out to the mall, where she talks me into buying a gray jersey dress for the dinner, more outfits than I could possibly need for the presentation day, as well as new boots—much like my old ones, only with two-inch heels. When I worry about what Mom will say about the credit card bill, she rolls her eyes and says she'll be thrilled at this evidence of normalcy. She's almost certainly right.

When we get back to Newton, we decide to exchange Christmas presents. I turn on the fairy lights around my window and stream music on the computer. Bex makes hot chocolate in the microwave. We've done this every year, and it's a little sad to think that this will be our last Newton Christmas.

Bex hands me a tiny box wrapped in silver paper. Inside is a necklace with a small circular pendant of hammered silver. In the center is one word: BRAVE. I throw my arms around her, and then she fastens the chain around my neck.

"I won't take it off until after Frontier," I say.

I pull my present for her off my desk. It is also tiny. Bex opens it and examines the ring box cautiously, looking up at me. She opens it slowly.

"Is this a joke?" she asks.

"No, no," I say. It hadn't occurred to me that she wouldn't get it right away. "Look inside."

It took the jewelry store almost no time to buff out the

saying on the ring her parents gave her and replace it with a single word: BRAVE.

Bex looks inside the ring and then laughs. "Thank you," she says.

"This way, you can wear it at home, and maybe it will help you tell them what you want."

She hugs me. "I love you, Evie."

"I love you too, Bex."

∞ ∞ ∞ ∞ ∞ ∞ ∞ ∞ ∞ ∞ ∞ ∞

Leo and I go back to our diner that evening to try to recapture some of our early magic—this part is not said out loud—before we join everyone in the media room for the *Battlestar Galactica* marathon. It's a Newton tradition to watch an entire season of a sci-fi show the night after finals. Leo and I are planning to go a little late, because I hate the whole depressing New Caprica sequence that dominates season three.

Because the night is unusually clear and cold, I spend much of the walk to the diner looking up at the stars. Leo seems content with the silence, swinging my hand and occasionally smiling down at me.

When we get to the diner, our usual waitress seats us, saying, "I could eat you two up with a spoon!"

I watch her as she walks away. "Contemplating some off-label uses for that spoon?" Leo asks.

I grin. "Maybe it's because I'm short, but I've never liked being treated as cute."

He leans forward and kisses me on the nose. "Your cross to bear."

After we order, there's a lull in the conversation, and it doesn't feel comfortable like on the walk over. Leo spins his fork on the table. "I know things haven't been . . . like they were . . . between us, but I think after Frontier, it will be better. Not only will we be less stressed, but we'll be able to talk about what's going on in our lives."

"That part's been hard," I agree. "And half the time I don't know where the boundaries are. What I'm doing in math right now isn't exactly what I worked on for Frontier, but it's close, so I don't feel like I can talk about that with you either."

"I know. And every time you mention Caleb, I bite your head off, and we don't have to go to humanities anymore, so we can't complain about Abbie. It's making it pretty hard to have a conversation."

"I think this is what Mr. Stein would call irony—our first real conversation in weeks is about how we have nothing to talk about."

He smiles but seems sad. "It will get better after Frontier."

Over dinner, we talk about the food and our families' holiday traditions, such as they are. Before we leave, we exchange presents. I'm pretty pleased with what I found for Leo. First, a copy of *Our Mathematical Universe*, which, shockingly, he has never read—in my opinion, this alone should disqualify you from Frontier—an orange T-shirt that says SCREW LAB SAFETY, I WANT SUPERPOWERS, and a tiny glass ornament in the shape of a cup of hot chocolate smothered in whipped cream.

He holds it up. "This is my favorite," he says.

"That's because you haven't read the book yet."

Leo gives me a little gold heart on a chain. It's pretty, and I fasten it around my neck so it can hang next to Bex's charm, but something about it makes me sad. As if Leo was shopping for his idea of a girlfriend rather than for the one he has.

CALEB

I'M HEADED DOWNSTAIRS FOR SOME SCI-FI MAR-athon action—I can't believe I'll have only one more after this—when I look into the lounge and see Bex standing by herself, staring out the windows into the dark. Matthew and Celia are in one corner, talking quietly, and David and Yanaan are in another, even more quietly engaged.

I go to stand next to Bex, leaning toward her a little. "You okay?"

"Just feeling sorry for myself," she says.

"Ah, yes, the tragic life of Bex de Silva. Beautiful, wealthy, talented. It's heartbreaking, really."

"And alone," she says with a little sigh, and I realize how hard Evie dating must be for Bex, who, unlike Evie, stays away from boys not because she wants to but because she was told to.

"You know you could go down to the media room, put your head on someone's shoulder, and walk out with a marriage proposal, right?"

She smiles up at me. "I don't want a proposal of any kind. I'm trying to keep the promises I made."

"What are those promises, exactly?" Bex has talked to Evie about this stuff, but she's never really done it with me. I've met her mom and dad, and although I know they're super religious and sort of old-fashioned, they love her, and they don't seem cruel.

"They hate the idea of me living in a building with all these boys. So I told them I wouldn't go out with anyone here and that if I wanted to start dating, I'd do it at home, where they could keep an eye on me."

"Did you ever?" Has Bex had some whole secret life?

"No. The boys at home . . . it's hard for me. If I talk about religion here, people treat me like I'm saying the world is flat. And if I talk about science at home, everyone acts like I'm throwing in with the Antichrist."

"I think guys here would take your faith seriously. Some of them, anyway. If you gave them the chance."

"Maybe. But I'd have to tell my parents first. And that's . . ."

"Terrifying?"

"Yeah. Especially when I have to talk to them about college stuff too. Not dating never really bothered me before. But since Evie and Leo got together, I can't help thinking it would be nice to have someone's arm around me every once in a while."

This is a problem I can solve. "I was on my way down. You want to hang out with me?"

"Can you do it and not get confused?"

"Trust me, I'm an expert at not mixing up friendship and romance."

"Of course," she says. "I've often noticed that about you."

Downstairs, Bex curls up next to me and puts her head on my shoulder. I put my arm loosely around her. Her hair smells like orange blossoms, which is nice, but it's not cinnamon.

Leo and Evie come in a little while later and occupy the other end of our couch. She's wearing a sweatshirt and leggings, and she presses her bare feet against my leg when she lays her head on Leo's shoulder. I want to wrap my hand around her ankle, but to give myself credit, it's not confusion I'm feeling.

Two episodes later, Bex is asleep, and Evie suddenly goes still beside me. I hear her draw in a slow breath through her nose and release it, and another, and another. I turn toward her. Her eyes are big and vacant, but she's locked into her breathing pattern, not hyperventilating. Leo's watching the screen. I search for the problem, and then I see it: a spider crawling up the back of the couch in front of us.

Gently, I withdraw my arm from Bex, waking her in the process, pull an old Post-it note out of my pocket, lean forward to squeeze the spider inside of it, and chuck it out into the hall.

Leo, who has finally noticed something is going on, looks down at Evie and asks if she's okay. She nods.

"You did good," he says. And it's true. This therapist must know what she's doing.

When he goes back to watching the show, Evie looks at me and mouths, "Thank you." I lean back, putting my arm around Bex again.

After we're settled, Evie reaches her hand toward mine. We link our pinkie fingers, and although the most beautiful girl at Newton is pressed up against my side, this tenuous contact with Evie feels like the center of my world, and I don't let go.

Which is why our fingers are still linked together when Blake comes into the lounge. He stops behind us, looks down, and says loudly, "What kind of freak show do you four have going on here? McGill, do you even know that little slut is holding hands with Caleb while she's cuddled up next to you?"

He's barely finished speaking before I am on my feet, focused on important questions like how fast I can get him out of here, how many teeth I can remove from his head, and whether I have any moral obligation to let Leo help.

But to my surprise, Evie shrugs Leo off, pushes me down on the couch, and whirls on Blake. I'm furious, and there's no way she could set me down unless I let her, but I'm curious enough to see where she's going with this that I back off. Some freshman in the front row pauses the episode so everyone can watch the real show. Bex stands, ready to support Evie, but Evie isn't paying attention to her.

"What is your problem?" Evie shouts over my head at Blake. "What possible difference could it make to you who I'm holding hands with? Did someone make you the morality police while I've been busy with Frontier?"

This is brilliant, because it reminds Blake—and everyone else—that she's smarter than he could ever hope to be. Most of us are here at Newton because we love this stuff, but there are a few, like Blake, who were pushed into it by their parents. And they can't keep up, because they don't have passion or natural talent. You can make it here with only one or the other, but not if you lack both.

Blake crosses his arms and tries to sneer, but he's having a hard time pulling it off. He doesn't like it when his victims fight back.

"I thought Leo might want to know where your hand has been before he got any cozier with you."

Evie gestures to me, and her hand is so close to my face that I jerk back a little.

"I have known Caleb since I was a child. And yes, sometimes I hold his hand. This is not news to my boyfriend, or honestly, to anyone else in this room. Grow up, for God's sake." She looks at me and then Leo and says, "Do either of you have anything to say?"

I hold up my hands in the universal sign of surrender and shake my head. "I'm good."

She turns toward Leo, who glances around the silent room. "Maybe not here?" he says, pointing toward the stairs.

She nods and leaves. He follows her.

After a couple of beats of silence, I say, "We are going to own Frontier."

Still standing, Bex looks down at me. "Yeah, that's the big takeaway here."

"Do you want to go check in with her?"

She shakes her head. "I think we'd better give them some time."

So I open my arms, welcoming her back. She sits down and leans her head on my shoulder again.

This enrages Blake, and it's so much better than hitting him.

"I don't get it. No one else is good enough for the beautiful Rebeca de Silva, but you're content to be Evie's understudy with Covic? What is it about him?"

Bex leans her head back against my arm and looks up at him. "Fuck you, Blake," she says. And the ugly words in her gentle voice are beautiful.

If my smile were any bigger, it would leave the confines of my face.

"I love strong women," I say happily.

From a few seats over, Sarah-Kate says, "Do you get it now, Blake? That's what it is about him. If you want girls to date you, it helps if you actually like them." Sarah-Kate looks at the freshmen in the front row. "Feel free to take notes."

Blake storms off.

"You're the best, Sarah-Kate," I say. "You want to come sit by me?"

"Check your ego, Caleb," she responds. "And someone turn the show back on. I want to see Starbuck kick Apollo's ass."

∞ ∞ ∞ ∞ ∞ ∞ ∞ ∞ ∞ ∞ ∞

Headed for home, Bex takes a cab to the airport early the next morning. Leo's flight to Baton Rouge isn't until later, so he walks Evie and me to the bus station. They seem very careful with each other, saying lots of pleases and thank-yous, and despite her little speech last night, Evie keeps her distance from me. I wait by the bus door while she kisses him goodbye. It's pretty quick, and the last thing she says before we get on is "See you in Chicago."

I go up the stairs first, and when she climbs on after me, I turn around and raise my eyebrows. She shakes her head in response. "Turns out us holding hands *was* news to him," she says.

"But you're still together?" I can't think of another reason for him to be here at the bus station.

"Neither one of us wanted to give Blake the satisfaction. So we're . . . What's that thing that happens to TV shows?"

"They get canceled?" I say hopefully.

"No, before that. Like a break?"

"Hiatus?"

"Yeah. He says we should go on hiatus until after Frontier. Leo seems to think that will magically resolve our issues."

"The healing power of math," I say.

Ahead of us, a woman is holding a suitcase in one hand and a toddler in the other. She has a second bag over her shoulder and is obviously wishing she were doing anything other than traveling by bus with her two-year-old. Gesturing Evie into a seat, I toss my bag and jacket in after her, then ask the struggling mother if I can help. She gratefully gives me her suitcase to stash in the rack overhead while she coaxes her son over to the window. I'm turning back to my seat to put up my own bag when the universe rewards me for my good deed.

Evie is totally checking me out. She doesn't know I caught her looking, because she is fully engaged in a comprehensive body scan that lingers over my shoulders before heading south.

Evie's thinking about *this*.

With me.

I take a little longer than I need to position my bag on the luggage rack. Then, just to see what happens, I reach up to dig something—it turns out to be an ancient ballpoint pen—out of the top pocket of my bag, and Evie's eyes immediately go to the skin now showing between my T-shirt and jeans.

I love this bus. I want to live on it forever.

"You want to give me your bag?" I say quietly. She brings her eyes back to my face with a jerk, and I suppress a smile. I slide my fingers over hers as I take the suitcase, and she blushes, but she keeps watching me as I put up her suitcase. She looks a little dazed as I sit down next to her and startles when I point out the window at Leo, who's waving from the curb. I watch, untroubled, as she blows him a kiss goodbye.

Because Leo is dead boyfriend walking.

EVIE

I PRESS MY FOREHEAD AGAINST THE COOL GLASS, my mind not on the boy I'm waving to but on the one beside me. He has his laptop out and is not paying any attention to me, but I am hyperaware of our legs and shoulders touching.

I don't know what just happened. One minute I was watching him help that woman with her suitcase, thinking what a sweet and wholly Caleb-esque gesture it was, and then I was noticing the muscles in his arms flex, and then everything else, and there was that flash of his abs and those intriguing indentations at his hips, and I can't believe the thoughts I'm having. About Caleb—*Caleb*.

I've felt a couple of these little flashes before, like after that first fight with Blake. But nothing like this. The intensity is a little frightening. Caleb and I—together—would be unlike anything before. Because of who we already are.

But if I start something romantic with Caleb, I will be all in. If it ends, Wunderlochen is going to look like a mental health retreat. I cannot, cannot, cannot lose him. The risk is unfathomable. I see now that it's not that you *can't* be physically and emotionally connected to the same person. It's that doing so is unbelievably scary.

"You okay over there?" Caleb asks. "You're pretty quiet today."

I nod but don't meet his eyes. This is part of what would be so dangerous. I can't have a thought without him reading it.

To distract him, I say, "Want to do Hogwarts Christmas?"

He smiles. "Thought you'd never ask."

Hogwarts Christmas started because of Joel, who asked over Thanksgiving our first year at Newton if our bus had a trolley witch. Caleb and I decided that it did. Each year before we go home, we order candy online, pack baked goods, and prepare each other's Christmas presents. Sophomore year, I found some kind of pumpkin drink, but it turned out to be awful. I'm better prepared today.

I pull a thermos out of my backpack and hand it to Caleb. This is my first present for him. He opens the lid, and the scent of coffee and cinnamon fills the air.

His eyes light up. "When?"

"Early this morning. I couldn't sleep."

"You're the best."

He gets out muffins and chocolate frogs. I find the thermos with my tea and his present. It's a big one, not in size but in importance—I've been looking for it for three years now. I was just about to give up and buy a still cool but slightly more generic version when one of the bookstores I'd been in contact with regularly called to say they had found what I was looking for.

His present for me is squashy and poorly wrapped. I open it to find a soft gray hoodie.

I look up at him. "Thank you."

He smirks. "Turn it over."

On the back, in delicate cursive script, it says THE WORLD IS EVERYWHERE DENSE WITH IDIOTS. I've never had a personal motto, but if I did, this would be it.

I throw my arms around him, and he makes a strangled sound as his coffee splashes. He growls at me. "Don't. Spill. The elixir."

"I love it," I say. "I am never taking it off." I shrug out of the sweatshirt I'm wearing and put it on.

"I saw it and thought of you."

"That's the nicest thing anyone has ever said to me."

When I'm settled again and he's closed his thermos, I hand him my present. I'm a little nervous.

"What?" he says.

"I wanted to give you this because we won't be at school together next year. I don't want you to forget me."

He ruffles my hair. "You're plenty memorable."

He unwraps it and looks down at a slightly battered copy of *The Hitchhiker's Guide to the Galaxy*.

"Open it," I say.

He does and finds that the title page has not only been signed by Douglas Adams but is inscribed *To Caleb*.

Caleb looks at me, his eyes wide. "How?" he whispers. This is a reasonable question, given that Adams has been dead since before we were born.

"You'd be amazed what three years of phone calls to used bookstores and a part-time job grading calculus exams can do."

"This is the most thoughtful gift anyone has ever given me."

"You've been suspended twice, run away from home, gone to boarding school, and broken up with girlfriends on my behalf," I say. "It seemed like the least I could do."

He hugs me, and I feel both this trembly new thing between us and the quiet certainty of our old connection. Tears based on I don't even know what emotion are forming in my eyes, and I'm grateful when he asks, "Should I read?"

"Please," I say.

I lean back in my seat and close my eyes, letting the familiar words and his even-more-familiar voice wash over me.

Given how little I slept last night and how entirely safe I feel in this seat next to Caleb, it's not surprising that I nod off before he finishes the first chapter. When I wake sometime later, he's reading to himself, and I am unpleasantly aware of the food detritus, wrapping paper, and excess clothing surrounding us.

He smiles when I stir.

"I need to get some of this cleaned up," I say.

He gathers garbage and takes it to the front while I reorganize things in my backpack.

Caleb pulls down my suitcase for me, leaving his hand on my back to steady me as I stuff my old sweatshirt and my laptop (because it's clear I'm going to do no work) into my suitcase. There is nothing unusual about this. But today I am so aware of his touch. When I finish, he lifts my bag back up and then slides over to take the window seat and return to *Hitchhiker's*. I pretend to look out the window, but really I'm watching him. My heart rate is up, and I have no desire to use my CBT tricks to bring it down. I'm enjoying being overexcited.

I know my thoughts are not fair to Leo, hiatus or not, especially since we just had (yet another) argument about this, but I'm not interested in making myself feel bad for wanting Caleb. We have been the two of us for so long that everyone else feels peripheral. Still, I need to be careful. Caleb kisses people based on *whims*. But that's not what this would be for me.

And there is Milo. I'm not quite ready to say goodbye to him. I need some time to think this through.

We're approaching Chicago now. This has always been my least favorite part of the trip because we have to go over an enormous bridge, but today I feel only the lightest brush of worry. Without looking up from his book, Caleb unlocks the window, cracking it just a bit. He knows I like to feel like there's an escape in case we go over the edge. (My fear of bridges is based on drowning, not heights.) Then he switches the book to his other side so he can take my hand. I put my head on his shoulder and close my eyes, all of this too familiar to be weird.

Caleb puts down his book. "You look pretty relaxed for a bridge crossing," he whispers. He's right, I am, and this is partly because of him but largely because my fears are under control.

I press a little closer, and Caleb lets go of my hand so he can put his arm around me. My head on his shoulder feels like home.

"Caleb?" I whisper back.

"Yeah?"

"I think I'm getting better."

He laughs softly. "I kind of figured that, based on your public flogging of Blake last night. Not to mention the way you dealt with the spider."

"I'm going to stop therapy in the spring. Anita says I don't need it anymore."

"I'm proud of you, Eves."

"My mother is going to hate it."

He shakes his head a little. "Don't you think that she wants you to be well? To be happy?"

I do. But I also think that she doesn't believe it's possible. She thinks that as long as mathematics is part of my life, I'm at risk. I also know that for whatever reason, she's a much bigger fan of medicine than talk therapy.

To Caleb I say only, "We'll see."

I dig into my bag to pull out *The Phantom Tollbooth*, rolling off the rubber band holding on the front cover.

"It's been a while since I've seen you with that," Caleb says, looking at me.

"I've been wanting to reread it."

"Any particular reason?"

I look up at him for a moment, my face very close to his. I've already shared my secret about therapy, and he knows what's going on with Leo. I'm a little tempted to tell him all the details about Milo too. It would be a relief, but there is this new possibility opening up for Caleb and me, and I don't want to crush it, so I say only, "I want to channel the Princess of Pure Reason for Frontier."

"Hmm," he says, and goes back to his book, leaving his arm around me.

CALEB

IF LEARNING BY OSMOSIS IS POSSIBLE, I WILL have no trouble in physics after this bus ride. Evie keeps her head on my shoulder as she reads, at one point draping her legs over mine. I feel like I'm trying to tame a wild animal, worried that any move I make could cause her to withdraw in panic.

Unable to resist, I release my hold on her shoulder so I can trail my fingers up and down her arm. Not only does she not pull away, she presses closer. A little while later, I let my fingers wander up her neck and into her hair. She smiles at my touch, and I have to look out the window to hide my smug expression.

I am a little concerned about the way she smiles occasionally as she reads *The Phantom Tollbooth*, as well as the involuntary moves she keeps making toward her phone. But the weird thing is, I get it. One of my first thoughts after opening Evie's present was that I wanted to tell Tess about my awesome gift.

The fact that I'm confused doesn't bode well for how Evie is going to feel when she finds out Milo's true identity. I need an exit strategy.

When the bus pulls into the station in Chicago, we separate and organize our belongings. Sometimes we catch a second bus or a train at this point, but today Dad—who has some time off—plans to meet us here. Normally, this would be a good thing. It means pizza in the city and an easier, quicker trip. But today, I just want to be left alone with Evie.

I'm even more disheartened when we get off and see Evie's mother waiting with Dad. This almost never happens because they usually share pickup responsibilities. Whatever the reason, it means separate cars the rest of the way home. I'm consoled by the look on Evie's face, which mirrors my own disappointment.

She hugs her mother and says, "What are you doing here?"

"I need to finish some shopping. I thought we could do that and have dinner before heading home."

Evie turns toward me. "When are you leaving?" she asks.

"In the morning." We usually spend the week before Christmas in Minnesota with relatives. "Check in tonight?"

I kind of want to hug her or kiss her cheek or back her up against the bus and make her forget her name, but with our parents watching, even squeezing her hand feels like too much, so I say, "Have fun shopping."

She makes a face, which I understand to mean *This is not about shopping.* I feel unreasonably guilty that I get to go home to my family. Later, Joel, Nolan, and I play video games and then Ping-Pong. Mom makes my favorite dinner—tacos and peanut butter pie—and afterward, we watch *A Christmas Story.* Dad is the only one who finds this funny, but he laughs so hard that it's worth it for the rest of us. When the credits roll, Evie is still not home.

I text her: *ETA?*

She responds: *An hour. Meet for coffee in the morning?*

But I have another idea.

She texts when she gets in and says she's getting ready for bed. I give her an hour to fall asleep, because it doesn't count unless I wake her up. Then I pull on a baseball cap, throw a jacket over my flannel pants and thermal top, and sneak out the back door. I go into her yard, make a snowball, and put it dead center in her window. Her parents' room is at the front of the house, so they won't hear.

I text her: *Panquake! Panquake! Panquake!*

She knows she has five minutes or I'm coming in. It takes her two minutes to open her window. "Really? Tonight? We just got home."

I give her a "what can you do" shrug and tap my wrist to indicate the clock's ticking. She closes her window.

The Panquake is a Newton tradition reserved for times of moderate trouble—breakups, fights with parents, or academic setbacks. The rules (in addition to the five-minute deadline) are these: Panquakes can only begin by waking someone; clothing can be added for the sake of weather or modesty, but nothing that you have been sleeping in can be removed; and sneaking out of the dorm (or house) is required. If you have permission, it's not a Panquake.

Evie's out three minutes later in leggings, boots, and her jacket. Though she'd been lying down for only an hour, her hair doubled in volume.

We live in a neighborhood of large older homes. This means they mostly have detached garages, so it's possible for us to use a car without waking our parents, which is good, because it's two miles to the nearest all-night diner. When I take Evie's hand to lead her to the side door of our garage, something flickers across her face. I'm guessing guilt about Leo. But she doesn't pull away.

In the car, I say, "What happened?"

"We went to Water Tower Place and did some window-shopping. She bought luggage for my dad. On the way home, we stopped for dinner and had a huge shouting match over salads about whether I should go on medication for Frontier. She felt guilty for starting a fight before I had even gone into the house, so then we had to get our nails done so we could pretend everything was fine. Mine have little snowflakes."

She holds out one hand in front of the steering wheel.

"Nice," I say. "Are you okay?"

"Right now I am. Could be a rough week, though. How was your night?"

I talk to her about Joel and Nolan, telling her that Nolan asked if Bex was going to visit three times.

"I kind of love that he thinks he has a shot," Evie says.

I smile. "Confidence is half the battle."

"What's the other half?"

I let my smile deepen. "Dimples."

"It's a good thing Nolan decided to stay here. I don't think Newton could take the two of you."

Inside the diner, she takes off her jacket, and she's wearing the sweatshirt I gave her. She keeps this zipped up despite the warmth of the restaurant, which means that for the rest of the meal, a good half of my mental energy is devoted to imagining what she might be wearing (or not wearing) underneath.

While we eat—I order pancakes, which Evie picks at—I ask her how big of a deal this thing with her mom is.

"I'm not sure. She can't force me to take the pills. But she can make my life pretty unpleasant."

"You need to talk to your father."

"Maybe," she says.

I know it's tricky. Evie's parents have divided up responsibilities between them, and human beings, including Evie, fall squarely within her mother's domain. Her father is in charge of motorized vehicles, cooking, and snow removal.

But he has a much more expansive view of normal than her mother does, which I attribute more to him being British than being a mathematician. From what I can tell, England's perspective on mental health is similar to its perspective on teeth: variation is expected.

We're quieter on the way back, both of us tired. I walk her to the door and say, "If you need me, I'll find a way to come back early."

She shakes her head. "Contrary to all evidence, I think I can survive a week without you."

I squeeze her hand before I go. "Not sure I can say the same."

∞ ∞ ∞ ∞ ∞ ∞ ∞ ∞ ∞ ∞ ∞

The time in Minnesota drags by. All my cousins are much younger, and the weather is on that unpleasant border between rain and snow. I pass the time by texting Evie and messaging Tess, barely managing not to mix them up. Since she must have Leo in the mix too, I don't know how she's keeping things straight.

More to amuse myself than anything else, I put together this video Christmas card for her. It has images of supernovas, entangled particles, thunderstorms, and error-correcting code, drawings from *The Phantom Tollbooth*, and quotes from physicists, all accompanied by holiday music and a little snippet from "A Valediction: Forbidding Mourning" read by some ancient actor. ("Dull sublunary lovers' love / [Whose soul is sense] cannot admit / Absence, because it doth remove / Those things which elemented it.")

This, I decide, is my exit strategy. The video is such a mix of Caleb and Milo that I don't see how she could see it and not figure it out. I'll wait until I get back to send it, though. I want to see her face.

We return late on Christmas Eve, and while I text her to let her know we're home, I wait until after lunch the next day to send the video, putting the link in a "Merry Christmas" message from Milo. Then I fly out the door, not bothering to put on a jacket.

"Merry Christmas," I say when Evie's mother answers the door.

"She's upstairs," she replies. I'm always struck by how much quieter Evie's house is than mine. Her father is in the kitchen, cooking on his own, and her mother returns to the office, where she was probably working. Sometimes I wonder if they speak only when I'm here.

I bound up to Evie's room. She's sitting at her desk, her laptop open, tears falling down her face. She closes the laptop when she sees me, but I catch the last image from my video.

Kneeling down beside her, I whisper, "What is it? Eves?" I'm looking around for a spider or some other familiar source of distress, but she shakes her head.

"It's not that. Not anxiety. I'm a little sad." Her eyes linger on my face. "And confused."

Uh-oh. What have I done?

Obviously, she hasn't put things together. Which means I've made a pretty big mistake. I could just tell her, but I'm afraid. After coming so close, I couldn't stand it if she got angry and stopped talking to me again. My brain's searching for pathways here, the way it does when I have to fix a program, but I can't see my way through this. It's all one big error message.

Pulling my sleeves over the palms of my hands, I wipe her eyes. "What do you need?"

"Bex." She looks at me. "Sorry. It's just . . . girl stuff."

I nod, thinking. "Stay here and have some tea or something." Evie's right—Bex is the solution. She can help Evie, and she can tell me what to do next. But she needs to know what's going on before Evie talks to her. "Let me find her for you. You know what her Christmases are like."

As soon as I get out the door, I call Bex. Texting is not going to be adequate for this conversation.

"Merry Christmas," she says. "I don't have long. Talk fast."

Speaking quickly, I tell her everything, from the first anonymous message to Evie's tears right now. I'm pacing the whole time.

"Darwin's ghost, Caleb!" she says when I finish. "What were you thinking? You're supposed to be the one with emotional intelligence."

I have to smile. "Darwin's ghost?" I ask. "Is that how biologists swear?"

"I'm at home. This is how the religious right swears. How did you think this plan was going to work?"

"It wasn't a plan. I was watching her with Leo freaking McGill, and I lost my mind a little. What should I do?"

"Nothing. You've done enough. I can be there tomorrow. I'll call Evie when we hang up."

"Your parents won't mind?"

"As far as they're concerned, my mission at Newton is to convert the unsaved, and so far, they're not impressed with my metrics. If I tell them I'm having a breakthrough with Evie, they'll let me go. They think she's too nice a girl to go to hell."

EVIE

WHEN BEX COMES OUT OF SECURITY, I THROW myself at her, just about knocking her over. She pats me on the back and asks, "Is he here?"

"No. I convinced him to let me get you on my own." It didn't take much. When he suggested I might not be okay driving to the airport alone, I merely looked at him, and he stammered, "Not—not because of, you know, Evie things, but because you've been all weepy and . . . girl-like." Then he'd shut his mouth like the sensible boy he is.

Yesterday was strange. I was a wreck after Milo's video, which did nothing to convince Mom I was stable heading into Frontier. Talking on the phone to Bex helped, although we had to do it in fits and starts since she was with her family and the existence of Milo and my confusion about Leo and Caleb were not easily explained. I was in the middle of describing the Bus Ride of Constant Touching when Bex said, "Wait a minute. What did you get Caleb for Christmas?" I explained the gift. Then she asked what I'd gotten Leo. After I told her, there was a full thirty seconds of silence on the phone.

"What?" I said. "I don't even know if Leo likes *Hitchhiker's*."

"A) He's a boy at a science academy. Of course he likes *Hitchhiker's*. And b) that's so not the point, it's a line," she replied.

After a couple of seconds, I said, "This is still Bex, right?"

"I'm trying to talk in a language you can understand. How much time did you spend finding Caleb's present?"

"I don't know. A lot. I've been looking on and off for three years." I didn't mention the hundred hours of grading exams that paid for it.

"And Leo's?"

"Twenty minutes? I shopped online."

Another pause, and then Bex said, "Embarrassed."

"You can't even see my face," I argued.

"I don't need to. Your homework tonight is to think about this. I'll grade your work tomorrow when I get there."

And so I thought about it. I thought about it while I was eating cinnamon rolls with Dad and trying to convince him to intervene with Mom. He, clearly uncomfortable, asked if I was sure I was okay, because I seemed a little emotional. I said that I was emotional because boys were confusing but that antianxiety meds were not going to change that. Then he didn't want to talk anymore.

I thought about it while I played Risk with Caleb and his brothers. So much so that Nolan lured me into attacking Africa before I was ready and knocked me out of the game, leaving me little to do but watch Caleb. I thought about it while I was on the phone with Leo, hearing about his Christmas, telling him about mine, wishing that I were still watching Caleb roll dice, and while I was in bed, messaging with Milo until I fell asleep with the phone in my hand.

After all that thinking, what I know is this: I am falling in love with two people, and neither one is my boyfriend. I'm not sure how it happened. I suppose I should have figured out how I felt about Caleb a long time ago, but I didn't. Not until that bus ride.

And even though I've only been messaging Milo for a few weeks, somehow he's become one of the most important people in my life. And he's the one who made that video. The person who did that gets me in a way I can't even put into words.

I can't imagine giving up either one of them.

∞ ∞ ∞ ∞ ∞ ∞ ∞ ∞ ∞ ∞ ∞ ∞

When Bex and I get into the car, she tells me to take her somewhere quiet for lunch. "The last thing we need is Caleb hovering around while we figure this out."

I know the perfect place, a restaurant that's all little tables and lamplight and pink walls. The bakery counter has twice as many items as the menu. Bex smiles when she sees it. "Order a salad," I say, "because for dessert, we're getting one of those giant éclairs."

We order and talk about the holidays with our families. "I missed you," I say. "Did you tell your parents about Columbia?"

She shakes her head. "Chickened out. How about you? Did you do your homework?"

I nod. "I need to break up with Leo. For good. But I have to do that in person, right?"

"You really should."

"It's weird still texting with him. It's like light traveling from a dying star. We're over, but he doesn't know it yet. Although I think he suspects."

"Well, that's the hard part decided," she says.

"That wasn't the hard part."

I tell Bex about Milo's video. How it was weird and wonderful and full of all these words and pictures that tapped into something at my core. And romantic in a way that I'm not sure my sunny, pragmatic Caleb could ever be. I feel tremulous just thinking about it.

Pulling out my phone, I play it for her. When it's over, she sighs. "This boy. Why opt for simple when complicated is an option?" She sighs. "Okay, Evie. I know you think you have learned nothing in four years of English classes."

She raises her hand to halt my attempt to confirm this. "But I am about to prove you wrong. I want you to go back through every conversation you've ever had with Milo and write down the words that call out to you. Then we are going to talk."

I make the face that I usually reserve for Anita's wackier ideas.

"In the meantime, I am going to get one of those éclairs and maybe some cheesecake, and if you want to share, you'd better get started." So I do. My list is long and includes, among other things: tollbooth, Tegmark, Noether, girl-space-friend, entanglement, Schrödinger's cat, practical, hacking, MIT, normal's overrated, flirting, and soap bubbles.

I'm about to hand the list over to Bex when my eyes stick on the last phrase. I think of Caleb blowing bubbles at the science museum and me lifting my hands to catch them. Then I remember the first object Milo talked about tossing—a baseball.

But what about MIT? That's not Caleb's plan. Except that MIT is a secret from everyone in Milo's real life. I look up at Bex, who is eating a piece of éclair and watching me.

"So tell me, Evie," she says with a smile, "did you learn anything about textual analysis in your four years at Newton?"

"It's him," I say. "Caleb is Milo. But how? And why? And does he know that I'm Tess?" And then I realize that he does, because I told him about Bex. (*"Can you pretend that's a pseudonym?"* *"Um, no. I really can't."*)

"Oh my God, Bex. I talked to him about Leo. And about him."

"Let's watch the blasphemy, please," she says. "But what did you say?"

I shake my head. "Everything."

I told Caleb—while he was being Milo—about Leo helping me see the point of kissing and about how I felt that night with him by the campfire and about my boy-space-friend being the most important person in my life, which of course he knew, but still. And on top of all that, I told Milo—when I was talking to Caleb?!—that I had feelings for him and that I might want us to be more than friends.

I am never, ever going to be able to look Caleb in the face again. And also I am never going to meet Milo. Because there is no Milo. Which is a little sad. And pretty confusing.

But also sort of wonderful.

∞ ∞ ∞ ∞ ∞ ∞ ∞ ∞ ∞ ∞ ∞ ∞

On the car ride back, Bex tells me everything she knows about Milo. Caleb set up his profile hoping I would find him. He knew all along that I was Tess. Thinking back, I realize he sat in that study room and asked me what I was working on *while* I was messaging with him. He listened to me confess to finding Milo adorable. He wanted to know why I was rereading *The Phantom Tollbooth*.

I am going to kill him.

But then I think: Caleb made me that video, Caleb knew the Noether quote, Caleb told me to leave my understanding boyfriend, and Caleb wants to kiss his girl-space-friend. (A lot.) I am not in love with two people. It always was, always would be Caleb.

I thought that having Caleb as a friend meant I couldn't have this too. But now, as the full magic of what we could be washes over me, I decide that, whatever the risk, I don't want to walk away. I might not be strong enough to lose him. But I'm brave enough to take the chance.

So I make a new plan: First, I'm going to kiss him. And then I'm going to kill him. That way I won't have to worry about him leaving me when he gets bored.

Bex has something more complicated in mind.

She says, "We are going to spend a few days torturing Caleb, because he deserves it. Then you will go to Frontier and break up with Leo and make Caleb the happiest boy in the world."

Bex tells me to text Caleb to say we're doing a girls' night because we have a lot to talk about and that we'll see him for an early lunch tomorrow before we leave for Frontier. Bex gets a series of texts moments after I send mine, which she holds up for me. They say: *Do. Not. Tell. Her.* I grin. Then I tell Leo that I'm spending the night with Bex, who came in early, and that I'll talk to him in person tomorrow, so that gets that awkwardness out of the way.

We bundle up to go for a walk, eat cheese, crackers, and

carrot sticks for dinner because we're still full of éclair and cheesecake, and then finally I message Milo, telling him that I can't stop thinking about his video, that no one in my real life gets me the way he does, and that I'm so happy to have found someone I can be totally honest with and who would never, ever lie to me.

Bex looks at it and laughs. "You're surprisingly good at this."

"I feel highly motivated."

Mom comes into my room and says, "You're very giggly all of a sudden." She studies me, probably assessing whether I seem manic, although this has never been one of my issues. I feel like she's constantly on the lookout for new diagnoses. "How are things going with that Leo of yours?"

The doorbell rings, sparing me from responding. I open it to find Nolan, who is like a diet version of Caleb—all of the looks and charm with none of the nutritional value. The differences between them make me think Caleb might be right about me being good for him. He learned to be brave by defending me and grew ambitious trying to keep up. Nolan could use a few obstacles in his life.

"Hey," Nolan says. "I was wondering if you wanted to do something."

"Me?" I say.

"You and any guests you may have?" he says hopefully, looking over my shoulder.

"Right. Does Caleb know you're here?" His eyes flick

toward his house, and I figure it out. Caleb sent him to check on me, probably using Bex as the incentive. I'm sure he figures Bex will be less likely to spill his secret if Nolan's around.

"Tell Caleb we will see him tomorrow," I say, and shut the door.

The next day, we take Bex to lunch at Ella's, because she likes to see the carousel even when it's not on. Caleb spends the car ride watching me covertly, trying to figure out what I know. I spend the car ride thinking about kissing him.

After lunch, we'll drive down to the train station in Kenosha and leave the car because it's so expensive to park in Chicago. Our parents will come to Frontier in the morning for the public presentation and stay for the stage show if we make it. I've refused meds for what I hope is the last time, but I suspect Mom will make one more push if we get that far.

I order a peppermint shake and a veggie burger, pleased to make Bex happy with my lunch choice after everything she's done over the last twenty-four hours.

When the waitress brings our drinks, Caleb says, "Ready for tomorrow?"

"For the math part."

"Are you still worried about the talking?"

"No, I think I've got that too."

"Then, what?"

I take a deep breath and then look down at the table. "I

need to break up with Leo." Then I pull my straw out of my milkshake and lick it. Caleb is frozen, staring at me.

"Why?" he finally whispers.

"I'm falling for someone else. It's not fair to him."

Caleb and I spend a long moment looking at each other, and I almost break down and tell him. The way he feels about me is all over his face, and I don't know why I couldn't see it before.

But Bex kicks me under the table and says, "It's someone she met on the internet. Tell her it's not a good idea to trust boys you meet online."

Caleb cuts his eyes to her.

"Don't you think that might be situational?" he asks.

"I think you have to assume anyone you meet anonymously is lying about something."

For maybe the first time ever, Caleb blushes.

Bex is right. This is fun.

CALEB

THE HOTEL HOSTING THE CONFERENCE IS OFF Millennium Park, so it's a short walk from the train station. I'm desperate for quiet. Bex and Evie were effervescent on the train, but what with our performance tomorrow, Milo's impending doom, and Santori's email letting me know I'm sharing a room with Leo, I'm a little on edge.

Tess messages me regularly, counting down each hour. This would be cute if it didn't also feel like a time bomb. I've convinced her that we should not meet until after the poster presentations tomorrow. It would probably serve me right if I lost my chance at MIT because Evie was too angry to go through with our session, but as much as I want this to be over, I can't bring myself to risk it.

While we're checking in, Evie looks down at her phone and says, "Uh-oh." Both Bex and I turn to her.

"Leo's plane is delayed. He might not make it to the dinner."

Bex and Evie exchange a long look before Bex says, "You have to wait until tomorrow afternoon. You can't do it right before the presentations. That's not fair to either of you."

Evie nods. "Okay. Sure."

Maybe this is just as well. While our relationship drama is at the top of all of our minds, this is Frontier. It deserves our full attention.

I decide to take a little time to be in the moment. After dropping off my stuff, I visit the ballroom that's set up for the poster session tomorrow. The space holds fifty gunmetal-gray stands, each about my height, with room for a poster on the front and back. Dividers have been placed between each one, which will make it difficult to chat with our neighbors. Curtains cover the wall of windows, and while the room feels cavernous tonight, it will seem crowded tomorrow.

We don't know yet where we'll be, so I walk up and down the rows, trailing my fingers over the rough fabric and smooth metal of each stand, making the space my own. Like checking out the field from the pitcher's mound before I play.

I have a while before dinner, so I head out into the city, looking at my reflection in that weird metal bean and watching the ice-skaters. Everything is decorated for the holidays, and people—tourists with cameras, parents managing small children, and office workers swinging briefcases—are everywhere. I could live somewhere like this, I think, but I try hard to keep the thought generic, squashing down images of me in Boston.

Coming into the lobby after showering and changing my clothes, I see Evie, and every resolution I had about focusing on Frontier evaporates. She's gorgeous in a soft gray dress with her hair piled up on her head in a way that's just an invitation to take it down. Bex is clearly responsible.

I pull out my phone.

Caleb: *Are you trying to kill me?*

Bex: *Who is this?*

I pocket my phone and approach Evie. When she senses me behind her, she turns, her shoulder brushing my chest. All words flee my brain when her eyes meet mine.

"Caleb."

She's so happy to see me.

I'm starting to suspect Evie has been teasing me about Milo. Every signal she's giving off is saying *yes* and *more* and *closer*, not *I'm in love with an anonymous boy I met on the internet who is not you (except that he actually is)*. Before I can figure out what to do about this, Bex appears and says, "For goodness' sake, you two, look away before you set something on fire."

Evie drops her eyes, blushing, and I grin, happy to have caused this reaction in her. Then Santori and Chandran are there, and we follow them into the hall. As we're walking, I say, "You look lovely as well, Bex."

"Close your eyes!" she says with such authority that I do. To avoid injury, I also stop moving.

"What color am I wearing?" she asks, a smile in her voice.

I have no clue. It's a pretty formal event though. "Black?"

"Open," she says.

Her dress is bright orange.

"Save your compliments for when you mean them."

We're seated at a table with the principal of a public high school in Minneapolis, the dean of an East Coast boarding school I've never heard of, and their two students. Neither the dinner nor the speech is memorable, and Bex sits in between Evie and me. I don't know if this is an accident or if she's trying to prevent trouble in case Leo gets in early.

After Santori finishes a dessert the rest of us ignore— tasteless chocolate cake drowning in raspberry syrup—he urges us to go to our rooms and get some sleep. He's almost as nervous as we are.

We agree to meet for breakfast at the bagel place across the street. As I get off the elevator, Bex says, "Be nice to Leo tonight. Don't make things harder than they need to be."

"Do I ever?"

Both she and Evie roll their eyes. I'm offended.

It's early, but I get ready for bed. In the spirit of making things easy, I want to be able to pretend to be asleep when Leo gets in, which is what I do when he comes through the door an hour later. He cleans up, checks his phone, and gets into bed.

I can't quite keep still, but I think I'm convincing enough that if he wanted to avoid talking to me, he could. Instead he says, "It's over, isn't it?"

"Um," I say, not sure what the humane response even is at this point.

"She's not responding to texts."

"Her phone's probably on do not disturb. She's exhausted, and we have a big day tomorrow."

This is true, but we both know that if Evie were still thinking of Leo as her boyfriend, she wouldn't have turned off her phone until he got in.

"It was never going to last," he says. "She's in love with you."

I'm starting to think he's right, so I don't argue.

"Why did you make it so easy for me?" he asks. "In the beginning? You could have caused a lot more trouble than you did."

"You were what she wanted. So I got out of the way." I pause, thinking about Milo. "More or less."

He makes a sound somewhere between an exasperated sigh and a laugh. "Whatever you just remembered, I definitely don't want to know."

"No," I say. "Probably not."

EVIE

I'M AWAKE BEFORE DAWN, WORRIED ABOUT THE day ahead. Everything that was going on yesterday managed to occupy me, but the enormity of it all is hitting me now. I've already made it farther than I did last year. Anita would say to celebrate this small victory, but I can't help but think it doesn't count unless I follow through.

I stay in bed and do breathing exercises until Bex wakes, and then I let her shower first while I read our paper again, relieved to find that I still think it's good. If I can keep it together during the poster session, we'll be onstage later. This is even more important now that I know that Caleb is Milo. I will hate having him so far away, but if MIT is what he wants, I want it for him.

When I get out of the shower, I select the most traditional of the outfits I brought because I don't want to screw this up for Caleb. I put on khaki pants and a white button-down and slick my hair back into a ponytail. I think I look like a mathematician, but when I come out of the bathroom, Bex takes one look at me and says, "No, no, no," pointing to my hair, my shirt, and my pants with each negative.

When I argue, she cuts me off.

"No," she says again. "I know what you're doing. But you are not going to win this by pretending to be a boy. You are a mathematician and a physicist and a girl. You get to be all three. This," she says, gesturing at me with a little hand wave, "is not how you challenge stereotypes."

"Some girls dress like this," I say.

"But not you. If God—"

I open my mouth to interrupt again.

"—or the universe," she concedes, "sees fit to give you an hourglass figure, you do not put it in pleated pants."

She goes to my suitcase and riffles through it, pulling out a crinkly navy silk blouse that skims but does not hug my curves and a flippy black skirt. "This," she says. "And because of that atrocity you perpetrated on fashion, no tights. Now, go change."

"Bex," I say. "It's twenty degrees." I will make some concessions, but this is too much.

"Fine," she says, giving me my tights. "But I get to do your hair."

After I change, she puts my hair in a loose bun at the nape of my neck. Then I zip up my new boots. My only jewelry is the necklace she gave me, which rests in the hollow of my throat. I study myself in the mirror, and she's right. Before, I looked like a mathlete. Now I look like a professor on my way to class.

"Okay," I say.

Bex steps up to the mirror, next to me. She's wearing a pink skirt and a matching sweater. My guess is that this will be the only pastel color I'll see all day, and I love her for being so wholly herself, even in this environment. We grab our bags and head down to meet Caleb and Leo.

Breakfast is all the awkward. We're keyed up, and it's the first time I've seen Leo since he put Caleb and me on the bus, and everyone knows I'm about to end things. Even so, I kiss him on the cheek and sit next to him.

When it's time for us to leave, Bex says, "I'm going to wander around and look at the Christmas decorations for a while. I'll check in with you all when they open to guests."

I stand, and she wraps her arms around me. We hold each other for a long time. "I wouldn't be here without you," I whisper.

"Yes, you would," she says. We squeeze each other's hands, and she leaves.

I'm a little teary, and Leo puts his hand on my back. I lean into him, unable to figure out if it's selfish or kind to take comfort from him in this way right now. I hope that when all of this is over, he and I are still friends. On our way back across the street, I take his hand, and he looks down at me. I give him a little smile, trying to communicate: *I like you as a human being even though I no longer want to date you.* I've made some progress dealing with emotions during the last six months, but I suspect this kind of subtlety is beyond me.

When we get to the room for the poster session, we check in and get assigned to our stands. Caleb and I are in the row facing the windows. I take this as a sign of good luck, because it's the least claustrophobic place in the room. Leo's somewhere in the middle. At 10:00, there's an hour where anyone can come through, which is when Caleb and I expect to see our parents and Bex. Then there's a short break, and then the room closes to everyone but the judges and the presenters.

"Good luck," I say to Leo.

He touches my face. "Good luck, Evelyn Jane." Then he looks at Caleb. "You too."

Caleb nods. "See you on the other side."

Because he can reach the top of the stand, Caleb tacks up our poster while I look out the window at the traffic below. I'm so worried about the poster session, I can't even work up butterflies about Caleb, so I breathe and remember my success in the Math Genius booth.

Caleb comes to stand next to me. "Yesterday, I was thinking that there are only 132 kids who get to do this, and we're two of them. It doesn't matter what happens now. We're starting the day at awesome."

"Tell that to Santori."

He shakes his head. "I mean it, Evie. If you crash and burn, or if I do, it doesn't matter. Look around."

So I do. And I see what he's talking about. We are in a luxury hotel in the middle of Chicago. Kids buzz about, talking about some of the most interesting problems in mathematics and physics. In an hour, brilliant professors will be here to discuss our work with us. Tonight, we can go out for a fabulous dinner in the city. I look up at Caleb. "You're very wise all of a sudden."

And the doors open. Caleb talks to his parents and my mother, giving them a general explanation of what we've done, while I take Dad more deeply into the work. He's not familiar with adinkras, so I slow down and describe the meaning of each part of the diagram, connecting them back to the matrices and equations. He's less interested in the error-correcting codes, even though this makes the work more interesting. I'm explaining this to him when I notice that everyone else has stopped talking and is watching me.

"Everything okay?" I say, looking around.

Mom takes my hand. "You look beautiful, Evelyn. Ethereal."

I'm not sure if I'm being oversensitive, but I feel like her word choice has a hidden message—"not of this world," which I take to mean "bordering on madness." Either way, I gain nothing by reacting, so I just smile and say, "Thanks. Bex picked out the clothes."

From behind Mom, Caleb gives me an exaggerated once-over and mouths, "Thank you, Bex." His dad, who's standing off to the side, reaches behind his mom and smacks Caleb lightly on the back of the head. I grin.

Caleb offers to walk everyone over to Leo's and Chandran's posters so they can see the full Newton contingent. Before she goes, Mom kisses my cheek and says, "Text me if you need anything." She means drugs.

"You bet," I say. Because I'm trying to do cheery.

CALEB

WHEN I LEAVE MY PARENTS WITH LEO, I SAY TO Mom, "Your job is to keep Beth away from Evie the rest of the day."

"Okay," she says. "Your job is to tell that girl how you feel."

"On the agenda," I respond as I walk back to Evie.

She's talking to some guy who looks like a low-rent version of Leo. She gestures at the poster next to ours and says, "This is our neighbor. He's called Brian." She turns her back to him and says quietly, "He's an idiot."

This is something else I love about Evie. Not that she calls people idiots right in front of them (although I'm pretty fond of that too), but that she uses her father's British phrasing when introducing people. With her inflection, it always sounds like she suspects they've given her an alias.

Brian goes back to pointing at our poster, saying, "I was just explaining something to your lovely coauthor." Evie sticks her finger down her throat. "It seems to me that you would have been better off sticking with algebraic representations, because you give something up in terms of clarity when you move to these complicated models." He gestures at the adinkras. "They're pretty." He smiles down at Evie. "But unnecessary."

Confused, I say, "But without them, we don't get to the error-correcting code, and that's kind of the whole point."

"Don't bother," Evie whispers. And then she says more loudly, "Let's go see Brian's poster."

We step around the divider. His poster is some kind of long proof that, at least according to Brian's description, has implications for string theory. Evie looks at it for about two minutes before saying, "There's an error in line thirty-two." She tilts her head and studies it. "You might be able to fix it so it doesn't invalidate the proof. That's probably why it got in. They expected you to correct it."

Brian looks at her and then stares at his poster, gobsmacked. (Such a great word.)

Evie looks at me. "Time?"

I pull out my phone, wondering why girls' clothes never have pockets. "Ten forty-seven."

"You've got at least twenty-three minutes to think of something to tell the judges," she says to Brian.

She pulls me back around the divider.

I study her smug face. "Was there really an error?"

"Of course," she says, shocked. "I wouldn't do that to someone at a time like this."

"Even someone like Brian?"

She nods. "There are only about a thousand people in the world who do what I do. The better they are, the better my work will be for the rest of my life. I don't have to like him." After a moment, she adds, "Thank goodness."

"But don't you get sick of it? Being condescended to by people like him and Dr. Lewis?"

"Of course I get sick of it. But there are also people like you, and David, and Dr. Biesta, and Leo, and even Dean Santori—who, granted, didn't think I could do this but has been nothing but supportive since I did."

I know now why Evie told David that everything has always been easy for me. I get to live my life without having to constantly navigate who I am. Even today, how many people—even her own mother—have already talked to Evie about how she looks instead of what she does? I need to do better.

We spend the last part of the session chatting with Bex, and Evie visibly relaxes. When the organizers ask the guests to clear the room for the judges, I pry Evie and Bex apart and push Bex out the door.

The noise in the room drops noticeably, and suddenly there's lots of downtime, since there are a hundred posters and only five judges.

After about ten minutes, one of them approaches. David told us getting singled out for questions is good. Because the judges can't get to everyone in an hour, they only check in with people they're considering for the top five.

This first guy is the engineer. If I get coding questions, it will be from him.

He studies the poster in silence for a few minutes, then traces the adinkra with his fingers, lingering over the error-correcting code blocks. He looks over at me. "This is very interesting."

"We think so," I say.

His eyes go back to the poster.

"Your names are in alphabetical order?"

"No, sir," I say. "In order of intellectual contribution." This is the rule, and he knows it. Evie starts doing that deep breathing thing. She's not ready to speak, so I go on. "Evelyn did the mathematics. She wrote the equations and designed the models. I created the program to fold the adinkras and find the symmetries. I can also answer questions about Hamming code."

He looks between us skeptically.

"The work is plenty impressive on its own," he says. "But I understand the temptation to lead with her name. There'll be a lot of publicity if we award the top prize to a young woman for the first time."

Evie, toying with her necklace, finally says, "Do you have questions about the mathematics? It can be difficult to understand if you don't have the background." She gives him a deceptively sweet smile.

Evie's responses to his questions are long, detailed, and technical. I've been doing this work with her for months, and I can't follow them.

He pushes me on the programming syntax and the meaning of the error-correcting code, but David and Bex prepared us well, and he asks nothing I haven't answered before. He ends by saying that he'll send the mathematician on the judging panel over for an evaluation. His tone makes this sound like a threat, but Evie says, "That's a good idea."

He watches her, trying to figure out if she's being sarcastic, but she keeps her face blank.

As he's walking away, she says just loudly enough to be heard, "Hey, Caleb, you know what they call physicists who fail?"

The engineer looks back over his shoulder, making me wonder if he's heard this joke before.

Evie may have just destroyed any chance we had at winning, but I don't care.

EVIE

A FEW MINUTES AFTER THE ENGINEER LEAVES, another judge appears. He's not the mathematician but a physicist from the University of Chicago. I'm a fan of his work—so much so that I'm a little giddy. Dr. Singh has the kind of expensive haircut that looks like each strand was individually trimmed, and he's wearing a bright orange button-down shirt. Charisma seems to be a requirement for physicists in a way it isn't for mathematicians.

He smiles. "Ms. Beckham and Mr. Covic, I've been looking forward to this." Then he pulls reading glasses out of his pocket, puts them on, and looks down at his phone, shaking his head a little. "Sorry," he says. "I called a colleague ignorant, and he's taken offense. But ignorant is not the same as stupid, correct?"

"No," Caleb says. "It's not the same." We exchange an amused look.

"Well, then." Dr. Singh holds his hands out to us, his point proven. "Tell me about this project of yours."

I explain the motivation behind the project and the mathematical work that led to the adinkras.

"Yes, yes," Dr. Singh says, "I read all of that in your paper. Let's cover some new ground. You bring up Bostrom's simulation in your paper, but you don't spend a lot of time on it."

Caleb elbows me.

"Dr. Singh," I say cautiously, "you know there's no evidence for that theory."

"Not yet, but if our whole world is written in computer code, the theory would be more credible, wouldn't it?"

I smile back. "You're a troublemaker."

Dr. Singh looks at our poster. "So are you," he says. "Have some fun with your talk this afternoon. You've got a big idea here. Don't get bogged down in the weeds."

When he leaves, Caleb and I turn toward each other, our eyes big and our smiles wide.

"Our talk this afternoon?" he mouths.

I want to jump into his arms, but I'm trying to be a grown-up, so I just bounce up and down on my toes a little.

"You weren't nervous talking to him," Caleb says.

I shake my head. "No, but he loved us."

We see one more judge before the end of the hour—the mathematician. He is neither as hostile as the engineer nor as enamored as Dr. Singh, but I have no trouble with his questions. Then it's over.

There's a tense lunch. The decisions about the finalists will be announced at the end, so no one feels chatty. Neither Leo nor Chandran seems hopeful, and Caleb and I keep our excitement to ourselves. Dr. Singh is only one of the judges. Nothing is certain.

The guy who welcomed us last night takes the podium. I grab Caleb's hand.

We're told that everyone who made it here should be proud, that more than 500 papers were reviewed in selecting the 132 participants, and that the 5 papers selected as finalists showed innovative mathematical tools, meaningful contributions to physics, and original thinking. He names the finalists in alphabetical order, which means my name and Caleb's are read first. And then I'm in Caleb's arms, and I don't hear the other names.

It's Dean Santori who takes me away from Caleb, giving me a hug and saying, "I'm very proud of you, Evelyn. I know what you had to overcome to be here." Then he pats Caleb's arm. "Congratulations to you too, Caleb."

He recognized that our project is primarily my work. I blink back tears.

When I see Leo's and Chandran's faces, I can tell they didn't make it. From everything David said (and didn't say), I expected this, but it's not going to make what I have to do next any easier.

Leo hugs me, whispering, "Nice job" in my ear, and I'm surprised at how strange it feels. Not so long ago, I couldn't get close enough to him, but now it seems wrong. The talks start at four, and until then we'll have a room where we can practice, but because David pushed us to do run-throughs, we don't have to start right away. And I'll do a better job without this hanging over my head.

I look up at Leo. "Time for a walk?"

"Sure. Why not get all the bad news out of the way at once?"

Rather than go outside, we head for the second floor, where there's an enclosed walkway over the street below. About halfway across, Leo steers me over to a couch facing out toward the street.

We sit down, and I say, "I guess you've figured this out, but I don't think we should see each other anymore. I'm sorry."

I study his face. He's not sad or angry.

After a moment of silence, he gives me a half smile and says, "Relieved. I look relieved."

"Why?" I ask. Even though I'm the one ending this and I don't want to hurt him, I don't like to think that he's happy to be rid of me.

"I tend to think dating is more fun if the person you're with isn't in love with someone else."

I look down at my boots. "It probably doesn't make you feel any better, but I didn't know."

"I believe you. But I think you were the only one."

Now that it's over, I feel a little sad. I'll always be grateful to Leo for all that fluttery excitement in the beginning.

"It never occurred to me to want to kiss a boy until you looked at me in physics the way you did," I say. It feels important that he know I wasn't just waiting for Caleb while I was with him.

"Thanks." He takes my hand and squeezes it. I squeeze back.

"And maybe it's not *just* because of Caleb and me that you're relieved?" I ask.

He shakes his head a little.

"There was some interest in a Princess Leia costume?"

"No, you don't get to blame this on me. Maybe I was a little Bex-curious, but that's as far as it went."

"But it could go further. Now."

"Evie. This is not your problem to solve. You broke up with me. Your responsibility ends here."

"I don't want you to be sad."

"You don't get to be in charge of that."

"Will we be friends? When we get back?"

"Maybe not right away. But yeah, I think we will."

Standing, I say, "I'd better get ready for this afternoon, then. Thank you for being my first boyfriend."

"My pleasure." He sounds amused. Which is a relief.

"And I'll still vote for your solutions in physics," I say, wanting to offer something else.

He laughs. "I'll still think yours are more beautiful."

CALEB

I'M IN THE LOBBY, LOOKING AT MY PHONE. PART of me hopes that as soon as Evie's done with Leo, she'll come looking for me—the real me—but odds are it will be Tess wanting Milo.

The longer I wait, the more I don't care who I have to be. I just want to hear from her. Is it possible she changed her mind? She took Leo's hand crossing the street this morning, and except for when they announced the finalists, she hasn't touched me all day. Or maybe she did break it off, but she's sad and needs time to recover?

When I can't stand it anymore, I open her home page. It says she's online, but she hasn't written anything in our chat. Of course, she now knows I'm here too, and I'm not saying anything either. I don't want to have a huge fight before this talk, and is there any way she can find out what I've done and not be furious?

We sit in silence until I can't stand the suspense.

Milo: Ready to do this?

Tesseract: I've been ready for a while now.

Milo: It's bound to be weird when we meet. I'm sure you have a picture of me in your head that's different from the real me. But I want you to remember that this was the real me too.

Tesseract: Except your name.

Milo: Yes. And I said I picked that because I wanted to meet girls, but that was only partly true. I wanted to meet you.

Tesseract: I hope you realize that makes no sense.

Milo: It did at the time.

Tesseract: Why are we talking online when we could be together?

Milo: Where are you?

Tesseract: If you take the escalators all the way down to the basement, there's a lounge in the middle of a bunch of meeting rooms.

Milo: You'll be the one with the single red rose?

Tesseract: So clichéd . . . I'll be the one with *Why Cats Paint*.

I look up from my phone, shock and joy fighting for control of my face.

Milo: Evie.

Tesseract: Less typing, more running.

I don't need any more encouragement. I jump up and

tear through the lobby, flying down the corridor toward the escalators at the back of the hotel. I'm two flights up from the basement. I don't slow down on the escalators, weaving around people standing by themselves and pushing through people standing together. I get some pretty ugly looks, but I don't stop, and I don't explain.

She's standing on the bottom floor, waiting for me, a huge smile on her face, which gets bigger as she watches me slalom through all the people. I'm still moving pretty fast when I leap off, taking her hand and pulling her to the side.

"How long have you known? Since Bex or before?"

But she shakes her head. "Later." She pulls me around the side of the escalator and into a little alcove underneath. I love that she figured out this was here before she summoned me.

"Evie," I say, looking into her big gray eyes. Brushing my fingers along her jaw, I tilt her face up toward mine. Then I force myself to stop, checking to make sure she wants this as much as I do. I don't want to get pushed away again. "You're sure?"

She nods. "I want you to kiss me. A lot."

I smile, remembering my confession to Tess. "When I said that, I was hoping you'd tell me to go do it."

"I'm telling you now." The echo of all my longing is in her voice.

So as slowly and gently as I can manage, I bring my lips to hers, a living memory of that imagined kiss against my garage so long ago. Then she grabs my shirt, to pull me closer, and the gesture—such a mix of trust and desire—makes me lose myself in her kiss.

When I pull back, I keep her face cradled in my hands and say, "Finally," unable to find a better word for how I feel.

"Caleb," she says, layering meanings into my name. What I hear most is the same fierce certainty I'm feeling. I have kissed a lot of girls, but this is the first time I've ever kissed someone I love. Kissed Evie. Because it was never going to be anyone else. And even though I've imagined this happening in dozens of ways, the reality is better.

I pull her down to the floor, and we sit curled together against the wall, kissing and getting lost in each other's eyes and smiling goofily. But when she reaches up to brush my hair back, whispering my name again, a disturbing thought hits me.

"You don't keep saying my name because you're trying to remember who you're with, do you?"

She shoves my shoulder. "God. No! Although if I were confused, whose fault would that be?"

Grimacing, I say, "Sorry."

"I can't believe it was you all along. And now I'm here. Doing this. With you."

Her excitement thrills me, but I'm also reminded of what she said to Milo, and I'm irritated enough to take my hands off her. "And you don't think I'm kissing you just because you're physically present and willing?"

She looks down at the ground. "No."

"And you're not worried I'm going to leave?"

"Not really."

I'd like her to be more certain about this. "Evie." I wrap her hands in mine. "I wasn't going anywhere when you weren't kissing me. You think I'm leaving now?"

"Well, I always figured part of the reason you stuck around was that we didn't do this stuff. Once you kiss a girl, the clock starts ticking."

I can't believe she doesn't get this. "Because none of them were you."

"But even with me . . . that time . . . you said it was a whim. That didn't inspire a lot of confidence."

"Right. Not like saying you didn't want to do this with anyone—*especially* me. That was a total confidence boost."

"You knew what I meant."

I shake my head. "No. I didn't. I tried to figure it out. But really I had—I *still* have no idea what you were thinking."

She searches my face, obviously not believing me. "Since kindergarten, you have been the most important person in my life. You were a safe space in a world that terrified me. I couldn't risk losing that." She shrugs. "Especially for something that seemed a little icky."

I have to laugh. "But now?"

"Now I'm braver," she says. "So we can be more."

Taking her face in my hands again, I kiss her softly. "Icky? Really?"

She smiles. "It was a long time ago." Then she slides her

hands into my hair, pulls me back to her, and thoroughly convinces me that she's gotten over her concerns about ickiness.

But only a few minutes pass before I can no longer ignore the chorus of buzzes from our phones.

"I hate to say this, but do you think we need to rejoin the real world?"

"Probably. If my mother doesn't hear from me soon, she's likely to start the process of involuntary commitment."

"And Santori will expel us if we don't show up on that stage."

She looks at me hopefully. "But we get to do this more later?" The eagerness in her voice makes me grin.

"Every available minute," I promise.

EVIE

CALEB AND I SPEND A FEW MINUTES TRIAGING
our messages. We have a text from someone called Isobel, who's organizing the talks this afternoon. She gives
us the name of our prep room and says to be there no later
than 3:30.

I write back and tell her we've been preparing somewhere
else but that we'll be on time.

Sitting right next to me, Caleb texts, *We've been preparing?? What are you planning to do in this talk?* And it feels
like Milo.

Mom wants to see me. She says it's to say congratulations, but it will be more complicated than that. We agree
to meet in the coffee shop. I give Bex the name of our prep
room so she can meet us there and tell her I've moved on to
the happiest-boy-in-the-world part of the plan.

Caleb pulls me to my feet, and we step out of our little hideaway. I almost drop his hand, but then I realize I don't have to and give a happy little skip.

Riding up the escalator in front of him, I kiss him again, because it's so easy to reach his mouth. And he says, "It's more convenient like this. Now I know why I was always finding you and Leo in stairwells." I'm a little blown away by how easy this is. I keep expecting us to be different, more careful about what we say to each other, but so far it's not like that.

Truthfully, it's not like anything before. Kissing Leo was amazing, but I felt it only in my body. Being with Caleb—this boy who knows me better than anyone in the world, who loves me even though he's seen me sobbing in fear and unable to speak, who finds joy in everything—is transcendent. I didn't know it was possible to feel this many different kinds of pleasure all at the same time.

At the top of the escalator, Caleb pulls me over to the wall. "Will you be done with your mom by three? We should go through our talk at least once."

I blink a couple of times, trying to focus. "Sure. That'll give me an excuse to leave."

"You're feeling okay about everything?"

I grin up at him. "Fabulous."

He shakes his head. "I don't mean about us. About the talk. You're good?"

"It's strange—I'm not worried at all."

"In some other universe, you're terrified," he says. For some reason, I find this comforting—knowing some other me is out there panicking so I don't have to. I turn to go, but Caleb grabs my wrist and pulls me back.

"I am your boyfriend now?" he says. "No more space?"

"No more space," I agree. Caleb is my boyfriend! And also Milo! I know I should be angry with him for what he put me through, but I can't help being thrilled I get to keep them both.

"Then you don't leave without a goodbye kiss," Caleb says.

"All we've been doing is kissing."

"I don't make the rules," he says.

I can't imagine why I'm arguing, so I throw my arms around him, pressing my body against his and sliding my hands down his chest when I pull back. The flaw in this kissing-goodbye plan is that it makes it very hard to leave.

"Do you want to know my favorite part about kissing you?" I ask.

"More than anything."

"When we stop, you're here, and I get to talk to you."

The side of his mouth turns up. "Did you really just tell me that your favorite part about kissing me is when we stop?"

"No. I mean, I guess, yes. My second-favorite part is when we start?"

"Nice recovery, Eves." He messes with my hair, so I know I didn't really hurt his feelings.

Mom is waiting at a table in the back of the hotel coffee shop. She's already ordered a cup of tea for me, which is thoughtful, but I am (ahem) a little overheated, and I'd kill for a Diet Coke and something chocolate, which is what I tell the waitress who approaches when I sit.

"Brownie?" she says.

"Perfect."

Mom makes a face. "You really want to put that in your body before something like this?"

"I'll drink some water later. I want to celebrate. I couldn't eat lunch, and dinner last night was sad. The vegetarian entrée was ravioli, and I think it may have come out of a can."

She slides the mug toward me. "At least drink this too. Make your mother happy."

I pick up the mug and take a sip, but the tea is strangely bitter, so I push it away and wait for my soda.

"Congratulations. You and Caleb must have done well with the judges."

I tell her about how it went, especially the conversation with Dr. Singh.

"You didn't have any problems?" she says.

My small freeze with the engineer doesn't seem worth mentioning, so I shake my head, taking a long drink of the soda the waitress puts in front of me and a giant bite of brownie.

Mom flinches at both and pushes the tea toward me again. "And how many people will be in the room this afternoon?"

"A couple hundred? The participants, their teachers, some families, probably a few professors and kids from local schools."

Mom makes a face. I wish we didn't have to do this. I'd like to have a conversation with her that doesn't feel like a clinical interview.

She takes my hand. "Saying this is not going to make me popular, but I'm your mother, and it's not my job to be popular. I spoke to the judges. You and Caleb will get the scholarships even if you don't go onstage. Why risk everything you've accomplished? What if something happens and you stop speaking again? What if it's something worse?"

Her fear is contagious. My heart rate picks up. And the litany of possible fates she's always warned me about spirals in front of me: madness, suicide, paranoia, hallucinations, catatonia. Is this talk worth skating closer to that border?

But I remember Anita's words: *They're your parents, but they don't own you.* Her fears aren't mine. I wonder how much of my anxiety has been produced by turning it into a Disorder instead of just seeing it as one of my traits. A problematic one, sure, but maybe not so much worse than my inability to catch a flying object or my allergies.

"Caleb will be with me," I say. "I'll be fine."

"Caleb is not the answer to every problem," she says. "He

cannot punch this audience into submission, and he can't prevent whatever trigger might send you into free fall."

"Wow," I say. And I can't manage anything else. I am genuinely shocked by this dismissal of both my own capabilities and Caleb's role in my life, but it's not me spiraling out here. It's Mom. This fear of hers is big and irrational, and it's interfering with her life. Somehow, this thought gives me enough empathy not to lash out. If I know anything, it's what it feels like to be that afraid. And it doesn't matter that the fear isn't logical.

"When I get like this, I breathe through my nose, hold it for three heartbeats, and exhale. I can feel my body calming down when I do."

"Evie, that's good, but it's not enough. Please. Please. If you're determined to do this, drink your tea before you go."

I look at her oddly. She is not the kind of person who puts faith in herbal teas and yoga. Mom trusts only two kinds of help: prescription and over-the-counter.

Oh.

She wouldn't.

Would she?

Watching her, I stick my finger into the cooling tea, stir it around, and then put my finger in my mouth. This time I recognize the strange bitter taste.

Xanax.

CALEB

WHEN I OPEN THE DOOR TO OUR PRACTICE ROOM, I find Bex pacing back and forth, talking to herself. With hand gestures.

"Everything all right in here?" I ask. I sort of thought she would be the one calming us down.

"No!"

"Okay, then."

"My parents came to Chicago for a 'business meeting.'" She does exaggerated finger quotes. "And they're staying in the hotel across the street. They want to come over to say hello."

"And that's terrible because . . . ?"

"Other than the fact that they couldn't stand the idea of me being in a city on my own for forty-eight hours even though I am an actual legal adult? And when you think about it, I'm not even on my own. I'm here under the supervision of my principal, who is a grandfather and runs a school and has a physics degree."

"Yeah," I say, working really hard not to show my amusement. "Other than that." Bex is flipping out, and though I do feel bad for her, I am also enjoying this little payback for the way she's played me the past two days.

"I promised myself that the next time I saw them, I would tell them I want to go to school in New York and study climate change and date science boys, and I haven't had time to prepare myself yet. So what am I going to say?"

"Um."

"And also, what if they say it's all right? Then what, Caleb?"

"Then you go to school in New York and study climate change and date science boys? Maybe not in that order, though. Your odds on the last one are pretty good at Newton, so you might want to start with that." I feel like I'm getting insight into Evie's world here. It's strange but a little freeing to talk to someone while having absolutely no idea of where their emotions are coming from.

"You should kiss me," Bex says.

"Damn it," I say, grinning. "I should have known. This whole day . . . it was a dream."

"I'm serious. I'm eighteen years old, and I don't know what I'm doing. You can't send me out there to start dating like that. It's irresponsible."

"Bex." I hold out my arms.

Her eyes get big, and she swallows. "Okay. I'm ready."

"Stop. I am not going to kiss you. But come here. You need to calm the frack down."

She lays her head on my chest, and I pat her back. "What is going on? This is not like you."

"I don't want to tell my parents about Columbia. They won't be thrilled about the climate science part, but I think maybe they can cope. But they will throw a fit about New York for sure because they'll be so afraid for me. Which means there's no space for me to be scared." She takes a deep breath. "But I am. It's just that I want to do it anyway. And I can't talk about it to Evie because I see how upset she gets every time I mention New York, and I don't want to make it harder for her."

I pull Bex over to the conference table, and we sit on top of it, my arm around her. "I don't know if this helps, but I've been scared too."

"About what?"

"I applied to MIT," I admit. Now that I won't have Tess, I'm going to try to be more open with Bex and Evie.

"You did? And you didn't tell us?"

"I didn't want you to feel sorry for me if I didn't get in. Or couldn't go."

"But we could have helped you deal with it. If we'd known."

"Yeah," I say, and give her a significant look.

She nods. "Like my parents can help me if I tell them."

"At least with the college stuff," I agree. "Maybe with the kissing you could go with a more need-to-know approach."

"I am worried about that too. It's weird to be eighteen and not know what I'm doing. People are going to expect me to be good at it because . . ." She flutters her hand up and down herself.

"Because you're beautiful and confident and have been good at everything you've ever tried?"

She smiles. "Yeah. Because of that. That's why I thought . . ." She gestures at me.

"I know."

"I'm sorry. I think I lost my mind for a minute." She looks away. "Evie's going to kill me, isn't she?"

"I think she'll understand. And don't worry about it so much. It's not about being technically proficient. If you find someone you want to kiss—and not for instructional purposes—you'll be fine."

"Thanks."

"You're welcome. I'm happy to still have one girl-space-friend."

"What does that mean?"

We're sitting pretty close together, so when Bex jumps as the door opens, her forehead cracks against mine.

"Rebeca!"

Bex's mom comes through the door, Santori and her dad right behind her. Bex springs off the table in a way that makes us appear much guiltier than if she'd stayed put. She does not make it better when I put my hand on her back to settle her and she leaps away. I give up on Bex and extend my hand to her mother.

"Nice to see you again, Mrs. de Silva." I nod at her father. "Reverend de Silva."

"What's going on here?" Mrs. de Silva asks, her face serious.

Reverend de Silva looks at Santori. "I thought you wanted her here to support Evelyn. Why is she alone in this room with this boy?" He turns his attention to Bex. "Is he the real reason you wanted to come?"

"Dad, no. Mama. Caleb's my friend. We were talking about college stuff. I came here to help Evie, like I said, not to hang out with boys. I need you to trust me on this."

The door swings open, nearly hitting Santori. "Hey, Bex," Leo calls on his way in. "I've got my camera. You want to show me that skating rink now?"

Every single person in the room except Leo starts talking at once. I have no idea what anyone, including me, is saying. Then Santori, showing the leadership he's paid for, grabs Leo and me by the arms and drags us out of the room and down the hall and points us to a bench in the lobby.

"Sit."

We do.

"And do not go back to that conference room for another fifteen minutes."

"Yes, sir," I say, so grateful he helped us escape that I'd agree to just about anything. Besides, that room's no good to me until Bex finishes pacifying her mother.

When I figure Leo's had enough time to process all the excitement, I say, "So. You and Bex?"

"Nope," he says. "I already talked to Evie about this. We're friends. That's all."

"Sometimes that's how it starts." I keep my voice very, very neutral.

Even so, the look Leo gives me could freeze helium.

"Just saying."

We're quiet for a bit.

"Or Sarah-Kate's fun," I suggest. "We could double-date again?"

Leo stares at me for several long seconds. "You're over there harboring the delusion that you and I are friends, aren't you?"

"Yeah. Evie approves of like eight people, and you're one of them. Plus, you and I already agreed on a stuffing recipe, so it seems like a waste not to follow through."

I love Bex and Evie, but sometimes I need other kinds of friends. Now that I no longer want to murder him in his sleep, Leo would make an excellent addition to my nights out with David and Dev.

Leo shakes his head. "You're like the human equivalent of a golden retriever."

"Impossible not to like?"

"Asking for a smack with a newspaper."

"You'll come around."

He looks down at his phone. "Chandran needs to see me."

"About what?"

He stands. "You got me. That was an excuse so I could leave."

"I'll wear you down," I call after him.

He looks back. "I guess when you find a strategy that works . . ."

Harsh.

But fair.

EVIE

I LOOK AT MOM IN HORROR. "DID YOU THINK about what might have happened if I had decided to take a pill on my own? Or if I'd had cough medicine? Or even if I'd felt the effects of that Xanax in my body but didn't know where they were coming from?"

She shakes her head. "Evie, I just wanted to help."

"Do you know who drugs people against their will? Date rapists. I have been trying and trying to understand this from your perspective. I know it hasn't been easy having a daughter like me, but this is too much. And today—I shouldn't have to think about this today. It's no wonder I had a breakdown with you last year."

"Evie!" she says, shocked.

She reaches across the table for me, but I shake her hand

off. Caleb peeks his head into the restaurant from the door leading out to the hotel, and I stand up.

"You need to explain this to Dad. Tell him why I won't be seeing you for dinner tonight."

I move toward Caleb, trancelike, vaguely aware of the way his face shifts as he gets a good look at me. When he came in, he was bubbling over with some joke, but now he's worried.

When I get to him, he wraps his arms around me, and I whisper in his ear what happened. He pulls back to look at me. "Evie! What if you had already taken something? She could have—"

"I know. I know." I'm starting to shake a little. I can't believe this. It's a step beyond anything that has happened before.

"It's criminal," he says. "Actually illegal."

Mom approaches us, and Caleb pulls me back, positioning me behind him as if she might physically hurt me. "I'm sorry," she whispers.

I shake my head and press into Caleb's back. "Not now," he says. "We have to be onstage in an hour." And he turns, keeping himself in between Mom and me, and propels me out of the restaurant.

In the hall, he gives me a questioning look. But I say, "Let's not do this now. I can't think about her. We have a Frontier talk to do."

When we get to the prep room, Caleb opens the door slowly, as if expecting someone to leap out at us, but the room is empty except for a basket of snacks. I open a plastic bottle of water, saying, "Don't tell Bex I'm depleting the earth's precious natural resources."

Caleb smiles. "Don't worry. Bex has her hands full."

We go through our talk, focusing on telling it like a story. In the middle of our second time through, a pretty, dark-haired girl with cat-eye glasses sweeps into the room.

"Hi! I'm Isobel, Dr. Singh's graduate assistant, and I organized the conference. I loved your paper. It was brilliant." She holds out a paper bag to us. "Pick a number to see what order you'll speak in."

I step back. Isobel is a little high intensity.

"Let me," Caleb says. "I am having a very good day." He pulls out a five. "As I said."

This gives us almost another hour to prepare, and it means ours will be the last talk the judges hear. Isobel says, "I'll come get you ten minutes before you're on. Be ready," and leaves.

"Should we keep going?" I ask, holding up my notes.

Caleb shakes his head. "Let's keep it fresh. I think it'll play better if it sounds more like a conversation." He flings himself into an armchair in the corner of the room.

I stack my papers into a pile and then curl up on his lap. He pulls me close, and we sit in silence for a long time.

Despite the fight with Mom and the performance ahead, I feel calm. I love Caleb for who he is, but also for the empty space he gives me. I feel most wholly myself when I'm with him.

I'd like to think I do the same for him, but I'm not sure that's true.

Without moving, I ask, "Why didn't you tell me about MIT?"

"I did."

"No. Milo told Tess. I realize that for you, that was the same thing—which we are not done talking about—but it wasn't for me."

"It seemed unlikely it would happen. And I didn't want to worry you."

At one point, I know it would have. I couldn't even admit the possibility to Anita at the beginning of the year. But I've faced strangers and spiders and bridges, and I'll do okay with this too.

"I don't have to go," he says.

"Don't be silly. Giving up what you want would be a lot more likely to break us than a few hundred miles."

"Okay."

"But I don't want you to hide this stuff from me. Especially once we're apart." I think back about everything I learned about him as Tess. It's going to take a while before I fully wrap all that into my idea of Caleb. "You don't have to be strong all the time. You can tell me if you're worried about something. Or sad."

I feel him nod. Then he whispers, "I'm worried about our talk. I know it doesn't matter so much at this point, but I don't want to screw this up."

"I know. Me too."

I rest my head on his chest and listen to his heartbeat. Almost effortlessly, I sync my breathing to it.

CALEB

ISOBEL COMES BACK BEFORE OUR TALK TO MIC us and take us backstage, where we watch a guy named Andrew Xiao finish up. With her head on my shoulder, Evie says, "He's the one to beat."

"How do you know? We've only seen two minutes of his talk."

"I saw the poster," she says. "The mathematics is nice, and it's got some pretty clear implications for space travel."

"Ah," I say.

"That's right, Milo. It's practical."

Her eyes move toward the audience, and I see her steel herself, so I link my fingers with hers. "When we're out there, I want you to talk to me. Forget about the audience. Forget about the judges. I'm going to ask you questions, and you're going to talk to me."

Her eyes are wide. She looks pale and a little frozen, but when we're onstage, I need her to do most of the talking. David was right. I can't explain all of our work.

Pulling her close, I whisper, "Do you remember the first time we played Can You Help Me Find?"

Her eyes refocus on mine, and she smiles. We were eleven, and Evie's therapist insisted it was time for her to learn to talk to unfamiliar adults. Her parents took her to the library a couple of times, but Evie flat-out refused to engage in the therapist's game. So the next time I went with her. I volunteered to go first, and Evie sent me in search of *My Very First Tea Party*, but when I returned triumphantly, she shook her head.

To encourage her, I stood directly behind the librarian seated at the reference desk, turning whenever he looked irritably over his shoulder at me and pretending to study a poster on the Dewey Decimal System while muttering things like, "It's fascinating, really. So very many numbers."

Finally, Evie relaxed enough to approach, and, meeting my eyes over the librarian's head, she asked for her book.

Now I tuck a stray curl behind her ear. "It doesn't matter who else is out there, Evie. You're talking to me."

She gives a small nod. "I won't let you make a mistake."

"We've got a plan, then."

Isobel clears her throat next to us and says we're up.

We turn on our mics and head out to center stage. Evie keeps her eyes on me. I'm focused on her, but I'm also tracking the audience (larger than I expected), the judges (in the front row), and the clock (now counting down from ten minutes).

I give Evie a big smile and say, "So, tell me, Evie, how did we end up here?"

This gets a little laugh from the audience, and as I hoped, Evie smiles back and then begins to talk about the initial spark of curiosity that led her to the adinkras, her conviction that they could be used to explore the symmetries in various states of helium, and the mathematical path she took to get there.

She skims over the Clifford algebras and doesn't mention the matrices at all, taking Dr. Singh's advice not to get bogged down. Then she says, "But I couldn't do enough with my paper models."

This is my cue. I talk about writing the program, Evie's idea to assign binary addresses, and my amazement when we'd folded the models and found the error-correcting code blocks. Worried about time, I rush it a little.

Evie opens her eyes wide. "There was C++ code right in the models?"

"No, of course not," I say, grateful that she slowed me down. We could have gotten in trouble both for inaccuracy and overselling. I explain the relationships between error-correcting codes in programming languages and binary. And then I toss it back to her. "But what could it mean that we're finding binary code in our mathematical models of atoms?"

Evie describes the fine-tuning problem and talks about how strange it is that mathematics keeps predicting discoveries in the material world. She finishes by saying, "But maybe it's not so unexpected if our entire universe is written in the language of mathematics."

"Maybe," I say, letting a little amusement show in my voice, "we live in a computer program. We could be in a simulation right now." And I talk about Bostrom's essay.

Evie rolls her eyes.

The audience loves this, and the judges are eating it up too—my willingness to believe, and Evie's science-based skepticism.

"It is hard to accept that binary code ended up in the mathematical representations of atoms by chance," I say coaxingly.

Evie talks about what physicists would need to do to test some of the hypotheses I'm throwing out.

We have forty-five seconds left. We didn't practice this part, but I give her a soft pitch to finish up. "All of this is very interesting, Evie," I say, "but is it useful?"

"Well, Caleb," she responds with exactly the right amount of edge to her voice, "we don't always know ahead of time what's going to be useful. If it weren't for quantum mechanics, we wouldn't have GPS, and then you'd spend even more time driving around in circles than you already do."

"No need for personal attacks," I say, but I love that she's relaxed enough to do this.

"But more importantly," she says, and her voice turns serious, "the goal of physics isn't really to be useful. The project is grander than that. Physics is about describing the world we live in, how it started, the way it works. The goal should be to write the language of the universe in words humanity can read. So I don't care if my mathematics is useful. If it's beautiful and it's true, then I've done my job."

And the green light on our timer turns red. I extend my hand toward Evie. She crosses the stage to take it, and I lead her off as if we stopped to have this conversation in the middle of a walk.

Noise fills the room. From offstage, we look out at the crowd. If the audience is any guide, we've put this thing to bed. The judges are harder to read.

"Wow," Isobel says, approaching us. "I didn't think your heads were in the game, but that was fab. Come on, we've got to get you to the back room with the other finalists. You need to stay out of the way while the judges deliberate."

Evie takes a deep breath, and I know what she's thinking. She just finished performing for hundreds of people, and now she's being led into a small room with a bunch of strangers, but when she looks up at me, her face isn't panicked.

"It's okay," she says. "I'm with you."

EVIE

ISOBEL OPENS THE DOOR TO A CONFERENCE room much larger than the one we were in earlier. Five boys, including two arguing in a corner, are spread throughout the room, and I'm struck by how difficult it would be for me to walk into this space on my own. I recovered from Wunderlochen, but I'll never really be over it.

One of the guys in the corner shouts, "Well, at least I didn't say anything that directly contradicts the laws of physics!" The combatants must be the other pair who made the finals. Caleb lightly touches my back, steering me away from them. "Other side, I think."

We stop at a table, get drinks, and consider where to sit. One of the three non-arguing boys looks up from his phone and waves, so we head in his direction.

"I'm Andrew," he says. "I wish I could have seen your talk."

We introduce ourselves, and I say, "We actually saw the end of yours, but I'd love to read the full paper."

"Ditto," he says. "I'm afraid I messed up onstage though. I hate being in front of crowds."

I smile. "I know. If it wasn't for Caleb, I never would have gone on."

Andrew says, "This might be obnoxious, but can I ask you something?"

"All right," I say, a little nervous about where he might be going.

But his question turns out to be about transforming equations to adinkra, which I'm happy to talk about. I spend a good fifteen minutes explaining, drawing little diagrams on napkins. Andrew asks some of the best questions I've heard all day. Then his phone buzzes. "My mom," he says. "I have to answer."

When I turn back to Caleb, he says, "You made a friend."

There's something not quite right in his voice. "Are you jealous?" I ask, worried. It's going to be a problem if Caleb flips out every time I talk to someone now. There are lots of boys in math.

He shakes his head with a smile. "Not like that. But, Evie, even after doing this project with you, I only understood about a third of what you said. I don't know if I'm smart enough. Maybe you'll get bored with me?"

"Caleb, you're brilliant."

He shakes his head. "Don't flatter me. I watch you and

Leo in physics, and there's no way I can keep up. You called Brian an idiot, but I couldn't have written that proof in the first place, even with an error."

"And if this were a gathering of coders, could I keep up? Solve the same problems? Create the same programs? And if I couldn't, would it mean I was any less smart?"

Even considering everything he said as Milo, I can't believe that Caleb has been carrying this insecurity around with him. He has always seemed so comfortable in his own skin.

"It's not the same," he says.

"Well, no. It's clearly misguided to spend your life on programming instead of mathematics. But that says more about your priorities than your intellect."

He looks at me for a long time, and I hold his gaze.

Then he smiles, and it's like the sun coming out. "You think I'm smart?"

I think about Caleb explaining error-correcting code, Caleb ordering Leo around in the lab, Caleb in the library with me, eyes lit up as the program we needed started to come together for him.

"I do. You were amazing on that stage. You created a ten-minute story from something that took us twenty-five pages to explain."

"Evie, you were amazing. I kept the trains running."

Without thinking, I lean toward him, but I stop when I remember we're in this room full of boys. Instead, I take his hand and squeeze it, wanting to communicate the intensity of what I'm feeling.

Then Caleb pulls out his phone with a grin. I get mine, and we turn away from each other on the couch and go into our chat room.

Milo: So how'd your talk go?

Tess: Really? That's how we're going to do this?

Milo: ☺

Tess: Fine. It went very well. I ended up onstage, but I did not make a fool of myself, thanks to my BSF.

Milo: I heard there was no more BSF.

Tess: I don't know where you got that idea.

Milo: Evie!

Tess: Caleb!

Milo: Fine. We'll do it your way. What do you want to talk about?

Tess: When did you first know how you felt about me?

Milo: You really want to know?

Tess: Of course.

He texts me a picture.

It's us when we were eight, sitting together on a hay bale with pumpkins in our laps during a school field trip. I'm looking at Caleb with some intensity, my mouth open, one hand holding my pumpkin, the other arm flung out wide. Caleb's head is thrown back, laughing at whatever I was saying, which was probably a lecture ranking the plausibility of the Great Pumpkin, Santa Claus, and the tooth fairy.

"No," I say. "We were children."

"I didn't have the words for it then. Didn't even really know what the feeling was. But look at my face, Eves—total joy. That's what you do to me. For a long time, I wondered if I should give up on us. But whenever I looked at this picture, I knew I couldn't, not unless I found someone else who made me feel that way."

"But you never did?" I'm so used to thinking of myself as someone Caleb takes care of, not as someone he wants.

"No."

"Thanks for waiting."

"Thanks for not making me wait any longer."

Then Isobel comes back and says they're ready for us onstage.

CALEB

HOLDING HANDS, EVIE AND I FOLLOW ISOBEL down the hall. I suppose this is not the most professional way to head into the finale, but I can't make myself let go.

Back in the wings, the seven of us gather around Isobel. Evie drops her bag so she can lean back against me, and I wrap my arms around her, enjoying the still-new feeling of her body pressed entirely against mine. It's not until the other pair goes out to center stage that I notice they've started the rankings.

In the end, it's down to us and Andrew Xiao, as Evie predicted. "Your work was beautiful," she tells him.

"And yours was wild," he says.

Then they call our names. I let go of Evie so we can walk out and accept medals and certificates commemorating our second-place finish. The audience is cheering with an intensity that suggests they think we were robbed. Looking at the engineer's face, I know who the holdout was, but I don't really care. Evie, a little overwhelmed by the intensity of the emotion in the room, takes a small step back toward me. We're not quite touching, but she turns her face toward my chest as if she'd like to hide. The clapping and cheering grow louder. Who'd have guessed the Frontier audience is a sucker for a love story?

I look down at her and raise my eyebrows. If I kiss her, odds are good that the audience will storm the stage and demand a recount, but she shakes her head with a little smile. So I lead her off the stage the same way I did after our talk.

When we go out into the audience we're immediately surrounded by hordes of people calling out and grabbing us. Evie hates it. She's trying to calm herself, but her breathing's getting faster and faster, and I'm worried she's going to tip into hyperventilation. Holding her close, I push toward the stage, and then I put my hands on her waist and say, "Jump." When she does, I lift her so she's sitting on the stage, looking out over the crowd. She gives me a look of so much gratitude that I feel it like a touch. Then I position myself on the ground next to her so we can greet our admirers.

Other participants tell us how much they love our work, a man wants us on a podcast on science for young people, a woman asks if we'll participate in some kind of junior TED Talk, and recruiters from universities invite us to dinner. I keep only the card from MIT Evie says "I've already committed," over and over again.

And then, finally, the strangers melt away, and Evie hops down from the stage. Dr. Singh hands us each a business card. "I look forward to seeing you on campus next year," he says to Evie. And to me, "Maybe we'll get you for grad school?"

"We'll see," I say. If anyone could get me into physics full-time, it would be Dr. Singh and Evie.

Dean Santori congratulates us, and Mom pulls me into a hug. When Dad takes her place, Mom kisses Evie's cheek and says, "And if this one gives you any trouble, let me know. I'll take care of it."

"Hey," I say, "how about a little loyalty to your firstborn?"

"Well, Caleb, I have two other sons, Evie's one-of-a-kind." She puts her hand on Evie's shoulder. "You remember that in case this doesn't work out. In a few years, the three-year age gap between you and Nolan will be nothing."

"Mom," I say. "Please stop scaring my girlfriend." This is the first time I've said it out loud. Evie looks up at me and grins.

Mom kisses my cheek. "Enjoy tonight. We'll see you tomorrow." And they're gone.

Evie's father holds her close and tells her how proud he is, and Evie cries, but she wipes her tears away when her mother approaches.

"You two were incandescent out there," she says.

"Thank you," Evie responds. "But do you see? Even if

the worst hadn't happened, you could have taken that away from me. From us." And she steps back into me again like she did onstage, this time turning her head to lay it on my chest. I put an arm around her, feeling the same mixture of pleasure and pride that I did holding her on the bus after Wunderlochen, knowing that this brilliant, beautiful girl chose me.

Her mother says, "I'm sorry. I want to do better."

Evie studies her mother.

"I can't do this tonight," she says. "But if you stay, we can talk tomorrow. At breakfast?"

"Why not when we get home?" her mother asks. "Your father has to be back tonight."

"Here," Evie says. I'm not sure why.

Her mom nods. "Okay. I'll stay. I can take the train back."

"I'll text you." Evie hugs her mother quickly.

Then it's just us and Leo and Bex. Bex grabs us and hangs on until Evie cries again and I tear up. I readjust so I'm holding them to me. I am going to miss them both next year more than it's possible to say, which is maybe how they feel too, because none of us speaks.

Eventually, Bex lets go, wipes her eyes, and says to me, "Can I talk to you for a minute?"

I nod, even though this means leaving Evie with Leo.

We move off to the side, and Bex says, "I want to apologize for earlier today."

"Asking me to kiss you was not a mortal insult."

"Thank you for not doing it, though. I'm glad I didn't waste my first kiss."

"Wouldn't have been a waste."

Bex shakes her head and presses a plastic card into my hand. I give her a confused look; a gift card seems overly formal for the sort of apology required here. Then I look down. It's a room key.

"My parents and I have a lot to talk about," she says. "They got a suite across the street, so I'm going to stay with them tonight."

"Bex, you are an excellent coconspirator."

"I'm not telling you the room number. That's up to Evie." And then she goes to find her parents, and I take Evie away from Leo, who looks amused at the role reversal.

When Evie and I are alone except for the staff cleaning up, I say, "So, what do we do for an encore?"

"You should go to the MIT dinner."

I shake my head. "Not unless you come. I don't want to leave you alone."

"No," she says. "I need to not be with strangers. I'll eat with Bex. Meet you after?"

"About that," I say, and I tell her what Bex did. Her eyes get big, then a little panicked.

"Relax. We've been dating for thirty seconds. We are not going to have sex. Not tonight," I add for the sake of honesty, and I'm pleased to see her panic shift into something like interest. "But I'd like to stay with you, if that's okay. As hard as this may be to believe, I think Leo needs a break from me."

"Give me your hand," Evie says. Then she reaches into her purse and pulls out a black marker. I grin.

Evie turns my hand over and writes her room number on the inside of my wrist. Then she takes my other hand, turning it over as well. I tilt my head at her curiously. On that wrist, in tiny letters, she writes, "Mine."

As the pleasure of being claimed by Evie sweeps over me, I say, "That I am."

EVIE

BEX'S PARENTS DID NOT COME TO CHICAGO solely to check up on her. Her father is in town for meetings about a possible television show. The collaboration has been in the works for a while, and the opportunity to take a business trip that overlapped with Bex's visit proved too tempting to pass up.

This works out well for us, because her mom and dad have a business dinner. The reverend doesn't want us wandering around Chicago alone, so he urges us to stay in their suite and order room service. This is an introvert's dream. You call on the phone, and they bring pizza and salad and tubs of ice cream right to your door. We live in an age of miracles.

Although the suite has a table, we picnic on one of the beds in Bex's room.

"How are you?" I ask. We've already talked about my day, which was flashier, but Bex's was equally important in lots of ways.

"I told them everything."

"And?"

"The climate science stuff went pretty well. My dad quoted some passage about having dominion over the earth, so Mom had to accept that."

"Good." That was easier than expected.

"But they really, really hate the idea of New York. They're going to be in Chicago a lot for the television show, so they want me here. They're so afraid they're going to lose me."

"How could that even happen?" I'm really angry with Mom right now, but we're not going to lose each other. Being someone's child doesn't go away.

"If I stopped going to church, it would feel like a loss to them. I wish they would trust me, though. I'd never give it up."

"You're sure?"

"Yes. There's so much beauty and comfort in it. And I need that. To do the hard things."

"I guess that makes sense."

Bex hears the doubt in my voice. "What is it? You can tell me."

"Doesn't some of it bother you?"

"There are problems. Definitely. But the things I don't like—how the church talks about women and sexuality and science—they're never going to change if people like me just leave."

"All that energy. I don't get where it comes from." I feel like it takes everything in me to live my ordinary life and do some math, but Bex wants to reform Christianity and be a soccer star and a fashion icon all while saving the world. I'll be happy if next year I can find food, get to my classes, and figure out what to wear without a uniform.

"I like to keep busy," she says.

"Too busy for boys?" I ask, wondering if she talked to her parents about that too.

"No." She smiles. "Not that busy."

"They said yes?"

Bex nods. "They asked me tons of embarrassing questions, and they wish I'd start with someone they know, but they say it's my decision now."

"What made them change their minds?"

"Well, I'm eighteen, and I waited a long time. Because of them. And my mom says the ring wasn't really supposed to be about not dating but about making sure whoever I chose was worthy."

"Uh-oh," I say, feeling guilty. "Are you mad I got rid of their saying?"

Bex laughs and twists her ring. "No. I'm glad you did it, especially if we're going to be apart next year."

"You're going to keep pushing for New York?"

"I am. It's important to me."

College on my own. I'll have to think more about that, but tonight I want to focus on fun. "For the dating thing, do you have someone in mind?" Despite everything Leo said, I can't help hoping it's him.

"Maybe."

"Well?"

"What do you think of Chandran?" Bex asks.

"I don't think of Chandran."

"Start. We hung out a little bit today while you were practicing and Leo was wallowing." I wince. "He's funny. And because he's not in our year, he doesn't do that I'm-about-to-get-with-Bex-de-Silva thing when I laugh at his jokes."

I know what she's saying. Boys in our grade can be weird about Bex. "I mean, he's at Frontier as a junior. So that has to be good."

Bex twists her hands together. "And because he's a year younger, it feels a little less scary that I don't know what I'm doing."

"Okay. Chandran. I can get used to that."

"I said *maybe*. There's also Caden. He's a really good striker."

"Is that an important quality in a boyfriend?" I know *striker* is a soccer word, but I'm not totally sure what it means.

"And I think he prays before games."

"He does? Why? Does God care who wins Newton soccer

games?" I know from Abbie that God's got a lot of little side hustles, but even so, prep school soccer doesn't seem worth His time.

Bex shakes her head. "It's not about winning, Evie. It's about being grateful for your speed and strength and the chance to play."

"Oh," I say, feeling chastised.

"But then, he's had a couple of girlfriends, so maybe he's not a good idea."

"It's not like calculus, Bex. You don't have to test into the advanced class."

"Two boyfriends, and you think you're an expert."

"I do. I'm going to start an advice column."

Bex giggles. "Will all the advice be 'Get your parents to move in next door to your soul mate'?"

"Yes," I say, but this makes me think of Mom. Bex was incredulous when I told her the story of the Xanax, but we didn't get as far as making a plan. "I can't go back home tomorrow. I'm not ready." Because of all this, I might need therapy for a little longer than Anita and I thought. But I'm okay with that. It feels different to choose it for myself.

Bex offers to take me to D.C. for the rest of the break. I'm grateful. Given the choice of an airplane with Bex or a week with my mother, I'm going to opt for the airplane, and I have the pills Anita prescribed if I need them.

When her parents return, they say they'd be happy to have me visit and enlist me in trying to talk Bex into U of C.

Silently, I promise Bex that I will take her side. When she walks me to the door, she hugs me and whispers, "Enjoy your evening, Evie."

"Thank you, Bex," I say, squeezing back, hoping she can hear how grateful I am.

CALEB

WHEN I LET MYSELF INTO THE HOTEL ROOM after knocking and getting no response, I hear the shower. The movie that's been running in my head since dinner, which features robotics competitions, Red Sox games, and measuring in smoots, is instantly replaced by a very different sort of story.

I rest my forehead on the bathroom door and tell myself to chill. Then I play music on my phone and turn it up loud so she'll know I'm here. Because if she comes out wrapped in a towel or worse (better?), I'm going to be in trouble.

A little while later, I hear the door open, and she says, "Caleb?"

"Evie?" I respond, my voice catching a little.

When she doesn't come out, I say, "Do you need something?"

"No. It's just . . . I hadn't planned on company when I packed."

My interior movie veers off in a dozen new directions. "Are you wearing cartoon characters? Or black lace? Please let it be black lace," I say, mostly to break the tension.

But when she steps into view, it's so much better than lace. She's wearing an old warm-up shirt of mine. The logo over her heart, the hem at mid-thigh, and, although I can't see it, my name on her back. She also has on these ridiculous pink polka-dotted flannel pants. Standing there with her hair down and her feet bare, she is heartbreakingly adorable.

Without thinking, I move toward her. "Why do you have that?"

She shrugs a little. "It rained at that game last year, and my T-shirt got all clingy. You gave it to me so I could cover up, and I kept it."

I smile at the memory. "Always so chivalrous." I take her hands. "But why do you have it here?"

"Pajamas."

"This is what you wear? All the time?"

"Not all the time."

I feel the same way I did when I read that poem—delighted and surprised by this evidence that Evie had a secret fascination with me. "Did you wear this even when you were with Leo?"

She nods.

"Why?" I think I know, but I would like to hear her say it.

"It was comfortable," she says, but she isn't meeting my eyes, and there is no way I am letting her get away with this.

"Evie. You were dating someone else and sleeping in my shirt. It wasn't because you liked the cotton blend."

She bites her lip in that way that makes me want to join in. "It made me feel closer to you. The more involved I got with Leo, the more I missed you. Is that awful?"

"I'm probably not the right person to ask. If it were up to me, you'd never wear anything else." After a moment, I add, "Except maybe that gray dress from last night."

She pulls me over to the couch and sits next to me, cross-legged. "Bex says I've always been in love with you. And I think she's right. I'm sorry it took me so long to figure it out."

My heart is cracking open, but I say only, "Recognizing emotions isn't really your thing."

She laughs. "True."

"But why did you fall for Leo?" I can't not ask.

The suspense while she thinks this over is terrible.

"What he did in physics made me notice him. It made him different from most people, who usually fade into the background for me. And once I was noticing, there were all the obvious reasons." She gives me a sheepish look. I decide I don't want to hear her list them. "And I think maybe I was just ready?"

"For a while there, I didn't think I had a chance. The girl never ends up with the funny best friend when there's a dark and brooding stranger around."

"Leo's not dark and brooding."

"He's more dark and brooding than I am."

She grins. "Frosty the Snowman is more dark and brooding than you are."

"It's that corncob pipe," I concede. "When did you first think you might want us to be more than friends?" I expect her to say the bus. I like that I got to watch it happen.

She needs no time to think about this. "The first time it crossed my mind was after that fight with Blake outside the study room."

"That was almost two months ago! Right after you started up with Leo." I am outraged. "And you were so scared. You were looking at me like you didn't know who I was."

She climbs onto my lap, facing me, which I am strongly in favor of. "Not because I was scared, you idiot," she says as she slides her hands up my chest. "Because I was pressed up against you and having all of these *thoughts*. About my best friend. It was confusing."

I love hearing this—that she was moving toward us without me pushing her. That she was having *thoughts*. Then something else occurs to me. "I didn't need Milo, then?"

"No! Milo was stressful."

But I was there, so I know that's not all he was. "Only stressful?"

She smiles. "No. He was fun. I liked the idea that I might fall for someone who got me so completely."

"Because there were no other options for that around."

"By the end, I thought I was falling in love with two people."

"Don't you mean three?"

She shakes her head and looks me in the eyes. "No."

EVIE

CALEB IS IN THE MIDDLE OF KISSING HIS WAY UP
from my collarbone to my jaw when he stops, inhales, and
says, "You smell like cupcakes."

Laughing, I say, "Leo always says—" and then I stop,
horrified.

Caleb pulls back to look at me. "French toast. I know."
Thankfully, he seems amused. I cannot believe I did that.

"I'm sorry," I say. "I'm so used to saying anything that
crosses my mind with you. Now that we're different, I need to
work on my boyfriend filter."

"Eves. We're not different." To emphasize his point, he
tightens his hands on my waist, pulling me closer. I can't
help a little gasp at the rush of pleasure caused by all the
points of contact.

He gives me a slow smile. "Okay, we're a little different," he says, and kisses me in a way that he clearly intends to be a quick side note to his speech, but I derail him with my response.

"But differences aside," he continues a little while later, "we're still us. That's kind of the point. I can stand to hear about whatever kind of sugary goodness Leo compared you to or anything else you want to tell me. But I will hate it if you start keeping things from me."

I would hate that too. I want to become more than what we were, not less, and I know part of the reason things didn't work with Leo and me is I had all of these rules about what was okay to say to him. So I nod.

"Although we're going to work on your verbs."

I frown. "That sounds like less fun than other things we could be doing."

"He does not 'always say.' He always *said*. For you, Leo is past tense."

Then he lies back, pulling me down. "Now. Tell me about these *thoughts* you were having."

∾ ∾ ∾ ∾ ∾ ∾ ∾ ∾ ∾ ∾ ∾

Sometime later, I wake, my head on Caleb's chest, his hands on my back. After a few minutes of lying still, enjoying the way he makes me feel both safe and reckless, I whisper, "Sorry I fell asleep."

"It's okay," he says. "I was out for a while too, but if we're going to sleep, there are two beds in this room, and we're in neither of them."

I crawl off of him and walk over to my bed, look down at it, then back at Caleb, then at the bed again. He comes up behind me, wrapping his arms around me and resting his chin on my head.

"Don't freak out now. Three minutes ago, you were asleep completely on top of me." He kisses me right below my ear and whispers, "I liked it very much."

Neither the kiss nor the huskiness in his voice is making me less nervous about getting into that bed. I've only ever slept by myself. This feels like a big step.

When I don't respond, he says, "You've fallen asleep on the couch next to me lots of times."

This is true. I find only about one in three of the television shows Caleb and I watch together interesting.

"But if you want, I'll sleep in the other bed. We have lots of time."

I turn in his arms so I can look up into his eyes. "No. I want you with me," I say, suddenly certain. "Caleb, I love you." This isn't the first time I've said this to him, but it's the first time it's meant so much.

"And I love you. For always."

He rests his forehead against mine, and we stand like that until I sway a little. It's been a long day.

He laughs. "Definitely time for bed. I need to brush my teeth and stuff, but I'll be back."

I crawl into bed and fall right to sleep. When I wake in the middle of the night, I prop my head on my hand so I can study Caleb. He's lying on his side, his back to me, one arm wrapped around a pillow. It seems strange that until now, I never knew how he slept, and I wonder how many other little secrets there are to discover.

Looking at his profile, I can see the boy he was when we became friends, the person he is now, and the man he's still becoming. More than anything, I want to take care of him. I've had so many different feelings about him today, but this tenderness is a physical ache.

As I listen to his even breathing, I want very much to slide closer, but I don't want to wake him or suggest that I'm ready for something I'm not.

Then Caleb says, "Evie?" in a sleepy voice.

"Yes?" I answer, feeling caught even though he can't see me.

"Don't overthink it. Do what you want."

So I scoot over to him, putting one arm under my pillow and wrapping the other around him so I can rest my hand under his T-shirt and over his heart. Then I kiss his back and sigh contentedly. I can hardly believe I get to sleep like this.

"For future reference," he says quietly, "my vote is always for you as close as possible."

∞ ∞ ∞ ∞ ∞ ∞ ∞ ∞ ∞ ∞ ∞

The first thing I notice in the morning is how warm I am. The heat is coming from the body next to mine. I'm in bed with Caleb.

I'm not sure what should happen next. I want to curl into him, kiss him again, and run my fingers along his jaw to see how it feels first thing in the morning. But I also want to talk to him about my mother, and Bex, and what it's like to wake up with someone beside me. I'm not sure how to do all of these things at once. It's a little strange to be my best friend's girlfriend.

Suddenly, Caleb kisses my forehead. "When you figure out how you want to play this, let me know," he says, and springs out of bed, reminding me, not for the first time, of Tigger.

"How did you know I was awake?" I ask.

"I could see the gears turning in there. I'm surprised smoke wasn't coming out your ears." He crosses the room to grab his shoes. "I'm going to go exercise, and then we'll figure out what to do about your mother."

"I forgot to tell you last night—I'm going to stay with Bex for a few days. I can't go home right now."

He comes to sit on the bed beside me. "But I'll miss you. You could stay with us."

"Where?" I ask. With three kids, their four-bedroom house is full.

Caleb raises his eyebrows and smiles.

"Your mom would love that. It would set an excellent example for Joel and Nolan."

"Honestly, Nolan would probably appreciate our leadership in this area."

I take his hand. "I'll miss you too. But I'll make it up to you at spring break. I think we should take a road trip."

"Where?"

"You pick."

He grins. "Cooperstown it is." I'm not sure what he's talking about, but as far as I'm concerned, the destination is irrelevant.

"And hopefully by this summer, I'll feel safe living at home again."

"If you don't, we'll figure something else out."

∞ ∞ ∞ ∞ ∞ ∞ ∞ ∞ ∞ ∞ ∞ ∞

We're sitting in the hotel restaurant with our food when Mom arrives. She looks at Caleb, clearly surprised to see him here, but doesn't comment.

"I wanted someone to keep an eye on my drink," I say. This is only half a joke.

"I'm sorry, Evie," she says. "I don't know what I was thinking."

"Me neither. But it wasn't okay."

"I was up all night thinking about it, and here's my best guess: I thought getting hit with all those things that are dangerous for you—the math, and the social pressure, and the other kids—would be too much. I thought you were overconfident."

"I'm sure that was part of it," I concede. "But you have a lot invested in the idea that medicine is the only solution to my anxiety. Because that way, we don't have to talk about how bad things were for me in elementary and middle school and why we never did anything about that."

Caleb squeezes my hand under the table. He knows a lot more than she does about what going to school back then was like for me.

"I'm so sorry, Evie," she says.

"I don't blame you," I say. "I didn't tell you half the things until they were over. And you got me medicine so I could get my anxiety under control. And you sent me to Newton so I could recover. And you taught me to get help if I need it." She's crying now, and that makes my own tears start. "And you're right, dealing with all those people and being onstage was hard for me. But the math wasn't. It's never been part of the problem. It's one of my ways out."

"I'm sorry," she says again.

I nod. "Here's what I need. I'm going home with Bex today, and over spring break, Caleb and I are going somewhere together."

"Cooperstown," Caleb says, interrupting.

"Why do you keep saying that? I don't know what that is."

He smiles. "You will."

I return my attention to Mom. "I want *you* to go to ther-apy. The real kind where you talk to someone. And then in June, we'll see if me staying at home seems possible."

Mom sits back. I know this is a lot to take in. She looks between Caleb and me. "Are you sure you two should be making plans for what you're going to do three months from now?"

I'm a little surprised that this is what she wants to focus on, but I guess this part makes her feel like a typical mother. I'm thinking about how to respond when Caleb says, "I know we're seventeen, and I wouldn't expect most people to get this. But you saw us grow up together. Do you really think we're going to be done with each other in three months, or six, or a year? Or a decade?" I turn toward him. The certainty in his voice rocks me.

"Oh," I say softly, because I understand. Not in my head, but bone-deep in my body. Caleb isn't going anywhere. Even if the worst happened and we couldn't be together like this, we'd find a way back to being friends. It would be horrible, but it wouldn't end us. Nothing can do that.

Caleb smiles, because he sees I get it.

Unlike Mom, who says, "I know you care about her, and you have a history. You're a good kid. But it is not your responsibility to look after her for the rest of her life because you happened to grow up next door."

I would not have guessed that it was possible for her to hurt me more, but I feel her words in my organs—my heart, my stomach, my lungs. My own mother thinks I am an obligation for Caleb.

Caleb lets go of me and puts his hands on the table, leaning forward.

"You think Evie is my charity project? Yesterday, I stood on a stage and accepted an award that means I can go to a school I thought was completely out of reach. Because of her."

My tears fall hard. I turn away from Mom and toward Caleb.

"And that was a bonus. Being with her is making toys out of the laws of physics, and playing games in libraries, and racing through hotels to—"

"Caleb!" I say, somehow managing to be embarrassed amid all the other emotions.

He grins. "Sorry." Then he turns back to Mom. "Stop thinking of her as broken. Because she's not."

Then he kisses my cheek and stands. "I'm going to bring our stuff down and check us out."

Mom's eyes widen a little at this, and again I'm surprised that this is the part she's thinking about. We both watch him leave, thinking, I suspect, very different thoughts.

"You know I love you, Evie," she says.

"That's not an excuse. I'm going to ask Anita to recommend some therapists for you. Give it a real try. Some of it is silly, but it worked for me."

She takes a deep breath. "If that's what it takes to make this right, I'll look into it."

"It is. We'll talk on the phone, and you can visit me at Newton, and then we'll see what's next."

She stands, and after an awkward pause, we hug, and I go to find Caleb.

After dropping off my things with Bex, I walk him to the train station. It's too cold for this to be pleasant, so we wait inside on the benches. I'm glad to be going home with Bex, but the week ahead without Caleb seems very long.

"Do you think Frontier will shut down its website now that the conference is over?" I ask.

"Probably. Why?"

"We're going to be apart for a while. Maybe Milo and Tess could chat?"

Caleb gives me a look. "The last time we did that, you didn't follow the rules."

"We were sitting right next to each other. It was strange. But I miss Milo."

"I went through a weird couple of weeks there where I thought I was going to lose you to him. It was surreal."

"How did you know I'd find you on that site?"

"I was trusting quantum entanglement."

"Your favorite physics concept," I say, remembering his home page.

"Everything else on there was for you, but that was for me. Even when separated by great distance, entangled particles always recognize each other."

This description is romantic, but not exactly true. Still, I resist the urge to correct him.

"Are you saying we had no choice but to fall in love because we were entangled as children?" This sounds too much like what Mom was saying.

He shakes his head. "No. I think we entangle ourselves every time we choose each other, whether we're in the same room or on the computer or halfway across the country. I trusted you to choose me."

I remember all of the times I have chosen Caleb in the last few months: to be my Frontier partner, to be my online friend, to comfort me on Thanksgiving, to tell about ending therapy, to be the last person I spoke to at night, and today, to be the first person I saw in the morning. I see what he's saying. Entanglement, like love, isn't something that happens to you. It's a choice you make.

Taking his hand, I lace our fingers together. "Wherever I am," I say, "I will always choose you."

He smiles. "At least in this universe."

EVIE

Five months later . . .

CALEB LEADS ME OUT TO THE ALLEY, POSITIONS me against the wall of his garage, takes a few steps back to study me, and then moves me to the left.

"What are we doing?" I say, laughing.

"I want to make sure it's right. This was the first one."

"The first one what?"

"The first almost-kiss."

He steps closer and presses his hands against the wall on either side of my head. I still have no idea what's going on, but I like where this is headed.

"What's an almost-kiss?"

"This, Evie," he says, smiling down at me, "was supposed to be our first kiss." He moves his mouth toward mine but stops before our lips meet. "Is this ringing any bells for you?"

I shake my head. "Sorry, no."

"I was shorter then, so we were closer to the same height."

"When?"

"We were thirteen."

"Thirteen!"

"We were playing hide-and-seek with Joel and Nolan, and I caught you here, like this, and I almost kissed you."

"Why didn't you?"

His mouth quirks up. "You ran away."

"I must have been out of my mind."

He leans toward me, and I close my eyes, but instead of kissing me, he stops again and says, "You know what? We're going to reenact them all."

I open my eyes again. "All?"

"This will be our summer project. We'll turn all fifteen almost-kisses into the real thing."

"There were fifteen?" I say wonderingly. I will never get over the idea that Caleb has been in love with me for as long as he has. That the one almost-kiss I knew about was one of many. Not a whim at all.

"It'll take some time. The county fair, a picnic at the beach, three separate trips to Newton, and we'll have to figure something out with sledding. Cardboard and cooking spray, maybe?"

He looks off into the distance, considering the problem, but I decide to let this part go. "We can't get all three Newton ones out of the way on the same trip?"

"Evie! Our almost-kisses are not chores," he says with mock severity. "They are sacred, and we will do them in order. Three trips."

"Can we drive?"

"No," he says, nuzzling into my neck. "I like our bus."

I sigh, but then he whispers in my ear, "It leaves my hands free."

In response, I slide my own hands up his chest to his shoulders and pull him toward me, going up on my toes to close the distance.

But he shakes his head, saying, "No," and gently takes my hands and puts them back against the garage. "It wasn't like that. You were much less friendly then."

"I'm doing my best to make up for that."

"I know." He laughs. "I almost ended up in Illinois coming home from work today because I was thinking about last night . . . and how friendly you were."

We smile at each other, remembering, and then I say, "Caleb, there have been three separate almost-kisses in the last five minutes. If we're going to do fifteen, it's time to take some action."

"But the almosts make me feel so philanthropic."

"What do you mean?"

"Many-Worlds. For every decision I make in this

universe, there's another universe somewhere out there where the opposite thing happens, right?"

"Theoretically, yes," I agree.

"So every time I almost kiss you but then decide not to, another universe's Caleb is very happy."

I don't like where this chain of reasoning leaves us, so I say, "It's only a theory. And I'm convinced it can't be right."

"Why?"

"If Many-Worlds is true, then somewhere in the multiverse, there would have to be an Evie who didn't fall madly in love with you. And that's not possible."

"Then there's no reason for any more almosts," he says, and kisses me.

AUTHOR'S NOTE ON THE MATHEMATICS

I think of the mathematics in this book as an Impressionist painting of the discipline. Caleb and Evie's story captures the spirit of mathematics—I hope—and draws on some recognizable problems and representations, although often softened for artistic effect.

Spinning top and particle-in-a-box problems are assigned in physics. Tangents are in fact lines that touch curves, and physicist S. James Gates Jr. has actually used geometric models that he calls adinkras to describe relationships among subatomic particles.

Gates has also found error-correcting code inside those models and has said, perhaps somewhat playfully, that this finding provides some evidence that our universe is a simulation. Similarly, physicist Max Tegmark has, along with others, made a convincing argument that we live in a multiverse that includes other versions of ourselves. Like Evie, I truly believe everyone should read his beautifully written book, *Our Mathematical Universe*. Unlike Evie, I also believe everyone should read Nick Bostrom's brief and delightful essay that argues that we are likely living in a computer simulation. If you're curious about adinkras, S. James Gates Jr. has some relatively accessible pieces that are easily findable with an internet search.

I let these real mathematical ideas inspire Evie's project in this book, although I definitely took some liberties for narrative effect. It was easier to talk about building a model of an atom than to get into weight-space diagrams and fermions, bosons, leptons, and quarks. While Evie certainly could have made an adinkra that would have revealed error-correcting code when manipulated, the process would have been quite a bit more complex than the one portrayed here. And in real life, the ways in which she was extending Gates's work would need to be more carefully demonstrated.

Beyond the adinkras, I had a lot of fun playing with the mathematics and physics metaphors, both the obvious ones like entanglement and a few more subtle ones. The problem Evie solves in the Math Genius booth about the figure eight is a callback to Caleb's reflection on Evie's model of boyfriends and friends. The figure eight comprises of two nonoverlapping sets, connected by a single shared point.

Overall, what I wanted to do in this book was not so much to portray a real solution to a real problem as to offer a glimpse of what mathematics can be. In school, too many of us learn that mathematics is about executing memorized steps to get correct answers as quickly as possible. But this is not how people who love it see the discipline. I wanted to write a book about a character who sees mathematics as beautiful and creative and bound up in our natural world.

Because I know that much is true.

ACKNOWLEDGMENTS

First, my most sincere thanks to my agent, Elizabeth Bennett. What I appreciate most about you as an agent is the way you keep faith even when mine falters. What I appreciate most about you as an editor is the way you insist my characters talk like themselves, even when it means leaving something hilarious on the floor. Thanks also to Barbara Miller and Amy Tompkins at Transatlantic for helping to get Evie and Caleb's story out into the world.

Lots and lots of thanks to my brilliant editor, Maggie Lehrman. I'm so appreciative of your ability not only to suggest specific changes in the text but also to name the broader principle motivating them. I'm a better writer because I worked with you. (Also, thank you for not letting Caleb get away with being slick and easy. The whole story is better because you pushed on that.) Thanks also to the rest of the

Abrams team, especially Emily Daluga for the fabulous catalog copy, Hana Anouk Nakamura for my pretty cover, Marie Oishi for steering the whole process, and Alison Cherry for the careful copyediting that fixed my mistakes and improved my comic timing. Finally, I will be forever grateful to illustrator Andrea Poretta for capturing the heart of my characters.

Heaps of thanks to physicists James S. Gates Jr., Max Tegmark, and Brian Cox for building a playground for Evie. I hope I didn't break too many of your toys.

Math and physics aside, it delights me to say that One Direction is largely responsible for this book. Without "Last First Kiss," I'd have a single POV story with the wrong love interest, and without "Happily," I'd have no bus ride scene, a fate too terrible to contemplate.

In fairness, the book probably would also not exist without the Okemos Panera, which supplied me with the only acceptable iced tea in the North while I wrote all the words. Thanks to all of the friendly folks there for knowing my name and not mocking my constant presence.

Thank you to the academic friends who let me show up as my whole self—a scholar who writes kissing books. I am especially grateful for Stephanie Jones, Mardi Schmeichel, Hilary Conklin, Mark Vagle, and Hilary Hughes (I miss you all every day); Cassie Brownell, Kristen White, Jon Wargo, and Lynette Guzmán (Why? Why did you leave me? Jobs are no excuse); and Anita Wager, Mandy Jansen, Marcy Wood,

AUTHOR BIO

Amy Noelle Parks is an associate professor at Michigan State University. When she's not using One Direction lyrics as a writing prompt, she's helping future teachers recover from the trauma of years of school mathematics. She lives in Michigan with her husband and two daughters.

Sandra Crespo, and Beth Herbel-Eisenmann (your authenticity feeds mine).

Thank you, always, to my mom and dad, who are much more models for Caleb's parents than Evie's, and to my sister Molly, my brother Josh, and all the members of their wonderful families for all the love, laughter, and support.

Sophie and Chloe, Evie's bravery comes from yours. It's such a privilege to watch you take on the things that scare you. I love you both.

And Perry. You are the reason I wrote a love story about a girl falling for a boy who makes her smarter and braver and stronger than she ever could have been without him. Thank you for thirty years of chasing dreams with me.